DOWN IN THE FOREST

Lucy Walker's vivid novels of the Australian outback, which authentically
portray a fascinating life unknown to
most town-dwellers, have become in-
creasingly popular and are in constant
demand. In this new and colourful
story we read not only of the adventures
of a young English girl, Jill Dawson,
when she takes a job with a wealthy
Australian landowner, but of the activities of a whole community in West
Australia as they prepare for a great
international event. Just as Jill's growing love for her attractive but stern
employer undergoes many vicissitudes,
so are the plans of the organising committee subjected to cruel setbacks
through the onslaughts of nature. This
is the story of the *real* Australia: the
" sunburnt country " of vast open
spaces; of blazing noonday heat and
wide and starry skies.

NOBODY READS JUST *ONE* LUCY WALKER!

Down in the Forest

Lucy Walker

BEAGLE BOOKS • NEW YORK
An Intext Publisher

Published by arrangement with the author and the
author's agent, Paul R. Reynolds, Inc.

First printing: May 1971
Second printing: September 1971
Third printing: April 1972

Printed in the United States of America

BEAGLE BOOKS, INC.
101 Fifth Avenue, New York, NY 10003

CHAPTER ONE

JILL DAWSON stirred in her seat in the bus. She glanced up to the rack overhead to see if her carry-all and coat were safely afloat on the wire mesh.

They must be getting very near to Darjalup now. It was the next main town on the Great Southern Road, and was her destination. For an hour past the bush had become thicker, the trees taller, the undergrowth dense and green. The great sweep of road wound away ahead and behind like a wide blue snake; and for miles there had been no sign of the wide paddocks with sheep grazing that Jill had seen earlier in the day. It was summer and this forest country, hazed with heat and fine smoke, perhaps from some bushfire in the far-off distance, was very beautiful in its strange, austere, almost frightening loneliness.

Jill was a little frightened herself, not of the bush but of her first job away from home, which lay ahead in Darjalup.

She had finished her training two months earlier and she was now on her way to join the staff of Darjalup High School as sports' mistress.

How, she kept wondering throughout that day-long journey, would she be able to manage the older girls—girls who weren't really so much younger than herself?

When Jill thought about these unknown girls she herself felt very young and inexperienced. When she thought of being twenty-three years of age, and going out of the city, away from home into the distant bushlands, she felt very old indeed.

Spinster—she had had to write against her name in connection with her appointment form.

"And that's about *it*," she had thought ruefully.

As she could not look into the future she did not know she was destined never to see that school at all.

The bus was now passing cottages. They stood on small blocks of land that had been hewn out of the forest. The trees around them were tall and black-trunked, very still and wise looking in their silence as if they also were very old, like the rest of this grey ancient land. How quiet, secret, yet lovely was that forest bush !

Jill had a sudden wish to turn round in her seat and see if the sophisticated and very beautiful young woman who had got on the bus at Perth, as she herself had done, was still there. This was a silly inclination and Jill knew it was, for she also knew the young woman in question had not got off the bus. Neither had she evaporated into thin air. Her name was Vanessa Althrop and she had only left the bus at the morning-tea and lunch breaks; as all the passengers had done.

Jill had been fascinated by her fellow traveller from the moment the latter had boarded the bus. Vanessa Althrop had a clear ringing voice, slightly affected but not unpleasant. It had a honey quality about it: attractive and inviting.

The bus conductor, and the driver had both known her.

" Good-morning, Miss Althrop ! " they had each said, one at a time, as if greeting someone well known to them and evidently very important.

"Has Darjalup got the red carpet out for you, Miss Vanessa? " the conductor had later asked with a cheery smile, as he clipped her ticket. " It's quite a time since we've seen you down this way. Been on your travels again ? "

So that is her name, Jill thought. *Vanessa ! How much more interesting than plain Jill.*

" Oh, here and there ! " Vanessa had replied.

" We've another passenger on board for the Timber Camps," the conductor had gone on. " The young lady up in the front seat." He meant Jill.

" Oh really ! "

That had been completely lacking in interest ! The voice hadn't even kept its honey quality for that remark, Jill thought ruefully. She wished the conductor hadn't mentioned her. She felt nervous about her new job and the last thing she wanted was to start off in Darjalup on the wrong foot—especially if Miss Althrop was a V.I.P. in that town.

At the lunch stop Jill had hardly been able to take her eyes from the other girl. She had seen that Vanessa Althrop's clothes must have come from Sydney or Rome. They were out of the world for the far west, and so was the beautiful green and red velvet swathed hat that sat with a kind of shining beauty on Vanessa's dark hair: also the dark glossy handbag with the large gold lettering on it, was very impressive. It told the world Vanessa's name.

All Jill's surmising about Vanessa, and her clothes, had been hours ago. Now as they neared Darjalup Jill had this odd compulsion to turn round and look at Vanessa again. She resisted the temptation and concentrated on what was passing by instead.

The bush suddenly thinned out into more open country; cleared land. There were veranda bungalows, each set in a half-acre of garden and orchard. They were pretty houses against the dark backdrop of smoke-hazed trees in the distance.

" The Timber Camps ! " the conductor called cheerily. Jill realised this was a little joke for Vanessa Althrop's benefit. They were entering a sprawling but lively country town.

Jill stood up and pulled her coat and carry-all down from the rack.

"Don't worry about your big luggage, miss," the conductor called. "I'll get it out for you."

Jill smiled as she thanked him.

The bus had run straight into the middle of the town and now pulled up alongside the kerb, outside the hotel. The conductor jumped from the bus first and was busy getting cases from the rear carrier as Jill and Vanessa Althrop stepped down on to the pavement. The dark girl with the lovely clothes took no notice of her fellow passenger whatever.

Jill looked around, a little unnerved by having "Arrived."

"Excuse me. Miss Jill Dawson?"

"Yes—that's me," Jill said in surprise. A young man with sandy hair and grey eyes—his feet planted wide apart, hands in pockets and a pleasant grin on his brown face—was looking at her. She wondered how this stranger knew her, and who he was.

He took one hand out of a pocket and with it a piece of notepaper. He put his head on one side and read from it.

"Medium to tall in height; fair-haired, green-eyed. Looks the kind that rides and plays tennis and golf well."

Jill's eyes widened.

"But who wrote that?" she asked. She hadn't expected anyone in Darjalup to know her. The headteacher of the school, Mr. Beckett, knew she was coming but he had never met her. His deputy had interviewed her in Perth . . . and the deputy had not been returning to this school after the holidays.

"Kim Baxter," the young man was saying. "He's just come in from the bushfire. He's taking off his charred clothes, and washing half the jarrah forest out of his hair. I had instructions from him to find, get, and bring into the pub one Miss Jill Dawson . . . *according to description in note.*"

The bus conductor had put Jill's heavy luggage on the pavement by the side of Vanessa Althrop's cases and she turned and thanked him. Vanessa, she noticed, was talking to someone through the window of the bus and took no interest in either Jill or this stranger meeting her.

The young man with a pleasant grin and a magician-like manner picked up Jill's cases, one in each hand.

"Follow me," he said with mock irony. "Destiny, in the form of Kim Baxter, awaits you."

"But please," Jill said. "You've got my right name. And I *have* got fair hair . . . ."

"And green eyes!"

"But I don't know anyone called Kim Baxter."

"He knows you—hence the note. Come along, child, through the door. That's right. Now turn left into the lounge and find yourself the most comfortable seat in the place. I'll check your name in for you."

Jill did as she was told. She sat in a large chintz-covered arm-chair and watched the mysterious young man carry her cases to the desk, put them down on the floor; then leaning sideways with one elbow on the counter, engage himself in conversation with the very chic girl behind the counter.

This activity was almost immediately interrupted by Vanessa Althrop who came in through the main door and advanced across the carpeted floor like an indignant but beautiful queen.

"Isn't there anyone to bring in my bags?" she demanded of the desk girl.

The girl looked at the young man, who straightened up and looked at Vanessa.

"Oh, it's you, Shane!" Vanessa said, surprised, but still haughty. "How you've grown up!"

"You too, Vanessa. Let's see, it must be all of three years ago. I was on my annual holidays the last two occasions you honoured Darjalup. Right me if I'm wrong but didn't you have . . . all those three years back . . . a gym tunic and dark plaits of hair down your back?"

"I never wore a gym tunic in my life—or black plaits," Vanessa said coldly. "We don't seem to have an official help here. Will you bring my cases in for me, Shane?"

This was a request and order, mixed together, but Jill could see from her arm-chair across the lounge and through the wide archway that divided it from the hall, that it was Shane's obligingness and not Vanessa's request-order that would get those cases inside.

Jill wished very much that she knew who was Shane, and who was Vanessa Althrop. Above all who was Kim Baxter, the man who had written that description of herself.

She had quite a long wait, sitting there in the lounge. Shane first brought in Vanessa's baggage, then took it up to the first floor for her. Jill's luggage remained on the floor beside the desk.

When Shane returned from his good-deeding he came straight across the lounge to Jill. He pulled up a chair so that he sat facing her, and smiled engagingly.

"I guess Kim Baxter's taking his time. Ah well, he's had quite a day of it! Have a cigarette? Good." He struck a match and lit both their cigarettes, then settled back and beamed in a friendly way at Jill.

"I see you have booked in here," he said. "So we'll leave what happens next to you to Kim—when he comes." His grin deepened. "You know what? If the pub had been burnt down the whole community would have turned out to try and save it. As it was the school—well, it just got burned down to the ground." He shook his head sadly. "*People!*" he finished deprecatingly.

Jill put one hand to her head.

" Please tell me what goes on ? " she begged. " First, I don't know Kim Baxter. I don't know anyone in Darjalup. And—did you say the school was *burned down* ? "

He raised his eyebrows.

" Sure. Didn't you know ? But, of course, what a clot I am ! You were in the bus all day. Well, Miss Dawson, here's a list of the facts. A bushfire, not uncommon to us, you know—swept through the south end of the town and licked off the High School in passage. Dear girl, you're out of a job. By the way, how come you don't look like a sports mistress ? No bulging muscles in unfeminine places ? In fact everything very petite and feminine indeed."

"You're thinking of Swedish drill and hardboard dragons of the past," Jill said with a smile. " Everything's different now. Sport-rhythm, the dance-music. That's how we do it now——' She broke off and a frown of worry creased her forehead. " Yes, of course, I'll be out of a job. But . . . ."

" But what, Jill ? You don't mind my calling you Jill ? "

" No, I don't mind you calling me Jill. But what will become of the children if they have no school ? What a terrible thing ! "

" They'll have one long glorious holiday while we're building another bigger, brighter, better school. There's nothing terrible about a holiday. Ask the kids."

Jill suddenly had an illuminating thought.

" Kim Baxter would be one of the staff members ? "

Shane gave a hoot of laughter that nearly made him tilt his chair far enough back to be at the danger-angle. He righted himself in time.

" Kim Baxter," Shane said slowly, dropping each word one at a time. " Is the biggest landowner hereabouts.

In Darjalup he's next to the Deity; and this is a pious town. So now you know what I mean."

" But why ask you to meet me ? And how did he know about . . . well, about what I look like ? "

Shane shook his head and spread his hands.

" No idea, but when I see him I'll ask him. Should be here any minute."

Jill looked over Shane's shoulder and saw a tall, well-built man walking down the carpeted staircase. He had shining black hair, wet from recent showering—and a cigarette in one hand. His clothes, a loose jacket and dark brown shoes, were casual but somehow looked as if they'd been cut by the best of good tailors. He was a lot older than Shane but how old Jill couldn't guess.

He reached the ground floor, said something to the girl behind the desk then turned towards the lounge where Jill and Shane were sitting. Jill watched him fascinated. There was no hint of a smile on his bronzed face. His eyes were a dark blue, Jill thought. They were intent and quite serious. He was very impressive.

At that moment Vanessa Althrop came down the staircase. She had changed her dress and now wore a beguiling pale blue dress of fine silk. She had a gold chain round her neck and from it hung a large embossed gold locket. Her gold ear-rings were small but lovely. With her dark hair swathed on the crown of her head she looked very beautiful.

" Kim—darling ! " she said.

The man moving across the lounge turned round quickly at the sound of her voice.

" Why, Vanessa ! " he said. His voice was resonant and soft, also *glad*—in a controlled way. Jill, from the distance, thought this man would be controlled about *everything*.

Vanessa came right up to him. There couldn't have

been more than two inches between them as they stood
there in the centre of the room. The man now had his
back turned to Jill and Shane in the corner of the lounge.
All Jill could see was his tall body, the excellent cut of
his jacket; and that his hair shone blue-black under the
overhead light; as did Vanessa's hair.

"A cigarette please, darling," Vanessa said. He took
out his cigarette case. Vanessa Althrop went on in her
clear-toned voice—all the honey in it now. " I told you
I'd be down in late February. I'm surprised you weren't
counting the days."

Shane had turned in his chair, also watching the scene.
Now he turned back to Jill.

" Leave them be till they get that ' darling-when-did-
I-last-see-you-act off; and Kim'll come and explain all
things to you, Jill. Meantime patience. The dark Vanessa
means business when she starts playing up to Kim that
way."

" Please," said Jill. Her pretty eyes were beginning to
be tired behind their veil of long lashes. " Would you
explain this whole situation to me. I don't even know
your name."

" Shane Evans," he said with a smile. " I'm sorry,
Jill, but honestly you swept me off my feet. In spite of
Kim's accurate physical description of you I didn't expect
anyone so young . . . or so well, downright pretty . . . ."
His smile was a little sheepish now. " You know, one gets
a sort of build-up in one's mind about school-teachers.
I never seem to remember any of mine being under
fifty . . . ."

" I'm not a teacher any more if the school is burnt
down," Jill said quietly. " I did my training as a private
student in the college so the Government doesn't have
to find me another job. Naturally, I'm worried."

She didn't like to add she had hardly any money with
her. She had understood her first pay day would be in

a week's time. She had exactly five pounds with her; and three pounds ten in the bank account which had been transferred to the Darjalup branch ahead of her arrival. A very humble account yet she had received a very pleasant letter from the branch manager welcoming her to Darjalup and wishing her a happy future in the town.

It didn't look as if she was going to have much future there now.

" That's the whole point," Shane Evans was saying. " I'd better not say too much or I'll get myself in the blue with Kim. He knew when that school went down it was likely one or two of the staff would be marking time for a month or so and he took just ten minutes to find out the only staff member who wouldn't necessarily be res-cued by the Government was someone who could ride horses, play tennis . . . and was generally speaking an out-door sort of person. He wants to recruit you himself."

Jill's eyes opened wide.

" But why ? " she said. " You said he was a land-owner."

" So he is. Look Jill, I can't say too much. Supposing he doesn't like you— that's not likely," he grinned. " Or you don't want the job. I'll be in pure trouble for mixing it up."

"Are you on his staff ? " Jill asked gravely. She had seen Kim Baxter and Vanessa Althrop move away towards the desk. They stood by it talking. Vanessa had actually leaned her arm on his shoulder. He was looking at her, right at her, listening to her intently. Jill had looked quickly away, back at Shane Evans.

" These days I think *almost* . . ." Shane said lugu-briously. He looked over his shoulder again and seeing that neither Kim Baxter nor Vanessa Althrop were coming their way he pressed the bell on the wall behind Jill's chair.

" We'll have a drink on it," he said. " Then I guess you'd like to go up and have a bath . . . or change—"

The girl from behind the desk came round its corner and crossed the lounge.

" Yes, Mr. Evans ! " she said. " Can I get you something ? " She was a pretty, rather pert-looking girl with berry brown eyes and a very red mouth.

" What do you like, Jill ? Sherry ? Gin and tonic . . .? "

" I think I'll have a sherry, thank you." Jill was beginning to feel very tired. How quickly Vanessa had managed to change her dress ! Jill felt dusty and forlorn by comparison.

Shane Evans was giving the girl whom he called " Dixie " the drinks order and for the first time Jill found herself looking round the lounge and taking it in.

It really was very comfortable with its maroon wall-to-wall carpeting, its gay chintz-covered chairs and its heavy dark red-wood beams in the ceiling. It was half modern, half old, yet somehow managed to look attractive in its mixture.

" Let's have another cigarette on it," Shane said when Dixie had gone away to get the order.

Jill shook her head.

" Not just yet," she said. " Thank you all the same. But please have one yourself."

" Don't sound so formal, Jill," he said, smiling at her through the match flame as he applied it to the end of his cigarette. " You don't look the formal kind. Do you know what ? You look the jolly kind to me, and this town's going to look twice when you go walking down that main street."

Jill had to smile. Her face lit up and there were lights in her grey-green eyes.

" I'm sorry," she said. " I expect I'm a little tired. And worried too . . ."

" Not to worry," Shane assured her. " Kim's the great man round here but he's got a heart of gold under that chassis of polished steel. Now what were we up to . . . "

" You said you thought you were *almost* on Mr. Baxter's staff."

" Mr. Baxter ! Who's Mr. Baxter ? Oh, you mean Kim ? "

" Please," said Jill gently. " Please explain everything to me in one piece. I'm very bewildered. Could we possibly begin with you because—you see—just now I'm in your hands ? "

Vanessa Althrop and Kim Baxter were still talking that half-acre away across the lounge. Vanessa's arm was still on his shoulder and she was still being looked at with that steady interested wholly good-mannered pair of inscrutable blue eyes.

Dixie came back with the sherries and placed them on tiny sea-grass mats, one in front of each of them.

Shane thanked her.

" What goes on over there ? " he grumbled to Dixie. " Kim's got a date with this young lady and it looks as if he's clove-hitched to the other . . ."

Dixie lifted one eloquent shoulder.

" Well, look who she is ? " she said airily. " Miss Vanessa Althrop, come home specially to get clove-hitched to him, by the look of it."

" Not while you're around, beautiful," Shane told her. Dixie tossed her head and walked away on her high heels across the deep maroon carpet. Shane laughed as he turned back to Jill.

" That's the Irish in me," he said knowingly. " But don't be anxious. I had a perfectly good Welsh father to leaven out the blarney." He lifted his glass.

" Here's cheers, and happy hunting with Kim Baxter." Jill lifted her glass and sipped her sherry.

" I'm not hunting with Kim Baxter . . . whom I haven't

even met . . ." she said, looking over the top of her glass at Shane. " But I would like a job if he's got one. There's not much fun in being unemployed. You said he was a land-owner ? What sort of a job could he have for someone like me ? "

" Off-sider. Left hand or right hand or whatever it is a man as busy as he is, wants."

Jill was perplexed and she looked it. She had done a shorthand-typing course before she took a college training in physical education. She had undertaken the typing course because her parents, not long out from England, had not been able to afford to send her on to further education. Then, in the small business they had taken in a suburb of the city, they had suddenly had a very good year. Jill had always been good at dancing and there had been a riding-school just over the way from her home, as well as a public golf-course half a mile up the road. The owner of the riding-school had willingly used her services after school and in the week-ends. This way she had learned to understand horses and ride them very well. She saved her pocket money to buy golf balls to play on the public course and had also played tennis in her school team, later being the seeded player in her college team.

She had always wanted an outdoor job in this country, where the sun shone almost all the year round ; but had agreed to do the shorthand typing course for her parents' sake.

Then they had had their good year.

" You're an outdoor girl, Jill," her father had said. " Now I'm going to send you to college to get a training. I suppose you'll be a sports mistress, or something like that."

" For two years after college, until I get my certificate confirmed ! " Jill had said gaily, nearly delirious with delight at this turn in fortunes. " Then I'm coming back

to help Mr. Jukes run his riding school and Mr. Stanton
manage the golf course."

All heaven had shone for Jill on that day !

Here, three years four months later, was someone of
whom Jill had never heard—in a town she had not yet
really seen—contemplating giving her a job as an " off-
sider." Whatever that really was !

She looked up, past Shane Evans, to where Kim Baxter
stood talking to Vanessa Althrop. Or was it rather that
Vanessa talked, and he listened?

What kind of a person was he ? What kind of an off-
sider did he really want ? And why ?

If he wanted one, well—here she was; but why didn't
he come over and find out about her for himself?

Perhaps he was terrifically important, and terrifically
important people deputised other people to do their
selections of staff for them.

Jill took her eyes away from that tall well-built man
on the other side of the room and looked at Shane. Her
own eyes sparkled for a moment.

" In addition to collecting me from the bus and planting
me in this chair, were you told to look me over too ? "
she asked with a smile. " Is that what you are really
doing, Shane ? Getting to know me so you can recommend
me—or *not*."

He had the grace to look slightly shame-faced.

" Well, not exactly . . ." he broke off and grinned.
" The minute you stepped off the bus I said to myself—
This is it! I wouldn't have told you about the job if I
hadn't been certain straight-off. Believe me ? "

" Thank you. But how did Mr. Baxter, or anybody
else in Darjalup know I had done a shorthand-typewriting
course ? Or didn't they know ? "

" The bank manager, dear child. Don't look surprised.
In this country, the minute you put so much as

one shilling in a bank account the bank manager not only knows the location of your immortal soul but its colour and size. No secret from him, the doctor or the padre. They find everything out back to before you were born."

" What a country ! " Jill said, dazed.

"All for your good. Service with a capital S. Want a dentist appointment ? The bank 'ull fix it. Want a job ? The bank 'ull help you."

" I see," said Jill more soberly. "As a matter of fact I had a very nice letter from the manager, Mr. Outram, before I came down."

"And, unless you're unlucky you'll land a very nice job—with his help—before to-morrow's sun rises and you've even met the bank Galahads."

" I do hope I do," said Jill, more fervently than she intended. Though she had more than one shilling in her account it still wasn't a very big account at three pounds ten shillings. Mr. Baxter probably wanted someone very badly and perhaps off-siders were hard to get in Darjalup.

She looked across the room at him again.

At that moment a man, who looked as if he might be a stockman or farm employee of some kind, came in through the glass doors at the front of the hall and walked straight up to where Vanessa Althrop and Kim Baxter were still talking. Vanessa dropped her arm and looked round at the man as if he was an impertinent intruder. Not so, Kim Baxter. He listened to what the strangely clad man had to say, looking at him with a kind of unflinching gaze as if he were paying great attention to every word. His face was suddenly both stern and grave.

He spoke to Vanessa then turned and came abruptly across the room to where Shane and Jill were sitting.

Jill thought he had more personality than any other person she had ever met, yet at the moment that he came across the room she had a feeling of nervousness. He had a stern face; in a way it was a nice face, except for the hard concentrated expression in those dark blue eyes.

To hide her nervousness—because she wanted that job so very badly—she lifted her sherry glass and her fingers were not quite steady. She quickly put the glass down without drinking.

That was a silly thing to do, she thought. What an awful impression she must have given—drinking sherry when her possible future employer was about to speak to her ! He glanced at Jill. In dismay, she read a restrained indifference in his eyes.

Bang goes the job, she thought, and wished she'd never heard of sherry in her life.

" Excuse me," Kim Baxter said, very formally, in a quiet voice but which nevertheless had a razor-edge of annoyance in it. He had taken in Jill but he spoke to Shane.

" I have to leave now. They want me out at Buckman's place. I'm sorry to have kept you waiting, Shane."

Shane was on his feet.

" This is Miss Jill Dawson—the young lady who was on the bus, Kim."

" How do you do ? " he said. His voice was even ; its tone unaltered. " I must ask you to excuse me. Is it possible for me to meet you in the morning ? Shane will arrange it."

He doesn't even like me, Jill thought, aghast at her folly in picking up that wine glass.

" Thank you," she managed to say.

Kim Baxter's eyes turned to Shane again.

" You'll arrange it ? Make it eleven o'clock, will you ? In the bank . . ."

" Okay, Kim," Shane said nonchalantly. Jill felt quite unnerved by Shane's ability to talk to Kim Baxter this way. "I must say at the pace you go, you *need* a secretary," Shane added.

Kim Baxter's eyes were suddenly two pieces of ice. He looked at Jill again. Her heart sank. There was a cold forbidding antagonism in them.

When he turned and walked rapidly away, taking Vanessa by the arm as he went and leading her through the glass doors and out into the growing twilight, Jill looked at Shane reproachfully.

" I feel I've lost the job before I started. I shouldn't have been sipping sherry and you shouldn't have told him he needs a *secretary*."

Shane laughed.

" He needs one all right, though it's a new dose of medicine for Kim Baxter. Probably thinks secretaries are like bank managers, the keepers of a man's immortal soul. But you'll teach him otherwise, sweet Jill. I've a feeling in my bones."

" Is that what an off-sider is ? A secretary ? "

" More—by a long gap: and different." He stood up. " Look, you're tired. You caught that bus at eight o'clock this morning and that meant you must have been up around five. It's stupid of me to keep you hanging around this way. Come on . . . I'll get your luggage up for you and I'll explain as much as I can over dinner. Right ? "

CHAPTER TWO

JILL WENT to bed very early that night. She was exhausted, not only by travelling but by the sudden topsyturvy world into which she had been thrown.

Her room was not big but it was a nice one, well furnished in a modern way. In addition to the usual hotel bedroom furniture, all in light blond-wood, there was a modern-type writing table with a lamp, and plugs in the wall above it for a radio, or even a radiator. She felt she would be happy if this room was to be her home, except she was terribly worried as to its costs in relation to this new job—she *might* get.

She knew that if she didn't get the job she must go home as quickly as possible. The thought of facing her parents, after their expense in giving her that college training, made her feel sick at heart.

If only she hadn't picked up that glass of sherry? Who ever heard of a girl, longing for a job, sitting with her knees crossed in a chintz chair sipping sherry while her potential boss made the first approaches?

She must have been mad! No, not mad—*nervous*.

Jill was inclined to be as angry with Kim Baxter for making her feel nervous as she was for herself being so inept.

At dinner Shane Evans had explained to her very briefly what the job was. Kim Baxter was a very important person in the Darjalup district and he had taken over the responsibility of turning the town and the surrounding areas of forest, timber cutting and milling as well as the farming and stock-breeding, into a show place. In November . . . nine months away . . . people from all over the world were coming to the state primarily for the Inter-

national Sporting Contest. They would descend on Darjalup on a look-see visit so that they could get a better
understanding of how things were done in the " outback "
of Australia: and to see the wonderful karri forest.

Not only the Government but the local Shire and the
residents wanted the best possible front to be presented
to these international visitors. They felt their national
pride was at stake.

A committee of the land-owners had been formed to
operate in conjunction with the Shire Council, and Kim
Baxter was the chairman of that committee. Shane Evans
was the Shire secretary and so his job was to help this
new committee and make things as easy as possible for
Kim Baxter. After all, Kim had his own big property to
run as well.

" We've been desperate for staff, and into our arms . . .
bang off a bus . . . you walk," Shane had said cheerfully.
He obviously had no doubts that Jill would get the job
in spite of that look in Kim Baxter's eyes which said he
disliked young women sitting about in hotels, drinking
sherry.

The next morning, shortly after breakfast, Jill received
a telephone message from the bank manager. Would she
please call on him about ten forty-five ?

Jill remembered that Kim Baxter and Shane Evans had
talked about meeting in the bank at eleven o'clock. This
extra quarter of an hour meant she would get some brief-
ing. Thank goodness for that. But what did she wear ?

Would a simple but smart office-girl jumper-suit be
right for the country ? What about shoes ? High heels or
low heels ?

Perhaps she should wear something casual. After all,
both Kim Baxter and Shane Evans had worn casual
clothes. Yet Vanessa had been super-elegant; so elegance
wasn't wrong for the country.

But then Vanessa wasn't looking for a job. Only a clove-hitch whatever that was—to Kim Baxter.

Jill decided to wear what she had intended wearing on her first day at the school—a shirt-maker linen . . . and yes, the high heels. The low didn't look a bit nice with a straight up and down linen dress.

She had already walked round the balcony of the upper story of the hotel and looked at the town. The smoke haze was still in the trees and there was a glorious smell of burning gum leaves. The wide street before and below the balcony was alive with the intermittent kind of traffic that made Jill's heart leap. This was a new place, different from anything she had ever seen before. One moment a great luxury car sped down the bitumen road, the next huge lumber trucks boomed down it. Some men came in on horseback and rode through the town, jog-trot, holding their reins high. Their faces were dark weathered brown, expressionless yet alert about the eyes. They were unconcerned about the townswomen already out with their shopping baskets.

The railway tracks gleamed silver on the other side of the road. Beyond them brown roads wound like snakes away into the forest.

And the forest ! It was so still, so ancient in a timeless kind of waiting. It seemed so old; older than anything Jill had dreamed about even in her own birthplace thousands of miles away in the northern hemisphere. She didn't feel afraid of the bush any more. It was too lofty, too ancient to be dangerous to mere humans.

At ten forty-five exactly Jill presented herself at the bank, which was only two blocks away from the hotel. As soon as she came in the door a fresh-faced pleasant young man came round from behind a counter and smiled at her.

" Miss Dawson ? " he asked. " Please come this way, Mr. Outram is expecting you." He opened a dark red-wood door at the side of the main office and with great good manners showed her into the manager's office.

So much, Jill thought bewildered, for a three-pounds ten-shillings account !

The manager, a heavily built middle-aged man, rose from his chair from behind an enormous jarrah desk and beamed on Jill. He had a kind, almost fatherly face, and pleasant light brown eyes.

" Miss Dawson ? " he said. He came round the desk and shook hands with her, then placed a chair for her opposite his own.

" You know what this is all about ? " he said as he went back to his own chair. He put his hands on the table and smiled across its polished surface at her. "You've heard of the tragedy at the school ? It was burnt down in yesterday's fire."

" Yes," said Jill quietly. " I'm terribly sorry about it. What will the children do ? "

" Well, it's early days to forecast. The head-teacher was out with us yesterday trying to save it. They'll do something, rest assured."

He offered Jill a cigarette but she declined.

" Too early in the morning," she said with a smile.

" Well, back to business," Mr. Outram went on. " I want to cover this as quickly as possible. Kim Baxter and the Shire Secretary are coming in at eleven o'clock." He glanced at his watch. Then he looked up at the girl, taking her in carefully, but unobtrusively.

" You are a client of ours, Miss Dawson, so I was concerned on your behalf yesterday when the headmaster of the school mentioned, when the gym hall went up, that he was afraid you would be out of a job. Meantime I happen to know there is a very good job offering here in Darjalup district. I took the opportunity of mentioning you to Mr. Baxter. He's the man with the job."

" I'm very grateful to you, Mr. Outram," Jill said. " I *am* looking for a job." A slow flush mounted her cheek. She looked at the bank manager with some embarrassment. " You would know the state of my bank balance," she added shyly.

He smiled at her reassuringly.

" We all have to start off," he said. " I started with sixpence in the school bank. It's our business to treasure you as a client and help you to build a big account—to our mutual benefit."

Jill laughed. He made it all sound so easy.

" So, if there's a good job going, you'll take it ? Good."

" Could you tell me exactly what the work is ? " Jill asked. " Shane Evans speaks of an off-sider and I'm afraid I don't know what that means. My parents and I have been in Australia seven years only, so we don't know all the *expressions* . . ."

" In straight dictionary sense it means a help to the boss. We usually use it in terms of the help-man in a stock muster, or when two mates are working together on a job, and one is the leader and the other is his off-sider. Possibly helpmate as a word would explain it better."

" I see," said Jill. She didn't really see. How could she help a man run a property ?

Mr. Outram saw the doubt in her eyes.

" In plain facts a busy man's wife and his secretary are his off-siders. One looks after his domestic life and the other his correspondence. In this case Kim Baxter has neither wife nor secretary and he wants someone more than a caretaker of correspondence. I think I'll have to leave you to find out for yourself. I doubt if Kim Baxter will explain it in straight terms, at the moment. I've got to tell you, however, he's desperate for the help but quite allergic to the idea of it coming from a young lady. He would have got a man—if a man had been available."

Mr. Outram smiled at Jill encouragingly. " I dare say you will be able to help him to appreciate you as much as he *needs* you. By the way, having lived in England is a great advantage. We expect most of these international visitors coming down here to be British. You couldn't possibly learn to type? The two-fingered job will do."

" I can type," Jill said. " I learned shorthand and typing before I went into the college."

" Good heavens ! " Mr. Outram said. " The man's got himself a gold mine."

There was the sound of men's voices in the outer office and as Mr. Outram stood up he leaned, slightly conspiratorially, towards Jill.

" Don't mention the word ' secretary '," he said. " It makes an outdoor man like Kim Baxter change colour. ' Off-sider ' is the word. Right ? "

There was a knock at the door and the young man who had shown Jill into the office appeared.

" Mr. Baxter and Mr. Evans, sir," he said. " You asked me to bring them straight in . . ."

" Right, Ralph." Mr. Outram was half-way across the office and he now lifted a hand in greeting.

" 'day Kim. 'day Shane. Come right in and sit down. I have the young lady here. Miss Dawson, I think you've met Mr. Baxter and Mr. Evans ? "

Jill turned her head and smiled politely. Her back was straight and she was trying desperately to live down yesterday's sherry impression. When she met Kim Baxter's eyes her own faltered. He was looking at her, his eyes inquiring, but still hostile.

Perhaps it wasn't the sherry, Jill thought, remembering the bank manager's advice. *Perhaps he just doesn't like the idea of having a female off-sider. But pressure of work has forced one on him. If I try . . . if I'm good at it . . .*

She wondered how he had known her hair was fair and that she looked the " out-door " type of girl. How he had been able to describe her to Shane Evans ?

They all sat down and the manager passed an opened box of cigarettes to Shane and Kim Baxter. They talked about the bushfire while they were busy lighting up.

Jill looked at Kim Baxter's hands rather than at his face. They were quick lithe hands with strong fingers; the hands of a strong man. Having acknowledged her with a polite but frosty nod of the head he did not look at her again.

" Well," Mr. Outram said peaceably. " Miss Dawson is anxious to accept your job, Kim. Do you think a three-months' trial might be a happy arrangement ? "

Kim Baxter's eyes flicked up quickly.

" I think that's a very good idea," he said.

Shane Evans smiled at Jill encouragingly as much as to say . . . " After three months he will want to stick to you for ever."

" If it doesn't work out," Shane said aloud. " I can give Miss Dawson a job in the Shire office. We can't get stenographers and last night she told me she has done a typing course . . ."

Kim Baxter looked quickly at Jill.

" Is that so ? " he said. " Could you handle correspondence, do you think ? "

Jill didn't know, she had done a course but never taken a job, but she wasn't going to show her diffidence to everyone in the office.

" Yes," she said. " That wouldn't be any trouble." Then because, after all, she had her own pride to think about, she added: " Three months would be a very suitable time, Mr. Baxter. By then they will have made some arrangements about the school and I may be able to go back to my post."

Jill expected him to show some slight reaction to her spirit of independence even if only by silence. Instead he said:

" Quite. A very good arrangement." He then looked past Jill to Shane Evans.

" Did you explain it would be necessary for Miss Dawson to live out at the homestead ? My mother would also be glad of her services."

It was Jill's turn to be taken aback.

Live out on the homestead ? In somebody else's house ? She had never been on a farm, let alone one of these large Australian properties. Ordinarily the idea would have thrilled her but now . . . well, this was different ! How did one get on with the boss, if one lived in the same house with him ?

Evidently this arrangement was not odd to anyone else in the office. In fact they had taken it for granted and assumed that Jill herself would have taken it for granted. Had she expected Kim Baxter to have an office in town ? Their manner seemed to ask this when they read the surprise on her face. Kim Baxter was a grazier and property man ; not a business man. What he was doing now was a community job in the interests of the district and strictly because he was the district's leading pastoralist.

All this was clear in their manner as both Shane Evans and the bank manager turned to her.

" You won't have much trouble packing up after only one night in the hotel, Miss Dawson," the manager said kindly.

" Thank you," was all Jill managed to say, a little bleakly.

Kim Baxter stood up and walked abruptly to the door.

" Well, that's that," he said. " Thank you for being of

assistance to me, Miss Dawson." He held the door open and looked at Shane Evans. " Could you get someone— from the agency preferably—to take Miss Dawson out this afternoon? I'll give my mother a ring and let her know to expect her. Meantime, I've an appointment."

The door was wide open and the outer office could hear this last remark as well as those in the inner sanctum. It wasn't a very big bank.

Vanessa Althrop's voice came laughing but clear through the doorway.

" I'll say you have an appointment," she said. " Coffee at eleven-fifteen. And it's eleven-sixteen. Kim, you used to be a stickler for punctuality."

Jill noticed Kim's face relax imperceptibly. There was even a hint of a smile.

" I apologise, Vanessa," he said. " I'll be with you immediately." He turned as if to take leave of the bank manager but meantime the latter had risen and gone round to the door. He now went into the outer office with Kim. Jill imagined him shaking hands with Vanessa and she could certainly hear him speaking to her.

" Why, Vanessa ! It's great to see you back again. I heard last night that you were in town. So you're taking the great man off for coffee, are you? Well, don't keep him to yourself all day. We've a citizens' meeting at two o'clock and I expect he wants to do something about his own property some of the time this week." His voice was jolly—that of the bank man talking to important clients.

Shane Evans stood up and held out his hand to Jill. " This is where you and I slide out of the side door," he said. Then added jokingly: " The forgotten ones." Taking Jill with him he opened a side door leading out to a gravel square at the side of the bank.

" Everyone else is forgotten when Vanessa Althrop's about," he said. " Good job it didn't occur to us to take the bank swag with us. Would have been easy, wouldn't it ? "

Jill laughed.

" There wasn't even a safe in that room, and only a box of cigarettes on the manager's table. He doesn't run any risks."

" Not with fair strangers like you around anyway. Let's go and have coffee ourselves."

It was three o'clock in the afternoon when a car from the agency, with a driver, called at the hotel for Jill.

She had had a lovely morning. After coffee with Shane Evans, he had driven her round the town and two miles out to the first of the sawmills. It was all new and exciting to Jill, enough to banish the feeling of anxiety she had about her new job and about living in Kim Baxter's homestead . . . under his eyes, as it were, day and night.

Nevertheless she couldn't quite banish him, as a man, from her thoughts. There was something about his personality, his air of strong-minded preoccupation while the bank manager had been speaking to him; and for one instant a look of *tiredness* quickly conquered.

He probably did have too much to do and did need an off-sider. Already Jill loved that word. She meant to be a good off-sider and prove to Mr. Baxter that a mere girl, if efficient, could be a very real help indeed. For Jill there was a real challenge in his attitude—and in the man too.

The agency driver was a slim, wiry man, not very communicative, but he did tell Jill one or two things that helped her as they drove along a narrow gravel road through the tall trees of the jarrah forest.

" The agency," he explained in answer to her tentative question about it, " is the pastoral company that handles the Baxters' affairs. We don't mind doing a small service for him like this. He's our biggest client."

"It wouldn't be so easy for three-pounds-ten-shillings clients, I suppose," said Jill, her eyes bright with a touch of mischief.

"Who knows?" he said. "Give 'em time and they might turn out to be a three-hundred-thousand-pound client."

"Goodness, is that what Mr. Baxter is?"

"Thereabouts. And then some."

Jill sat silent and watched the afternoon light shafting through the tall trees. How beautiful they were, she thought. They stood so straight and silent, like sentinels. Sentinels over what?

"Those trees seem to be so aloof, so old . . ." Jill said.

"Those big fellers . . ." the driver said, meaning the trees, "would be five hundred years old. But wait till you get into the karri forest, 'bout thirty miles west of Darjalup. You'll see age, and height too. Two hundred and sixty feet, some of them."

Jill looked around and took in a deep breath. She hoped she liked her job out at Bal-Annie. She had already learned Bal-Annie was the name of Kim Baxter's property and thought it was a very pretty name. When she'd been there long enough she would ask what it meant.

They swerved to pass a small dead kangaroo lying in the road.

"What was that?" Jill asked, she was filled with a burning curiosity about everything around.

"A wallaby, kinda small grey kangaroo. Got itself caught in the headlights of someone's car last night. They often get bumped off along the roads."

"Poor things!" Jill said sadly. The driver made a sound that was more a snort than a laugh.

"Damn' nuisances!" he said. "They eat out the pastures. All right in picture books with a joey in their

pouches . . . but out in the country they mean starvation
to the stock if you don't keep them under control."

After that Jill remained silent until they drove over a
railed stock-pit between two fences. This was the entrance
to Bal-Annie. She had read the name, painted in white
letters on the mail post. A young boy, in the paddock
adjacent to the drive which led away into the distance
towards the homestead, went past on a bay gelding. Jill,
in love with horses from the time Mr. Jukes had set up
his riding school near her home, turned her head to
watch the boy. He rode daringly but well, as most young
boys do. This she knew from her experience helping Mr.
Jukes.

"That's young Don Baxter," the driver said dryly.

"Don Baxter ! " Jill looked at the driver inquiringly.

"Yep. Kim Baxter's half-brother. Fancies himself
dandy with the horses. When it's blood stock. That gives
Kim quite a headache."

"Half-brother ! " Jill said to herself, half aloud.

"That's it," said the driver. " Old Mr. Baxter married
twice. Mrs. Baxter up at the homestead is his second wife.
And quite a one is she. Runs the town on the ladies'
side. President of the Country Women, President of the
Red Cross . . . something in the golf club. Mind you,
I'm not saying anything against her. She's really got
something. Keeps the town ticking over doing good.
Nice lady."

"Oh . . ." said Jill. She shouldn't appear to be too
curious about her future employer. Her *employers* in fact.
She'd been given a fortnight's salary in advance, and it
was the same as it would have been if the school hadn't
burnt down. Mr. Outram's doing, Jill had thought, mind-
ful of his comment that a three-pounds-ten-shillings
account could grow, to everybody's mutual advantage. The money had been paid into her account

and Mr. Outram had rung her at the hotel to tell her. " *We* are already affluent," he had said jokingly.

The driver sensed her unasked questions about Mrs. Baxter.

" She's not Kim Baxter's mother, only young Don's," he said.

There were no trees now except in the distant vistas. On either side of the drive were wide sprawling paddocks, dusty yellow after the summer's heat. Above, the sky was pure crystal blue, a lovely pale colour adding immensity to a land of infinities.

They drove two miles between these paddocks under that sky and came again to a belt of trees. Through the trees lay the lovely homestead . . . a wide sprawling building surrounded by gardens and lawns that took Jill's breath away. In the near paddock, smaller and with green grass instead of tired yellow stalks, was a bunch of horses, heads high, ears pointed, watching the arrival of the car.

The driver swung the car round and came to a stop below a flight of five stone steps. Above the steps was a veranda. Set, like a recess in the front wall of the stone house, was a double wooden door with stained glass ornamentation.

It was a beautiful home, gracious, big and old. Jill wondered why it surprised her. She had thought everything about this country was new. To-day the forest and now this homestead had told her she was wrong.

The driver got out and went round to the back of the car to take the cases from the boot. Jill opened her door for herself and eased herself out of the car so as not to show too much leg. Somebody might be waiting for her . . . up there on the dark cool veranda and this business of getting in and out of cars, even sitting in them, was the one grievous disadvantage of straight skirts and long legs.

She had just put her foot on the veranda when that massive door with the stained glass windows opened. Standing behind the wire screen was a tall slim woman, neatly and well dressed in a blue linen suit. Her hair was greying but well styled. Her face, slightly made up, was firm-textured and her expression was courteous though business-like. She was exactly the sort of person Jill could see standing in the chairman's place at the head of community affairs.

The lady pushed open the wire door with one very bejewelled hand and smiled pleasantly.

" Come in, my dear. You must be Jill Dawson. Kim rang me about you. I've told Tuffy to get the tea." She looked over Jill's head to the driver who now brought the cases up on to the veranda.

" Thank you very much," she said. " Just leave them there, please. If you would like a cup of tea it's already set on the side veranda. Tuffy will look after you."

She spoke in staccato sentences, managing everything deftly, kindly, but as a busy woman disposing of trifles.

Jill, holding her hat in her hand, watched her with fascination.

She imagined Mrs. Baxter disposing of the world with that jewelled hand and those incisive, conclusive short sentences of hers.

She now turned to Jill and motioned her to come inside.

"You would like a brush and wash-up, I expect? Oh, here's Tuffy. Tuffy, please take Miss Dawson to her room, like a dear. When she's ready you might bring her to the front room. We'll have tea there."

They hadn't shaken hands and Jill hadn't opened her mouth. Mutely, somewhat in the manner of a sixth form girl, she followed an elderly, comfortably bosomed woman, dressed in the kind of grey alpaca her own great grandmother must have worn, through the wide cool hall with its stone tiles, down a carpeted side passage, past several doors into which Jill did not dare glimpse, to a nice square room opening with french windows on to the front veranda at the corner of the house.

" There you are, my dear," this " Tuffy " said, standing back and glancing round the room. Her face, round and smooth, was kindly. " Everything comfortable for you. There's a bathroom next door."

She smiled at Jill and suddenly Jill knew just how strange and even homesick she had felt since she left home early yesterday morning. She had the absurd feeling she would like this elderly comfortable woman to put her arms around her. Tuffy was the *comforting* kind.

The other must have sensed this for she went over to the bed and patted a wrinkle out of the coverlet. She came back to the door and put her small hand on Jill's arm.

"A lovely bed, dear," she said. " You'll get many a good night's sleep in that."

" It really looks like a guest room . . ." Jill said uncertainly. The furniture was old colonial cedar and it glowed in the light pouring in through the veranda creepers and the french door.

" So it is," the other replied proudly. " We don't have any servants in this house. All the rooms are guest rooms."

" What do I call you, please ? " said Jill, wishing she could say something simple to show how grateful she felt for this woman's little gestures of kindness.

" Tuffy. Everyone calls me Tuffy. I look after the house. Now you have your wash and brush up and I'll go and make the tea."

She turned to go.

" Oh . . ." she said as if it was a matter of world concern. " Have you got your make-up things in your carry-all, or would you like me to bring down your cases?"

" I've everything here," Jill said quickly, repentantly.

She should have brought her cases down herself. Tuffy
. . . whoever or whatever she was . . . had said there were
no servants in this house.

"Then we'll look after the cases later," Tuffy said
firmly. "Now run along dear . . . and make up your face.
Kim will be in any moment now and we do have to start
on the right foot with him, don't wo ? "

This joint-effort " we " both amused and perplexed
Jill. She shook her head slightly as Tuffy went out and
shut the door noiselessly behind her.

So this was Kim Baxter's home and these were Kim
Baxter's people ! Mrs. Baxter, young Don on the bay
gelding, and now Tuffy.

What next ? Jill wondered.

The only thing that really disturbed her was that
Tuffy had said Kim would be in—any minute now. Jill
had the most ambivalent feelings towards her new employer. She dreaded his coming in, yet she longed to see
him again. What was he really like ? What would he
be like to work for ?

She walked over to the mantelpiece and looked at a
group of family photographs hanging in a row of small
carved wooden frames. There in the centre one was a
group of tennis players grouped against a net on a court.
In the background the trees were tall, dark and sombre
but the two figures in the centre of that group were
smiling. They were Kim Baxter and Vanessa Althrop,
looking much younger, with linked arms, their tennis
rackets on their shoulders ; and they were smiling at
each other.

It was a very old photograph, Jill thought.

CHAPTER THREE

When, a little later, Jill went through the passage then the hall, to the front room, she felt happier about her appearance. Mrs. Baxter had had on a linen suit, so the simple linen dress she herself wore was the right thing. What a relief that was !

As Jill came into the room Mrs. Baxter, sitting behind a tea-tray laden with gleaming silver, waved her into a small straight-backed chair. Like Jill's bedroom this was an old room but beautiful with hand-made colonial furniture, perhaps a hundred years old and made by the original pioneering family. Framed photographs stood on the mantelshelf ; odd chairs stood here and there and, not out of place, stood some more comfortable wide-armed chairs, covered with chintz. They were just a little shabby with age.

The nicest thing about the room was the wide view from the french windows over the gardens.

" Let's get down to tin-tacks straight away," Mrs. Baxter said, having given Jill only the briefest inspection. She lifted the tea-pot and began pouring. " You're here to help Kim out," she went on at once. " What are your duties ? Heaven only knows ! You could begin by answering the telephone. That's the worst enemy in the house." She looked up as she passed Jill her cup of tea and followed it with a pretty little silver basket that held both the milk jug and the sugar bowl. " I think you'll find out what to do as the days go by. The thing is to *help* . . ." She paused and really appraised Jill.

" You look an intelligent girl," she said with a quick smile.

" Thank you," Jill said, returning the smile eagerly.

There was hope, and a quick anticipation of liking Mrs. Baxter, in that smile.

Mrs. Baxter had poured her own tea and now took the proffered milk and sugar.

" I'm frantically busy myself," she said. " You could perhaps open and sort my correspondence for me in the mornings. I'm president, or chairman, of several organisations and on a host of other committees."

She sipped her tea, preoccupied with the thought of her many duties. Jill felt a touch of anxiety. How did one serve two masters ?

It was the Bible, surely, that had implied that that way lay disaster. A heart divided ! Who was to be her boss ? Kim Baxter or Mrs. Baxter ?

" You know, of course, we're expecting thousands of visitors down here in November ? " Mrs. Baxter's questions were as imperative and staccato as her statements.

Jill nodded.

" I understand it is something to do with the International Sports Contest."

" Yes. It's not the sportsmen who come here, of course ! Or not many of them. They're interested in other things. It's the tourists who follow in their train. Journalists— and people who write-up a state . . . sometimes adversely. Anyhow, it is a very sound opportunity to improve our roads and amenities. Not to mention putting signposts all over the country. Something we have ignored, to our confusion, in the past. Quite an excuse to bring us up to scratch. You see that ? "

Jill felt a little breathless, not from tea-drinking but from trying to keep pace with Mrs. Baxter's ideas.

She nodded.

" Yes," she said, hoping she was telling the truth. " I do see." What she was afraid of seeing was that she would turn out to be Mrs. Baxter's off-sider. Not Kim Baxter's.

In this slightly disorientated state Jill heard the sound of a big car drive up. Mrs. Baxter lifted her head.

" That's Kim now," she said. " I hope Tuffy kept some of the scones hot. Poor darling, he's been bushfire fighting for two days ; and struggling with small politicians in Darjalup on other matters."

She stood up, the picture of a woman in entire control of herself who had important things to do. Yet in spite of this appearance there was a hint of appeal in her very anxiety to appear publicly poised. Jill could sense it.

Mrs. Baxter walked quickly across the carpet to the doorway leading into the hall. In a way Jill admired her. Mrs. Baxter didn't look so much like a country woman as like a polished woman of the town. She was tall, slim and young looking for her age, and her linen suit was beautifully cut.

Jill's thoughts were shattered apart by Mrs. Baxter's next words. She had gone right into the hall towards the front door.

" Why, Vanessa ! Dearest girl, where did you come from ? Come in at once. How clever of Kim to have thought of bringing you out."

"Another ' guest room ' for Tuffy to pat down coverlets," Jill thought with dismay. Mrs. Baxter and Kim were going to be headaches enough. But Vanessa too !

So far, in their short acquaintance Vanessa had ignored her. With wild hope Jill prayed that Vanessa was not going to stay. Perhaps people in this part of the world took thirty mile trips out into the bush and thirty mile trips back, just for afternoon tea.

Mrs. Baxter came back into the room with Vanessa.

" You must have some tea first. If you leave it another minute you won't want Tuffy's lovely dinner. Don't worry about your case. Kim will see to it."

A case ? Vanessa was going to stay ! Kim had not yet come in.

"Oh dear," thought Jill, trying not to stare at the other's lovely cherry and white striped dress and big droopy hat. Vanessa looked straight out of Ricci, and was a lovely sight. Who would ever dream this house was thirty miles from the nearest small country town and two hundred miles from the nearest city!

"You have met Miss Dawson, of course," Mrs. Baxter was saying. "You must have come down on the same bus. Vanessa, tell me, they say those big land-train buses are as comfortable as real trains. Now what was your experience?"

"Boring but comfortable," Vanessa said in that clear voice of hers. She nodded to Jill and did not wait to have the greeting, or a better one, returned. She sat down in the chair indicated by Mrs. Baxter and crossed her knees. She had beautiful slim legs. Her stockings were pure, fine silk, Jill noticed; not nylon. And her shoes were dreams.

"Here's your tea, dear. You do take milk and not sugar. You see, I remember. Go on, Vanessa, what were we talking about? Oh yes, the buses. And of course Kim met you . . ."

"Kim did not meet me," Vanessa said with a laugh. "I didn't tell him I was coming. I wanted to surprise you all."

Jill began to feel she had no place here and would like to tip-toe away but she didn't know how to do it without a valid excuse.

She passed Vanessa the silver dish with the scones, and at that moment Kim came in.

He stood a moment in the doorway looking at the scene—three ladies sitting in the light of the french window, drinking tea. At least two of them were in the kind of conversation-piece that excluded, temporarily, the rest of the world.

Jill saw that sudden tired look cross his face. He shook

it off and came across the room and drew up a chair.

" Tea, Kim dear ? " Mrs. Baxter said. " But, of course. Tuffy will have heard you come in and bring you some more—*hot.*"

" Thank you, I should like some very much." Kim smiled. He turned to Vanessa. " Have you got everything you want, Vanessa ? " again he looked at her, waiting for her answer, as if it mattered very much.

Vanessa put out her hand and touched him. Only a person who knew another very well could do that, that way. She looked at Kim with lively amusement.

" Don't interrupt, old thing," she said. " I'm hearing about all the ding-dongs in Darjalup."

Kim turned his head a fraction and glanced at Jill. The antagonism his eyes had held for her earlier in the day had gone, but there was no friendliness.

He needs an off-sider but he doesn't think I can do it, Jill thought.

He would rather have had a *man,* or less to do and so nobody at all. Vanessa and Mrs. Baxter had returned to their absorbing preoccupation with what had been going on in the district during the last twelve months. Jill smiled at Kim and spoke first.

" I hope you will tell me about some of the things I can take off your hands, Mr. Baxter," she said. Then unexpectedly she felt confused at making the opening gambit.

At that moment the young boy she had seen riding in the paddock beside the main drive appeared in the open french window. He was very dusty.

" There's one of my troubles," said Kim, looking up and taking in young Don Baxter. " He's on holiday and he's got two of his fellow ragamuffins down from school staying with him. No one can keep them out of my stud-paddock when I'm away from the place."

He looked at Jill quickly.

" Can you deal with boys ? " He was sceptical, prepared for little co-operation.

" Yes," Jill said simply.

His eyes came to life and he appraised her with the first glimmerings of interest

" You can ? You don't know what that particular bunch of boys is like."

" I know boys, and I know horses," Jill said. " Will you leave them to me ? "

A sardonic smile eased the corners of his mouth.

" The best I can do is let you try," he said. Jill felt he was challenging her. She lifted her chin.

" Then there is correspondence that comes in in bushels," he said. " The yes-or-no stuff that clutters me up for weeks. Not the important mail, of course. Outram told me you could type ? "

" Yes, I can type," Jill said. " Have you an office, Mr. Baxter ? I haven't been here long enough to see the house. If you have an office, perhaps I could come straight away—after you've had your tea—and go through the correspondence with you."

Don Baxter had merely looked in at the french window and scampered away. From the veranda came the thump and laughter of boys struggling together.

" That can be your first assignment," Kim said, nodding his head towards the veranda. " How about trying your hand on St. Trinian's straight away ? "

Yes, the challenge was there. He didn't quite believe her.

Tuffy came in at that minute with fresh tea and another silver dish of scones. Jill made Tuffy's entrance the excuse to stand up. Kim unwound his long legs and stood up with her.

" If you'll excuse me, Mrs. Baxter," Jill said, feeling impelled to interrupt that other conversation which was mostly a monologue in earnest tones from Mrs. Baxter.

" May I go out with Tuffy now ? Between us we could give those boys a hefty afternoon tea. That is, if you approve. It's what boys mostly want at this hour of the day."

" Oh, by all means, Miss Dawson. We've only two more weeks of them, thank goodness. Their school goes back later than the government schools. Yes, feed them please. Tuffy dear, will you help Miss Dawson ? "

Vanessa was looking searchingly at one of her own long, silk-clad legs as if suspecting a ladder. She was not only totally disinterested in Jill as a person : she was going to demonstrate the fact.

It did not hurt Jill's feelings. Instead she gave Kim a fleeting smile, did not wait to see if there was an answering one and followed Tuffy out of the door.

The house was full of people, big and little. She saw it at once. It could possibly be bordering on confusion if Mrs. Baxter was as preoccupied with her duties in the town as she sounded. Jill's heart lifted. She saw now what it meant to be an off-sider, even in one or two small affairs. The yes-no correspondence; the boys who got into the horse paddock where the stud stock was grazing; the telephone. Well, here was something with which to begin.

Afternoon tea on the back veranda, with the boys, was an uproarious affair but Jill enjoyed it.

" Don, Dick and Harry ! " she said, teasing them. " In my day at school we used to talk of *Tom*, Dick and Harry. They were names for just anybody. Noisy bodies, or untidy bodies—not boys like you who can ride——"

She smiled at the three boys quaffing down orange juice and huge slices of cake at top speed.

" Good job my name's ' Don '," said Don Baxter. He had said he was twelve years old but his eyes were wickedly wiser than those years. He was beginning to come down favourably on Jill's side but he still had his reservations.

The way she had downed that orange drink and those huge slices of cake ! That made her one of them.

" It's a good job your name's got Baxter added, too," Jill said through her last piece of cake. If it choked her she would eat the lot.

" Baxter ? " the other two boys hooted. " What's that got to do with anything ? "

Jill, her cheeks bulging with cake, looked at them with raised eyebrows.

" Horses ! " she said. " Beautiful horses. The best cared for horses in the state. Why, international visitors from all over the world are coming to see *Baxter* horses."

" That's what Kim says ! " said Don, his dark eyes sceptical.

" I'll bet you a bet," said Jill. " If you and I take on some horses and groom them and groom them, then pace them and pace them, you and I'll have a better horse show than anyone else in this district. After that we can find out how the world looks at them." She looked at the expression lurking in Don's eyes. Was it a good idea ? She held her breath on the last of the cake and nearly choked on a crumb. This was how Mr. Jukes handled boys in the riding-school who treated good horses carelessly.

The other two boys, disinterested in this talk, were scuffling together on the edge of the veranda. Suddenly they fell off. They weren't hurt and Jill could hear them picking themselves up; each accusing the other of " pushing."

" We could do with some staff," Jill said, still looking at Don, keeping her eyes young, like his; mischievous, like his. " Do you think you can handle that pair ? " She nodded her head in the direction of the gravel path where Harry and Dick were still arguing. " They'd take some handling and you'd have to be *expert*—but . . ."

Her smile deepened. " It's worth it. Just what we could do at that horse show ! You and I ! Has your brother some horses to spare ? "

Kim Baxter's looks of scepticism no longer bothered her. Neither did her teacher training impose itself. Suddenly she was a young girl again, one who loved animals and now perhaps . . . yes, now with Don's help . . .

" He's got a bunch of brumbies no good to anyone yet, out to grass in the forest paddock," Don said.

Jill jumped up, scattering cake crumbs from her skirt on to the veranda. Tuffy had been watching the little scene from the shadows of the kitchen and Jill knew she wouldn't mind that little spate of extra mess.

" Come on ! " Jill said, challenging Don. " I want to see the best ones, first. Come and show me."

" Not in that rig-out," Don said looking her up and down unabashed. " You've got to have trousers—slacks, or whatever you call them."

" Wait for me. Don't go without me," said Jill, making for the door into the house. " I'll get them. I won't be one minute, promise you won't go without me——"

Five minutes later, Mrs. Baxter, who had led Vanessa through the french doors on to the veranda and down the five stone steps to look at her treasured garden, suddenly looked up in amazement.

Kim Baxter, hands in pockets, had followed his mother and Vanessa into the rose-garden. He was tired, but looking at the flowers pleased his stepmother. It also pleased her to think that on occasion she could say: " Come ! " to him, and he came. This was one of those occasions. He came because he was tired, because it would please his mother and because Vanessa had put out her hand, not really waiting for him to take it and had said :

" Come on, darling. We really must look at the rose-garden. Then I'll go and have a bath."

They were in amongst the roses when Mrs. Baxter, looking up, saw the flight of three boys, with Jill following, across the outside lawn towards the horse-paddock.

It wasn't so much the sight of Miss Dawson and the boys that amazed her. It was what Miss Dawson was doing. She was dragging on her slacks, hopping first on one foot then on the other in her effort not to fall too far behind the boys.

The slacks were on, hitched together with one button. Mrs. Baxter put her hand to her mouth.

" Good gracious. What is she doing now ? "

Jill was unbuttoning her linen shirtmaker dress. It was off and thrown to the ground. The thing that looked like a piece of silk she had tied around her neck was whipped off and in a flash it was on in place of the dress. It wasn't a piece of silk but a short-sleeved Tricel blouse that had gone over Jill's head and on, while she was still making for the fence.

" What *is* she doing ? " Mrs. Baxter said again.

" Showing off, I would say," said Vanessa.

Kim stood, hands in pockets, eyes narrowed against the westering sun, and watched the quartette mount the rails of the horse paddocks and stare out across them. Don was pointing out the different horses, talking emphatically. The other two boys were silent, muffled by being short-winded and by Don's superior knowledge of what went on in the yard.

" Do something about them, Kim," Mrs. Baxter said, turning to him, surprised at his stillness. " That is the Eden stock in there."

" Yes," said Kim very quietly. " I know."

He turned away and walked silently, not very fast, through the garden, back to the house.

Mrs. Baxter sighed with relief.

" He's gone to get his stock-whip, I've no doubt," she said. She looked at Vanessa with raised eyebrows.

" That girl ! Do you suppose he was wise to bring her here ? "

" He didn't bring her here," said Vanessa. " He'd never seen her before she walked into the hotel. Shane Evans and that bank manager wished her on him. They imagined he needed some kind of help with all that organising going on. And of course, not a *man* available. As if Kim hasn't enough to do out here at Bal-Annie without taking on the town ! "

" Well," said Mrs. Baxter, a little nettled and stooping to pick one daring weed from the rose-garden. " We do need help. What with my committees, and Kim's committees ! "

" *Help*, oh yes ! " said Vanessa with a laugh. " But not a children's picnic surely."

Mrs. Baxter straightened up. She had her back to the horse paddock, by intention.

" We must go and see what Tuffy is doing about the dinner," she said amicably. " Vanessa darling, you do want a bath, I suppose. Or would you rather wait until you go to bed ? "

" I'll have them both," said Vanessa with a laugh. " One before dinner and one before bed. Dear Mrs. Baxter, I know you don't dress for dinner but may I . . . just for once . . . put on my new Ricci dress. I bought it in Sydney. It positively scintillates, and it's time I knocked Kim off that frozen pillar of his."

Mrs. Baxter smiled as she patted Vanessa's arm.

" If you can't do it, my dear, no one can," she said. She looked at the girl admiringly. " I don't have to say I always hoped it would be you. But would you be satisfied here on Bal-Annie ? "

" Satisfied enough," laughed Vanessa. " I'm tired of Rome, Sydney and Melbourne and I never want to see the Prado again. I think it's time I settled down."

" You'll have quite a job cut out with Kim," Mrs.

Baxter said cheerfully. " He likes his freedom. Oh *Vanessa* ! Look at that new Mrs. Dornford Bell rose in bud. I shall pick it in the morning and take it to poor old Mrs. Sykes, the school caretaker's wife. She's in hospital. She was burnt . . . not very badly, thank goodness . . . trying to save, of all things, her clothes prop in the domestic science block of the school. Why the domestic science staff had to borrow her prop, I can't imagine. Remind me, Vanessa dear, when I get inside to make a note about it ! " She sighed. " If the school can't provide adequate facilities I must see if we can get the Parents and Citizens Association to do something."

" I thought the school was burnt down," Vanessa said as they mounted the steps and crossed the veranda.

" My dear girl, I'm thinking of the *new* school, when it is built. From a great deal of experience in this town's affairs I have learned one must always have vision; plan ahead . . ."

CHAPTER FOUR

KIM BAXTER had gone to his office, a small square room in the side wing of the house. It had a pinewood table in the middle of the room with two bentwood cottage chairs, one behind the table and the other at the side. On one side wall were deep shelves, filled with old files, accounts records, and pile upon pile of his pastoral company's monthly journal. There was an enormous pile of letters, opened and unopened, on the table. They were witness he had been away from the homestead fighting bushfires, instead of attending to his own affairs.

He stood behind the table and leafed through the un-opened letters, dropping some on to the table immediately before him and throwing others into a wire basket at the side. His hands moved quickly, his fingers flicking.

When he had finished this sorting he sat down and began to slit open the letters before him. When he had read the letters he placed them in a neat pile on the far side of the table from the wire basket containing the un-opened sheaf. The fingers of one hand beat a tattoo on the table as with eyes half-closed he stared out of the window thoughtfully.

He could see his beloved paddocks rolling away to the dark verge of the forest in the distance. It was a still warm late afternoon and already the shadows of that forest were stretching across the distant boundary of the paddocks. He looked a man, wearied from long hours of battling with bushfires to save other people's property, come home to be imprisoned by paper-work. The french window was open—but the paper-work was an invisible chain and cannon ball.

With a sudden movement Kim Baxter stood up. He went across the room and lifted the telephone receiver from the hook of a wall-cabinet.

He listened a minute, then spoke quietly, deliberately, as if he was a man who was never tired.

" Put me through to the stables, Tuffy. Or better still—can you tell me if Miss Dawson has come back with the boys ? . . . She has ? . . . I see. They're all eating again, are they ? Well, fill those boys up till they're immobile, will you, like a dear? And send Miss Dawson along to me. By the way, Tuffy. Is she *dressed* ? . . . What ? I mean Miss Dawson . . . Yes, I suppose slacks will do, as long as she's covered . . . 'Bye, Tuffy ! "

He put up the receiver and walked thoughtfully across the office to the window.

He was standing there, hands in pockets, staring out with eyes half-closed when Jill knocked at the open door.

He turned round slowly. His eyes were inquiring but

still hostile, she thought. Perhaps it was the slacks and the Tricel over-blouse. Tuffy had said she must go at once. Kim Baxter never waited for people to take their own time.

" It's his mind that matters," Tuffy had said, smiling. " Quick as lightning about things, is Kim. He expects everyone to go at his pace."

Already—per medium of the boys—Jill was at home with Tuffy and Tuffy's kitchen.

" Wash your hands at the sink," Tuffy had advised. " Don't wait to go to the bathroom. There's a roller towel behind the door."

" My hair and face ! " Jill thought aghast. "Ah well, not to worry. I'm here to work and not impress ! "

Now she stood inside the office door, very conscious of her ruffled hair, her unpowdered nose, and the slacks and Tricel blouse.

For a full minute Kim inspected her—not the hair, face, or clothes but her eyes as if trying to make up his mind whether this young woman really could help him. Like all landed men he was conservative enough to think that all women—and that included his stepmother—would be better off in the drawing-room and kitchen. That was their province.

He hadn't moved from the window except that now he stood with his back to it.

He nodded his head in the direction of the table.

" Do you really think you could tackle that wire basket of rubbish ? " he asked. " The unopened mail has to be dealt with and some sort of replies made."

" Yes, Mr. Baxter, of course," Jill said quietly.

" Then have a go at it while I go down to the stables," he said abruptly. He went towards the door as Jill moved towards the table.

In these clothes ? she thought. But then, of course,

Tuffy said Kim Baxter expected everyone to go at his pace. He was bathed and dressed himself but probably thought this a secondary matter for others when they had work to do.

Jill reached the table, and going round to the seat behind it drew the wire basket towards her.

" There's paper on the shelf on your right," Kim Baxter said. He paused and then added—" and an old typewriter on the floor in the corner . . ."

His voice was quite pleasant as he said this last and Jill lifted her head to look at him. " I'll be grateful for your help." He nodded at the typewriter. " If that thing goes . . ." he added, sardonically. Then he went through and Jill could hear his footsteps retreating at a firm pace down the passage.

Jill drew in a breath and looked around the room. It wasn't too bad, considering it was an estate office. She had enough imagination to know how little a property man would care for the indoor paper work involved in running a big estate. The room was without decoration, reasonably tidy except for those piles of ante-dated periodicals on the shelves. The typewriter in the corner was covered with an ancient cloth cover.

Jill certainly hoped it worked. She also hoped she could type accurately after three years' absence from the art. There was a door leading into another room ! Perhaps it was a further, more comfortable place adjacent to this work-shop. Presently, she would investigate.

As she sat down and drew the basket of letters towards her she tried not to think of Kim Baxter. He doubted her capacity to be of real assistance, partly because she was a " female " and partly because she wasn't a country girl. She was sure of that. He had known she could type and was " outdoor " but that was a very different thing from knowing anything about a grazing property. Jill had already found that out for herself as young Don and his companions had explained things to her.

Well, she could learn. And *would* learn.

She slit envelopes and placed the opened letters in a neat pile, and equally neatly she disposed of their covers in the waste-paper basket. Then she began to read them. "Dear heaven!" she thought. The things the man was supposed to answer. There were inquiries from prospective visitors to the district! Inquiries from business firms with wares to sell that had nothing to do with farming; insurance companies promoting their subsidiary activities; petitions for charity; petitions for his presence at pastoralists' meetings in Perth . . .

Jill stood up and after placing a pile of writing-paper on the desk went to the corner and lifting the typewriter carried it to the table. She removed the cloth cover and dropped it on to the floor beside her, and sat looking at the typewriter on the table.

The roller and keys were all right, she thought. Even the ribbon was not so badly used.

"Here's to hoping!" she said, inserting some paper and tapping out some letters experimentally.

She smiled happily.

"Hurray! It *goes*! Not well, but adequately."

An hour later Jill's head was still bent and her fingers still busily tapping. The sun had gone down beyond the jarrah forest in the west and the office was darkening. So intent was Jill in getting her typing accurate—not one single mistake or rub-out must be presented for Kim Baxter's inspection—she had not noticed the day dying or that now it was hard for her to see her work.

She only lifted her head when she heard footsteps along the passage and the little light coming through the open door was suddenly darkened. Vanessa was standing there.

Jill's mind had yet to come back out of the world of charities and requests, so for a minute she sat there looking at Vanessa and doing nothing about drawing in her legs which were stretched out in their slacks below the table.

Moreover, she was stunned, not only by Vanessa's appearance in the doorway, but by what she had on.

Poor though the light was, Vanessa's *gown*—it couldn't be called a dress—shimmered. The skirt was flared a little at the hem, in the latest fashion; otherwise it was figure-flattering in the fullest sense of the word and was made of some dark silver material. Her shoes had high heels, and not much more to them, but they were beautiful.

Jill blinked.

Vanessa stood poised in the doorway.

" I thought this was Kim's set of rooms," she said, drawling. " By the way. Where is he ? "

Her eyes took in Jill's long-legged slacks, the little inexpensive Tricel blouse, the dazed expression in her eyes.

She came into the room, switching on the light as she did so. She walked up to the table and looked at the work on Jill's typewriter. Jill closed her eyes. There was nothing either important or private in any of this correspondence but it was Mr. Baxter's. How did she put her hand over the work to shield it from Mr. Baxter's intimate acquaintances ?

She bent over, picked up the typewriter cover from the floor and began to fit it over the machine, leaving the unfinished letter in its place under the roller.

" I didn't know it was so dark," she said quickly. " Time I stopped, I suppose."

" You must be hard of hearing," Vanessa said quietly but pointedly. " I said—where is Kim ? "

" I don't know where Mr. Baxter is," Jill said, speaking with care. With Vanessa standing so near, looking at her, and asking her questions that way, Jill felt as if she was playing with gelignite. " Oh I think he did say something about going to the stables when he went out, but that was quite a while ago."

Vanessa pulled out the bentwood chair at the side of the table and sat down. She crossed her legs, showing again how nice they were and how delicately lovely were her shoes. The silver material of her dress rippled in the light and a blue sheen polished her dark hair. She was perfectly groomed and smelt, oh so faintly, of Dior scent.

" Don't be in such a hurry," Vanessa said lazily. " You'll never make dinner—*in the dining-room*. There's barely a quarter of an hour to go and though they don't generally dress for dinner here I'm sure you don't want to appear in that rig-out."

She looked at Jill with a lazy insolence. Jill made an effort not to return that insolence with what it deserved. She stood behind the typewriter, her hands on the cover and made a valiant attempt to smile naturally at Vanessa.

" I hadn't thought about dinner," she said with truth. " I wasn't watching the time as I worked. Besides . . ." she was determined to relieve the atmosphere with a little joke. " I'm afraid I've left my only ironed dress out on the lawn somewhere. I forgot it . . ."

" Yes, I saw the strip-tease act."

Jill remained calm.

" The boys were running—a long way in front. And I'm well covered underneath," she said.

Vanessa helped herself to one of Kim's cigarettes from the box on the table. She took out a blue and pink mosaic lighter from a silver chain bag, and flicked it alight.

" I didn't think it was for *their* benefit," she said. It didn't occur to Jill there was a double meaning in the words. " For half a minute I thought you'd come here on a holiday," Vanessa went on, glancing again at the slacks, and flat pointed shoes.

" I was anxious to make friends with the boys as soon as possible," Jill said. " They wanted to show me the saddling yard, and the horse paddock."

Then she bit on her words. Why should she explain herself to Vanessa ?

" If you will excuse me I'll go and do something about brushing up." Then she added with a smile, hoping to save peace, which suddenly seemed in danger. "And retrieve my dress from the lawn."

She moved round the table towards the door, hoping that Vanessa would follow.

" The boys brought it in and Tuffy has done things to it," Vanessa said idly, not moving. " I understand it has been pressed and is ready to wear."

" Oh, that was good of Tuffy," Jill said, then added laughing, " As a matter of fact it *is* a ready-to-wear." She had reached the door by this time but still Vanessa was not prepared to let her go. Jill realised that Vanessa might have come to the office looking for Kim but she had something to say; or to question Jill herself about.

" You seem to have an easy knack of attaching people to you," Vanessa said idly. She looked over the top of her cigarette at Jill. " Is this the professional skill of making friends and staying put in a job *long* ? "

" I didn't know I had attached anyone to me," Jill said. " I've only been here a few hours. But thank you for telling me. It was nice of Tuffy to fix my dress. I must go and thank her. Are you coming ? Shall I put out the light ? "

" No. I'm waiting for Kim. Oh, by the way. As his right hand I suppose you've already seen what a convenient set of rooms he has here ? So convenient for privacy. The office, the sitting-room, *his* room—So cut off from the rest of the house! I've no doubt it was your duty to look around."

Jill flushed. She had intended to look around to make herself familiar with where and how she was to work; but she had no idea Kim's own room, presumably his bedroom, was adjacent.

There was some kind of hidden implication in Vanessa's words and Jill was trying to puzzle them out. Or was she mistaken?

Vanessa had seen the flush, and taken it to mean that Jill had indeed been looking around. She stubbed out her cigarette and stood up.

She walked over to the shelves by the wall and started to flick through the top copy of one of the periodicals. "Don't wait for me," she said, not looking up. "As I said. I am waiting for Kim. He's expecting me."

"I will see you later then," Jill said courteously and turning went through the door.

It isn't anything that I've done that makes her dislike me, Jill thought. *She wasn't even average-friendly on the bus, or in the hotel.*

Vanessa dropped her periodical and going to the table lifted the cover from the typewriter. She glanced over the part-written letter. It wasn't interesting and it bored her, but she did not put the cover back. Instead she dropped it into a careless puddle of black cloth on to the floor.

She wandered restlessly round the room and was standing in front of an old large-framed picture of a racehorse when Kim came in.

"Hallo, Vanessa!" he said. "Haven't they found a comfortable chair and a drink for you in the lounge? I'm afraid I'm running late. How glamorous you look!"

He was smiling in a half amused, half serious way, admiring her.

" Heavens, Kim ! " Vanessa said, ignoring these remarks. " You really are tall. There's not much between
you and that door frame when you come in."

" Extremely uncomfortable in cinemas or buses," he
said. " That's why I never go in them."

Vanessa sat down on the chair again. Once again the
dress rippled silver lights and one very nice leg crossed
over the knee of the other.

" Give me a cigarette, darling, and don't tell me you
don't have a private cache of sherry, or something, in
one of those cupboards."

" As a matter of fact I have——" He looked at her with
a slightly quizzical expression. Then went to the cupboard. " It's for the kind of unexpected guest who should
be taken to the lounge and treated like royalty . . . but
who stays fixed," he added.

" Meaning me," said Vanessa. " Don't be tart,
darling. Besides, I like hardback chairs and loathe
horse-hair."

Kim poured a sherry for Vanessa and a whisky for
himself and brought them to the table. He moved round
and sat down in the chair where Jill had been working.
He glanced at the letter on the typewriter.

" Rather careless, don't you think ? " said Vanessa,
seeing what he was doing. " Really ! These working
girls of to-day ! Imagine leaving a letter unfinished, not
to mention the typewriter cover on the floor." She held
her sherry in one hand and leaned sideways and looked
at the letter over Kim's shoulder.

" Can she type ? " she asked, as if barely interested.

" Very well, it appears," Kim said quietly.

" I don't know why Shane didn't hang on to her himself.
They were almost in one another's arms when she got
off the bus," Vanessa said.

Kim moved his chair so as not to be directly in front
of the typewriter, and lifting the cigarette box, offered it

to Vanessa. When he had lit both their cigarettes he smiled at her.

" The Shire can't afford to give him more assistance, I expect. I didn't know they had met before she arrived here."

" Most obvious," said Vanessa.

Kim sipped his whisky and changed the subject of conversation.

" Very nice to see you, Vanessa," he said. " I'd like to ask you all about your travels except that we've got only ten minutes," he smiled at her. " Precious and all though they are ! I haven't very much courage about being late for Tuffy's dinners."

" The way you spoil Tuffy ! " said Vanessa. " You don't know it, Kim, but that woman rules you. She always has."

" She brought me up," Kim said. " Until my father married again, I had no mother for roughly twelve years . . ." he paused, looking into Vanessa's eyes. " Unless Tuffy was my mother . . ." he added, quite seriously.

Vanessa dropped her eyes as she shook ash into the ashtray.

" Dear old Tuffy ! " she said. " Of course, like you, I adore her." She swept up her eyelashes and smiled at Kim. " Who marries you will have to marry Tuffy too, won't she ? Well, why not ? Tuffy is a darling."

" I'm glad you think so. Hurry up with that drink, Vanessa my dear. Or we will spoil that dinner."

" Of course," Vanessa finished the rest of the sherry and stood up. " Darling, I'll leave you to put on your last dash of spit and polish—not that you look as if you need any. You always look marvellous. By the way, what with female help around the place you won't have so much freedom about leaving your doors open, will you ? I suppose that poor girl opened doors in error but she already knows your secret retreat. Hope you didn't leave your last change of clothes scattered about your bedroom."

Kim was standing too, his whisky glass in his hand.

" I never leave my clothes, or anything else lying about," he said with mock seriousness.

Vanessa reached up and pecked him on the cheek.

" Of course you don't, darling," she said. " I was only teasing." She let her hand linger on his hand a minute where it rested on the table, then went out—a shimmer of retreating silver.

Fifteen minutes later Kim walked into the dining-room. The boys, hair polished flat, were seated at the side of the table towards the end of it looking as if they had never eaten before. Vanessa and Mrs. Baxter were standing by the sideboard; Vanessa with another sherry in her hand. Tuffy, who had put a metal cover over the roast, was fussing with the vegetable dishes at the end of the table.

Mrs. Baxter in deference to her " guest's " wish to change into something exotic for dinner had put on an attractive blue silk dress; and wore her pearls. Tuffy, from mature wisdom and an understanding of the vanities of young ladies, had changed into a dark blue dress with pearl buttons running in a line over her ample bosom and straight down to the hem.

Kim, intent and preoccupied when he came in, glanced round the room.

" Where is Miss Dawson ? " he asked, looking down the length of the table to Tuffy. His eyes were inquiring. They meant he was not going to sit down until *all* the household was present.

" She's having a bath and changing her dress," Tuffy said amicably. " She'll be quick, don't worry. She was working late, poor child. I told her you wouldn't have her taking her dinner by herself, Kim . . ."

" Perhaps she'd rather not come in," Vanessa said, turning round and looking at Kim. "After all, she probably wants some privacy from the family. It's rather a pity, don't you think, that she has to live with her job? You shouldn't force her, Kim."

" This is the post she took on," Mrs. Baxter said firmly. " She'll have to take us along with the work." She moved round to her own place on Kim's right. "Vanessa dear, sit over there and then we can talk across the table. Kim wants you next to him, of course."

At that moment Jill came in. She looked at Mrs. Baxter apologetically.

" I'm so sorry," she said. " I wasn't watching the time. Tuffy said I must come in, so I scrambled . . ."

" That's all right," Mrs. Baxter said graciously. " You can't do everything perfectly on your first day. Sit down there on Tuffy's right, will you? Then you can help her with the vegetables."

"And look after us too," said young Don with emphasis.

" That she will," said Tuffy. " Now take your hands off the table, Don, and pay attention to Kim. He might forget to serve you with the largest helping. And don't monopolise Miss Dawson. She doesn't belong to you."

Jill had gone round the table to the place indicated. Kim had been so still, poised in a kind of waiting silence, standing behind that covered dish, she thought she owed him an apology too.

" I'm sorry I'm late," she said as she put her hands on the back of her chair.

He looked at her in that level unsmiling but intent manner of his.

" That is all right, Miss Dawson," he said. " You managed a great deal of work, I see, in a very short time."

Jill's eyes widened as she looked back at him. He had *praised* her. Or had he?

He was no longer looking at her but was taking the cover from the meat dish.

He had. He *had*—in his own way !

As she sat down Tuffy smiled at her.

"You serve the greens and I'll do the potatoes and gravy," she said.

Jill picked up the serving spoons and smiled back at Tuffy.

He had. He *had* !

CHAPTER FIVE

THE NEXT DAY things began to go at Kim's pace.

Breakfast was an all-change affair with everyone going to Tuffy's kitchen when ready. There was a veranda off the kitchen and there, sheltered by vines, now beginning to show yellow and bronze edges to their leaves, was a smaller edition of the dining-room refectory table, covered with a check cloth.

"Cook your own egg and bacon while I get this new bread out of the tins, there's a dear," Tuffy said. "The bacon's all cut on the board and the plates are warming in the oven. Kim had his an hour ago but he'll be back in the homestead about nine o'clock. Have a steak, if you'd rather."

It was seven o'clock so that meant Kim must have his breakfast at six. Jill would have to get up earlier to-morrow !

"When it's not bread-making day," Tuffy went on, "I'll be able to cook your breakfast for you." Her round smooth face was kind, but perspiration stood in beads on her forehead. Bread making was a job and a half. Thirty loaves a day—most of it for the men out-back.

"What about Don . . . and the other two boys ?

Shall I cook for them ? " asked Jill, anxious to help.

" Oh dear no ! They always cook their own. You'd be surprised how well they do it too. Of course I shut the kitchen door at eight o'clock, so if they're not up in time— they go without it. And well they know it; after the first two days of the holidays."

" Mrs. Baxter and Miss Althrop ? " Jill asked tentatively, still thinking she might help Tuffy.

" Mrs. Baxter had hers an hour ago and she's gone to Darjalup. Didn't you hear the car go ? It's the Country Women's street-stall to-day. She's in charge."

" Oh," said Jill contrite. " Perhaps I should have offered . . ."

" Kim'll be wanting to see you. You'll have plenty to do, don't you worry. As for Vanessa. She's on holiday, so she has hers in bed." Tuffy looked at Jill with wise eyes that said—"Vanessa's life is one long holiday but you and I won't say anything about that."

Jill sat on the veranda and ate her breakfast. The morning air was hot and sultry but the green shade cast everywhere by the vines, and the fruit trees a few yards away from the path below the veranda, made everything cool.

She was eating her second piece of toast when she heard the sound of footsteps and men's voices approaching from the garages. One she recognised at once as Kim's voice, the other was familiar, no more. She hurriedly swallowed the last of her toast, picked up her breakfast dishes and dashed into the kitchen. Against one wall was a two-sink wash-up bench with an enormous plate-rack above it.

Each person washed his own things and put them up on the rack to drain.

" It's as simple as that," Tuffy had explained earlier.

The smell of new bread in the kitchen was heavenly but Jill resisted the temptation to nibble. She must get to that office before Kim.

" Tuffy, am I dressed all right ? " she asked. " I don't quite know what to wear for this job."

"Very nice, Jill," Tuffy said. She had dropped the Miss Dawson by washing-up time last night. The boys, helping Jill wipe up and put away, had called her by her Christian name, and that was that.

Jill now wore a neat Terylene pleated skirt and a pretty mixed-blue and green over-blouse.

"You look a real charmer to me," said Tuffy. "And workmanlike too. Don't worry what Kim thinks, Jill. All he wants is *work* and I can see you're the kind to give it to him."

Last night Tuffy had told Jill, over the washing-up, how she had come to Bal-Annie to look after Kim when he was a motherless boy of four—twenty-eight years ago. "And I've never left Bal-Annie," she added. " Not even when old Mr. Baxter married again. But we've all got on well . . ." she had added.

Jill now hurried in the direction of the office. To whom had that other voice belonged, she wondered ? It was young, fresh, and vaguely familiar. One of Kim's men ?

She had just arrived at the office door when Kim came in with Shane Evans. Jill smiled with pleasure, her face suddenly aglow. She was relieved she was ostensibly on duty by the time Kim came in, and delighted to discover the owner of that other familiar voice.

" Oh Shane ! " she said with pleasure. Then she re-membered where her duty lay. Too late to apologise for not saying " Good morning ! " to her boss first. Why did she always do things wrong ? First that sherry, then those slacks—now Shane !

The frigid look in Kim's eye told her she had erred again.

" Good morning, Mr. Baxter," she said soberly.

Shane, who was looking at the typewriter as if some-

thing had rendered him speechless, now looked at Kim
with his eyebrows pointing upwards like a pierrot's.

" Mr. Baxter ? Does she mean you, Kim ? " he asked
with a grin.

Kim moved papers on the table and did not look up.
" Yes," he said shortly.

Jill had to do something about this early morning
atmosphere which looked as if it would choke Shane; or
that Shane would say something disastrous.

" I finished that correspondence before I went to bed,
Mr. Baxter," she said in a quiet voice. " The letters
are here if you will sign those you think can go off. If
you would mark the others how you wish me to alter
them, I'll do them straight away."

Last evening Kim had gone for a walk with Vanessa
along the boundary fence of the home paddock. Later,
when he had come in, he had gone straight to bed.
Jill had finished the work but she had not seen him after
he had walked down the front steps of the house, with
Vanessa taking his arm.

She had thought about the moonlight over the paddocks, and the heavenly smell of smoke still in the distant
trees, but she hadn't looked out of her open french door.

Time enough to see moonlit nights after Miss Vanessa
Althrop had gone home, wherever her home was.

" Thank you very much," Kim said formally. " I saw
you had done it. I'm afraid I will have to leave the
correspondence for the time being. I've some matters I
have to discuss with the Shire Secretary . . ."

" That's me," explained Shane with mock seriousness.

" Quite," said Kim. " We've got to get things on to a
formal footing when these international visitors come,
Shane. It's the only way to run things efficiently." He
smiled at the other man, softening his words. " We might
as well get some practice in early. Meantime . . . how the
devil am I going to get in to take that Junior Farmers'

meeting? The young chaps are in town for the pig market, and of course, they've ideas of their own about November."

" Can't leave them out," said Shane emphatically. " They're the group with the saucy ideas. We'll have to promote some of them, and suppress others."

He was suddenly struck with an idea.

He waved a hand at Jill.

" Why not let Jill—beg pardon, Miss Dawson . . . take your Junior Farmers for you ? After all, they're not much older than the High School students she was going to teach physical jerks." He beamed on Jill.

" How about it ? " he said. " I can take you in when I'm finished here and Mrs. Baxter can bring you back."

He looked at Kim.

" There's an idea on a plate for you, Kim. What's the good of having an off-sider, if she can't off-side for you at a Junior meeting ? "

The expression in Kim's eyes said that though his stepmother might be adept at conducting meetings Jill would be mincemeat in ten minutes amongst the Junior Farmers.

Jill didn't think she could take a meeting of strange young men either, so she had an idea herself.

" I did learn the principles of taking minutes and working to an agenda when I was in college," she said. " It was understood that out in the country we should give some kind of a community service. But I never have conducted a meeting . . . ."

She paused to see if Kim had any reaction to this. He was watching her and listening to her with that same intent look with which he looked at Vanessa, or Tuffy, when they spoke to him. Actually, Jill thought, it was a very nice look. It meant he was really listening. It was a form of courtesy.

"If . . ." she took in a deep breath and looked at Shane. "If Shane—I mean the Shire Secretary—will take me into Darjalup and if he will be the chairman, I will act as secretary." She glanced back at Kim. "You would save a day, Mr. Baxter. Then I could bring home the minutes and you would know everything that had gone on. That is . . . unless . . ."

"What? Me? Chairman of that kid's show?" expostulated Shane.

"Yes," said Kim shortly. "And they are not kids. They're young men—and women. As ratepayers in a few years' time they'll be your bosses, Shane. Time you got to grips with them."

He looked at Jill.

"Thank you for your idea, Miss Dawson. Now if you would give Shane and myself a few minutes, I'll release him as soon as I can."

"Yes, certainly." Jill moved towards the door.

"Oh, by the way," Kim said in a more human voice. "Thank you for those ' duty cards ' for Don and the boys. I've just seen the boys and though they're rather blasé about the cards, at the moment, I can see they mean business. I think that'll keep them out of mischief for the day."

"I'm so glad," said Jill, then a little confused—or was it plain happy—she went out of the room as quickly and noiselessly as she could.

Three-quarters of an hour later Jill was bowling at great speed down the long driveway of Bel-Annie, sitting beside Shane in his big Shire tourer.

"What's this business about ' duty cards ' ? " Shane asked her. "Don't tell me you can make that young bunch of hoodlums work ? "

"They're not hoodlums. They're just young boys with too much animal spirit to let them sit down and be good like little Mister Muffets," Jill said. " I didn't give them *work*. I suggested responsibility. That's quite a different thing. They're each going to have some horses to be responsible for . . . to make them show-worthy . . . and of course they have to begin by making the old disused stables worthy of their future occupants."

" Don't tell me Kim's going to let you and those kids play round with his Eden stock ? "

" Oh no ! " laughed Jill. " These are brumbies to be trained into ordinary farm hacks. At the show we're going to compete in the general class."

Shane threw back his head and laughed.

" You are a one," he said. Then he looked puzzled. " But when did you fix all this up ? You only got to Bal-Annie afternoon tea-time yesterday ? "

" I didn't fix it up. I gave the boys ideas and helped them write out the cards last night after dinner, before I finished Mr. Baxter's typing. The boys arranged it all with Mr. Baxter themselves. I had nothing to do with it."

Shane groaned.

" This Mr. Baxter business has got me worried. Nobody the length or breadth of the whole Darjalup district. calls Kim *that*. Look Jill, you've started something here——"

" But I'm different," said Jill. " I work with him. It's necessary . . ." she paused and then laughed. " It's necessary for him to keep me at arm's length."

Shane laughed too, then he stopped as suddenly as he had begun.

" Come to think of it I don't see why he should hog the whole of your life anyway. I claim my slice."

" That's very nice of you, Shane. I hope you have a slice."

He slewed his eyes round to see if she meant what she said.

They ran over the stock trap, then the boundary fence of Bal-Annie lay behind them. Now the road wound, brown and dry but gloriously shady, between the tall trees of the forest.

"Isn't this lovely," said Jill. "It's like a sort of cathedral of trees, isn't it?"

"Wonderful, except when the fire goes through It. It's still hot enough for fire hazard," said Shane. "Now let's get on with talking about us."

"Yes. I love talking about me," said Jill, smiling. She caught Shane's eye in the rear-vision mirror which he had deliberately fixed so he could see her face. "Shall I begin with my parents?" she asked. "They came out from England as immigrants——"

"I'll learn about your parents when I meet them," said Shane. "What I want to know about you right now is—how big is that slice I'm to have? Slice of your time, I mean?"

"It's you who is the *one*," said Jill. "Why Shane, you've only known me—let me see! Why, it's thirty-eight, no, thirty-nine hours, since I got off that bus."

"Time enough!" said Shane. "Do you know, when I drive down the main street of Darjalup in roughly thirty minutes forty-five seconds time, the boys in the bank, the boys in the pastoral agency and the boys in every other darn office commercial or otherwise—are going to have one long look through their respective windows? If their bosses aren't looking, or are deaf, they're going *each* to give one long wolf whistle. The plain facts of the situation are as follows—I got you first. Now are you going to run out on me?"

"I haven't met anyone in Darjalup but you—yet," said Jill, beginning to have fun at this way of doing things. A nice, and good-looking, young man wanted her company! What girl in the world was there, who didn't want a man to capture a slice of her time?

" Okay ! First in, first claim, you're mine till we quarrel," said Shane. "Agreed ? "

"Agreed," said Jill, nodding her head as she laughed. " Till we quarrel ! "

Their eyes, full of liveliness, met in the rear-vision mirror.

" We'll begin by parading the main street just to let the other fellows know," said Shane. " Then we'll have tea together."

" What about the Junior Farmers' meeting ? You're going to chair that. Remember ? "

" Oh-ho ! I'm going to chair that all right. I'm going to keep any of those future ratepayers from thinking they can have a slice of my secretary's time. From now on, Jill Dawson, you might be *Mr. Baxter's* off-sider, but you're my secretary." He took his hand from the steering wheel and tapped her hand where it lay in her lap.

" In fact—my slice of cake ! "

" Shane," begged Jill. " If you don't take your eyes away from that mirror and fix them on the road in front, we'll hit the forest."

" It can move over," said Shane. " It ought to look and see who's coming."

CHAPTER SIX

JILL HAD a very busy day in Darjalup. She felt so at home, with so much to do, she couldn't believe she was allegedly a stranger in the town. If the young men in the main street took notice of her she was unaware. She was happy in Shane Evans's company. As he parked the car under the pepper trees, outside the Shire Office and led her down the street, nodding here and there to passers-by, then to a shop for tea, she felt she had known him for years. Putting it briefly to herself she said, " We *click* ! "

She saw in passing where several women were very busy preparing their stall by the post office corner, but as Mrs. Baxter was not in sight Jill did not dally.

Time was getting on and that meeting was waiting.

At first Jill felt very nervous as she took her place at the side of the table on the raised platform of the Roads' Board Hall . . . still so named although the district had reached Shire status. But Shane was such a good chairman and on such good terms with all the robust young farmers, not to mention a sprinkling of young farm women, that Jill was soon at ease and pressing hard with her pencil in the notebook Shane had presented to her. She found herself becoming interested in the flood of ideas, some good, some zany, that came from all these ardent young people and she longed to add her modicum. Time enough another day, she thought, when they all knew her better.

The meeting was over by one o'clock and once again Jill was out in the brilliant hot sun walking down the wide street with Shane.

" We'll have lunch—same place as the tea-shop—then

I'll have to hand you over to Mrs. Baxter," Shane said. " To my sorrow, the Shire office calls. Jill ! Did I tell you you made a wonderful secretary ? "

" You haven't read my minutes yet," said Jill.

Shane leaned over the lunch table and beamed on her. " Now they all know," he said.

" Know what ? " asked Jill in surprise. Her thoughts had shamefully drifted for a moment, wondering what Vanessa was doing out there at Bal-Annie.

" What are they supposed to know ? " Jill asked, coming back to the table, the green plastic cloths and Shane's eyes smiling at her. " You mean the Junior Farmers ? "

Shane slapped the palms of his hands down on the table, tilted back his chair and laughed.

" Yes," he said. " The Junior Farmers, and their fathers and mothers in for the pig sale and a day's shopping. Also the normal lads and lasses round the town. They know, Green Eyes, that a very pretty girl has arrived and that Shane Evans—that's me—has got her under his wing."

Jill wrinkled her brow.

" I don't know that I'm very pretty," she said. " I wish I were. But I'm sure nobody in particular noticed me."

Shane shook his head at such innocence.

" Dear girl," he said. " They notice anybody who is new to the town; and there are special reasons why they would notice you. I won't turn your head by telling you why."

" Did they notice I'm your ' slice of cake '," Jill asked, her eyes sparkling.

" Till we quarrel," said Shane with mock seriousness.

" Till we quarrel," Jill imitated him.

" When that awful occasion arises I'll pick my successor out but I won't tell you who in advance. You might begin to get curious about him too far *in advance*," said Shane.

They were laughing together as they left the café. Jill now felt she had known Shane all her life, and somehow she liked the friendly way he took her arm as he escorted her along, under the verandas to the post office corner where the street-stall was being steadily thinned out of supplies.

Station waggons were zooming down the street and now and again big double-decker stock trucks rumbled steadily past.

The men about looked like farmers—brown-faced, powerful shouldered and wearing broad-brimmed dusty hats at odd angles. Their wives looked like farmers' wives, also brown-faced, kindly and anxious to get back, even at this early hour, to the hundred and one things waiting to be done out there on their stations, some of which were many, many miles away along dusty roads.

Mrs. Baxter greeted Jill pleasantly.

" Oh, you've been looking after her, have you, Shane? That's good of you. Now, let me see. Oh yes. You'd better take the far end of the stall. And look, dear, as the farmers are beginning to leave town already we'd better reduce those cakes by a shilling. And you can sell the jam at half price."

She had forgotten she had only known Jill a few hours; and forgotten to introduce her to the other stall-holders, but evidently they knew Mrs. Baxter well and they took that matter into their own hands in the kindliest way.

Jill had a busy hour and when everything was sold she helped the other ladies clear up the stall, find a man to come and fold down the trestle tables and take them back to the Roads' Board Hall where they were housed.

When all was over Mrs. Baxter hustled Jill along the road to the pepper trees by the old railway station to her car.

" I did my shopping instead of having lunch," Mrs. Baxter explained in her quick staccato way. " It's all in the back of the car. Get in the front with me, dear . . . oh, by the way, what is your other name ? I keep forgetting. Not Miss Dawson—the other name ? "

" Jill—please." Mrs. Baxter had forgotten she had already used it.

" Jill. That's right. The boys started calling you that straight away. I hope you didn't mind. Oh, I've just remembered another thing. How did you come to be in town to-day ? "

They were already in the big Buick and Mrs. Baxter was pressing the starter and warming up the engine.

" Shane Evans and I took the Junior Farmers' meeting for Mr. Baxter," Jill explained. " I took the minutes."

" Oh . . . you mean Kim ? Good heavens, I haven't heard anyone say *Mr. Baxter* since my husband died."

The car was being backed out and Mrs. Baxter swung it round, went forward, crossed the old railway line and made at top speed along the long stretch of gravel road through the forest.

She frowned a little as she thought.

" I suppose it's *right* . . ." she said, not quite having made up her mind.

" Oh yes," said Jill quickly. " When one is an off-sider one has to have very formal relations with one's employer."

" Off-sider ? " said Mrs. Baxter, wrinkling her forehead. She took her eyes from the road and looked at Jill. " Whoever thought of that name ? That foolish Shane Evans I expect."

" Well . . ." Jill said thoughtfully. " What am I ? I mean, what do you think I should be called ? "

Mrs. Baxter thought about that too, for quite three minutes.

"Do you know," she said at last, "I haven't the faintest idea."

She turned her head and looked at Jill as if seeing her for the first time.

"Managing the boys about the horses; typing letters, helping Tuffy, and now taking minutes at a town meeting . . ."

"And helping with the stall," Jill added diffidently.

Mrs. Baxter was watching the road again as the car sped along it, raising quite a dust cloud and running through the striped shafts of sunlight pouring down between the high-crowned trees. It was very hot but the cool shade of the trees seemed to make it less so.

"Well really ! When you come to think of it, I suppose that is what you are. If anyone asks them I shall tell them, 'Miss Dawson is my off-sider.' It sounds quite good, don't you think ? "

Again Jill had that faint feeling of anxiety.

Could she serve two masters ? What if activities conflicted ? Well, she would have to cross that bridge when she came to it.

"I hope Vanessa enjoyed the day," Mrs. Baxter said, her mind now switched from Jill to her guest. "Kim was going to take her out with him to the boundaries. I wonder if they took the horses. I can't remember whether Vanessa said she had her riding things or not."

"Vanessa is a very old friend of the family, I suppose," Jill said, trying to sound conversational and not curious.

"Oh yes. The Althrops have got a property down on the Albany line. Mount Sterling. A heavenly place. The best of everything. Of course Vanessa and Kim have been friends for years. Who knows whether it will ever come to anything. I keep on hoping."

" Your son seems quite attached to her," Jill said quietly.

" He *adores* her. She's so colourful, isn't she ? My dear, I really do believe there are useful people in the world other than farmers' wives and do-gooders like me. The decorative ones. We do so need decorative people, don't we ? There is nothing more exciting than someone who is nothing more than a beautiful woman."

" I do think Vanessa is very attractive," Jill said. " But you do so much yourself, Mrs. Baxter. It's not usual to hear someone like you praise someone who doesn't do very much. Or perhaps Vanessa does do things on her own property." She added this last apologetically for fear she had appeared to be criticising the other girl.

" Vanessa does nothing," Mrs. Baxter said shortly. " She'd do Kim a lot of good who does too much. As for me—well, there are reasons why I do what I do. When I know you better I'll tell you all about it. Nothing to do with Kim, of course. He's a dear."

She glanced at the clock on the dashboard.

" Oh dear," she said. " I'll have to step on it. With that house full of people we'll have to get home to Bal-Annie in good time."

Jill had a feeling that Mrs. Baxter needed to be soothed.

" I can manage the boys," she said. " That is, if Mr. Baxter doesn't need me. I'm sure Tuffy can manage the dinner. There are only five adults . . ."

" Five adults ? " said Mrs. Baxter with a touch of irritation. " There'll be about ten. Kim's got half the key townsmen out to-night to go through some of their plans. Better for them to come out than he waste time going into town. *They* don't have to run a property. Nine to five jobs. Quite a different thing."

" Oh dear ! " said Jill, with sudden sympathy both for Mrs. Baxter and for Kim. " Having an international visitation in the future really is a responsibility, isn't it ? "

" Kim didn't want to take the job on, of course. He was pushed into it." Then, rather proudly Mrs. Baxter added : " Of course he is the most important man in the district. I suppose it was his *duty*."

Stern daughter of the voice of God, thought Jill. But she said nothing.

There was quite a silence until after they'd run over the stock trap and were inside the boundaries of Bal-Annie.

" That is why I hope Kim marries Vanessa," Mrs. Baxter said out of a long silence. " He'd have family obligations and be left alone by the town, to run his own property."

" Besides having a decorative wife," Jill added slowly, but with the intent to cheer.

" Too heavenly ! " said Mrs. Baxter. " I really do believe in harems. You know—the kind of women that sit about in gorgeous clothes—doing nothing."

She sighed.

" I always did believe in doing nothing," she said. " Just because I can't."

Suddenly Jill, from having been a little intimidated by Mrs. Baxter, warmed to her. Bal-Annie was Kim's property, not hers, though she was probably still very well-off. Jill had realised that from the correspondence she had seen. Mrs. Baxter's husband, whom she had dearly loved, had died. That was the answer to the pre-occupation with other people's affairs . . . An escape. Her smartness in dress was a last-ditch stand against the dated drabness of dedicated farmers' wives.

There was no sign of Kim or Vanessa when Mrs. Baxter and Jill arrived back at the homestead. The boys were just coming up from the old abandoned stables which they had agreed to take over in their new venture to groom and train some horses of their own.

Jill was scarcely out of the car when they were upon her,

demanding she " Come down at once and see what we've done."

" Go along," Mrs. Baxter said, waving her hand in a general dismissal. " You started this, Jill. You'll have to see it through. At least they'll have kept out of Tuffy's hair for the day. Come up in half an hour for tea."

Jill felt there was no room in this life for tiredness, so she had better forget about being tired. She went eagerly with the boys down to the old stables, a wooden clutch of buildings weathered with time, and sporting a crazy roof as well as a jigsaw puzzle of stockrails around it.

The beaten earth floors had been raked and swept, a pile of old nails and bolts were witness to the cleaning up of the harness posts. On a bench, also recently cleaned, was a set of tools lying by a length of new timber-post.

" We're going to sink new posts to-morrow to bolster up that roof," Don said, pointing to the bench. "After that we're going to use the galvanized iron off the roof of the drying frames. No one dries fruit these days . . ."

" It's wonderful," Jill said, gazing round in admiration. She had no idea young boys, brought up on a property, could do so much with their hands. She looked at the tools dubiously. They were beautiful tools perfectly kept.

"Are they yours, Don ? " she asked. " Shouldn't they be put away ? In case of night dews rusting them, or something ? "

" They're Kim's," said Don. " He won't bother. He's too busy changing the cattle over from the forest paddock to the road paddock. He's got Vanessa with him so he won't be looking at anything but her."

Harry and Dick gave yo-icks of delight at this off-hand attitude to the grown-ups' goings-on with one another.

" You ought to have seen her go out . . ." Harry said. "All dressed up like a magazine."

" An' Kim brought in one of the Eden horses for her," said Dick.

" Shut up, you two," said Don. " I'm busy talking to Jill." Jill knew that this sudden turning on his friends was not so much that Don was busy talking to her as that this was his way of stopping his pals from being derisive about his brother.

" How about putting the tools away for your own sake, Don ? " Jill said. "A labourer is worthy of his instruments. They should be worthy of their master." She smiled at him, asking for wisdom even in youth. " We might as well keep on the right side of him too. Otherwise *I* might get the sack."

" You won't get that," said Don stoutly. " I'll see to that." He turned on Dick and Harry who were at the scuffling stage again. " Go on, you fellers," he said. " We can't get Jill in the blue. Put those darn tools in the case, then come up and get our tea." As the boys, somewhat sheepishly, went about doing as they were told, Don grinned knowingly at Jill.

" That'll keep them out of mischief," he said through the corner of his mouth—very stockman-like !

" What about the horses ? " Jill asked anxiously as she walked up towards the homestead with Don. " Is Kim going to allow you to have some ? "

" You bet," said Don confidently. " We're fixing that up to-morrow. Maybe if you don't go into town again to-morrow you can come with us. We're going to round up some of the young stuff from the forest. Brumbies."

" Oh, I'd love that, Don," said Jill. " You manage it for me . . ." then she hesitated. " I might have some work to do for Mr. Baxter in the homestead."

" Gee . . . you're funny, Jill ! " Don said. " One minute you call him ' Kim ' and the next you call him ' Mr. Baxter.' "

" Do I ? " said Jill suddenly alarmed. " I'll have to watch out, won't I ? "

" Yes. Just call him ' Kim ' like everyone else."

Jill didn't answer that one. Instead she said . . .
" Race you to the back veranda ! I wonder what
Tuffy's got for tea. I'm starving."

In the homestead, a gigantic tea over, Jill offered to
help Tuffy with the preparation of a big buffet dinner.
The refectory table had already been pushed to the end of
the dining-room and was now set about with neat little
groups of knives and forks, silver pepper and salt pots,
and a large bowl of Mrs. Baxter's lovely roses.

" No thank you," Tuffy said firmly. " Everything is as
near ready as it ever will be. No roast dinner to-night.
They get curry and rice and chow-mein. Very favourite
dishes with the people round about here. After that they
have fruit and cheese and biscuits. Tell you the truth,
Jill, those men when they come out from town spend most
of their time talking and drinking Kim's Scotch whisky.
You could give them anything to eat and they'd never
know. As long as it was hot, and *smelled* good."

There was nothing for Jill to do now until Kim came
home and gave her further instructions. She thought the
kindest thing would be to have her bath and change,
thus getting out of everybody else's way early.

This she did, then just before sundown she marshalled
the boys, now washed and polished themselves, on to the
back veranda where she agreed to take them on, one at
a time, at table-tennis.

She had finished her game with Dick and was watching Don and Harry making a welter of sending the ball
flying back and forward, the length of the tennis-table,
when she heard Kim and Vanessa coming up from the
stables.

Ages ago, it had seemed, she had heard the sound of
horses galloping up the rise towards the saddling paddock.
For some reason her mind had been on Kim and Vanessa

ever since she had come home and she kept wishing it was otherwise and trying to pin her mind on other things.

Now she looked out through the vines and saw the man and woman walk together through the back garden, come on to the cement path below the fruit trees and stand there talking a minute. There was something about Kim that held both her attention and admiration. His manner was so thoughtful as he listened to Vanessa, watching her with that intent expression that was so compelling yet attractive. He wore tight-fitting khaki trousers and his hat was slightly aslant on his head. Vanessa looked exactly as the boys had said . . . out of a magazine. She wore beautiful sand-coloured svelte jodhpurs: a chocolate brown silk blouse and a white hat that made a wonderful contrast with her glowing dark hair. She was indeed decorative, as Mrs. Baxter would have said.

Vanessa said something amusing for Kim suddenly smiled, and with that smile Jill's heart went out to him. It was a smile that shone and would have won any woman's heart. No wonder Vanessa put her hand on his arm and smiled too.

A minute later Vanessa had gone on round to the side entrance and Kim came on towards the back veranda. He came up the wooden steps and pushed open the wire door. He let it close quietly behind him. His smile for Jill was reticent, not quite at ease with a female off-sider yet. Once again she had the impression he was thinking about something, in connection with herself, that troubled him.

He looked at the three boys. Dick was leaning against the inside wall chewing a stalk from a bunch of grapes, watching Don and Harry who were playing murder with their long shots at the ball.

" Hallo, men ! " Kim said, with a touch of ironic amusement. " What's the tally of mischief to-day ? "

" Same to you," said Don, not very politely as he

smacked the ball down to Harry. " We've been working. Not riding out with ladies. Say, Kim, what sort of a Galahad do you turn out to be all of a sudden ? "

Kim looked at Jill and one eyebrow went up quizzically. Suddenly she saw that he was very human and that he understood, and was amused by, his young half-brother's banter.

" Did my mother bring the mail out from Darjalup, Miss Dawson ? " he asked, changing the subject and changing the atmosphere back to the more formal.

" Yes, Mr. Baxter," Jill said. " I've put it on your office table. The letters that look like obvious advertisements I put in a separate pile but I'm afraid I left the majority for you to open. Would you like me to go and do something about them now ? "

" No thank you. I've to bath and change. I've a sort of house-meeting on to-night. I suppose they've told you about that. But there is one thing . . ."

He looked doubtful for a moment then continued.

" Perhaps we had better go along to the office for few minutes."

" Yes, of course," Jill said.

The boys were too intent on this mammoth match to be anything but indifferent to the departure of their elders.

Kim stood aside to let Jill precede him down the passage towards his office door, which was past the kitchen, past the sewing-room on the right, to his office at the far end.

Jill went straight to the table and picked up the sheaf of mail.

" When you are free, if you would open these, Mr. Baxter, I could do the yes-no answers."

" We will leave them for a moment," Kim said, following her into the room. He put his hat on the shelves along the side wall, and at that moment the telephone rang. Jill walked to the window so as not to appear to be listening-in to his conversation. Kim picked up the receiver and stood, looking at the top of his hat with the same concentrated intentness with which he had looked at Vanessa.

"Yes, Tuffy, put me through," he said. "Oh yes, Bill ... No, that's all right ... You'd better leave the brumbies for the boys to-morrow. And ..." He looked round at Jill, then back at the phone. "You'd better have Sir Palfry or Gem for Miss Dawson ... Okay, see you in the morning. I'll be down about seven o'clock."

He hung up the receiver and turned back to the table. He stood beside it, a small frown on his forehead.

"You do ride?" he said, looking at Jill.

"Yes," she said.

"You started those boys on that project so you'd better go through with it, if you don't mind. That was my rouseabout and he'll bring in some horses for you to-morrow. The boys can round up the young stuff from the forest and begin their schooling of them." The smile creased his face again. "I'm thankful to keep the boys away from my Eden stock. And ..." he hesitated, then added—"and grateful to you for the help."

Jill's heart lifted. In so short a while—he thought she was useful. He didn't think a *girl* as an off-sider was so hopeless, after all!

"By the way," he said, not waiting for her to answer. "How did the Junior Farmers go?"

"Very well," said Jill quickly. "Shane was wonderful as chairman."

"He would be," said Kim shortly. "He's an able fellow, when he likes." He had a disconcerting way of looking at her thoughtfully too. "You get on quite well with him?"

"Oh yes," Jill said eagerly. "I really think we could do that job—to relieve you, of course. I think Shane enjoyed himself and would be quite willing. Of course . . ." she hesitated and then added: " It's not the same for the young farmers as having you there, but we explained you would see all the minutes. And offer suggestions—perhaps come to the more important meetings."

" Yes. I'll take an odd meeting now and again . . . as often as possible. The young farmers are the most important people of all. They're the coming generation. You seem to have found a soft spot with Shane . . ."

He glanced across the office, out of the window, and then back at Jill.

" I'd be glad if you could help my mother with her correspondence—when you have time."

" Of course," said Jill eagerly. " I'm so glad you mentioned it, Mr. Baxter. I rather wanted to offer."

" I'd be grateful," he said. "And . . ." There was a touch of embarrassment, an unexpected shyness in him now. He moved, and picked up his hat, looked down at it and then looked back at Jill.

" Do you think you could look distraught with over-work to-night?" There was a sudden flicker of a smile in his eyes. " That way the gentlemen from the town won't think they can borrow your services? They'll try, you know."

The flicker had become a real smile.

" I need you myself," he added. " For some of the time—when those boys and my mother deign to spare you."

It was capitulation. He needed her. *He had said it.* Jill smiled and her eyes sparkled lovely green lights.

" I'll work very hard at looking overworked," she said.

Kim had reached the door that led into his inner sanctum. He opened the door wide.

" This is something in the nature of a small sitting-room," he said. " Rather bare and masculine I'm afraid. But you could retreat here if you're too badly pestered by

other people . . . specially when the heat's on in a few
months' time. We're only just beginning organisation
now." He glanced at Jill.

"Nobody in the household dares to open this door,
except Tuffy, of course. She looks after it for me. It
means that once at work in here no one will interrupt
you."

Jill could see into the room. It was larger than the
office, was carpeted and had three big old arm-chairs,
nicely covered with some dark floral chintz. There was a
table beside one of the chairs with a desk lamp on it.
There was a desk against one wall and a gun rack in the
corner. On the far side another door opened into a
further room. Probably the one Vanessa had spoken of—
Kim's own bedroom.

"But, of course you saw all this yesterday," Kim said.

"No," said Jill, a little surprised. "I haven't seen
this room, but it is very comfortable. I hope I won't
have to intrude in it too much. It must be your holy of
holies."

She wondered why Kim was looking at her so directly
again. She was puzzled but determined not to forget the
wonderful uplift of heart she had felt when he had said
he needed her. She would be able to keep her job.
Mum and Dad wouldn't have to worry. She wouldn't
be out of work.

"I'll leave you to look round now, if you will excuse
me," Kim said. He went on into the room, seeming to
expect Jill to have the freedom to look round this room
now. His hand was on the handle of the far door, his
bedroom. He turned, "I'll have to go and bath and
change," he said. Again there was that short smile, half
shy, half ironic.

"Don't forget to-night," he said. "You're overworked,
and not available."

"I won't," said Jill, smiling.

"I'll see you later," he said, the smile gone and his mind back on other, distant affairs that had nothing to do with Jill.

He closed the door quietly behind him as he went out.

Jill stood quite still, looking round the room again. She was not seeing it. Her heart was singing a paean of praise for all things wonderful.

She had lost a job, then found a job. And he wasn't going to be hard to work for. He *needed* her.

She had not heard Vanessa come into the outer office. The girl was still in her riding things and she stood and looked at Jill with something more than dislike in her eyes.

Jill retreated from the inner room and closed the door behind her.

"Mr. Baxter asked me to look around . . ." she said, slightly confused, mad with herself that she had to explain herself to Vanessa.

"You seem to have got on to very confidential terms with Kim very rapidly," Vanessa said with a touch of insolence in her voice. "I thought that was Kim's room."

"His sitting-room," Jill corrected her, trying desperately to sound natural.

"How long have you been here?" Vanessa asked. "Twenty-four hours?"

"About thirty-four," Jill said. Her eyes met Vanessa's at a level distance across the floor. "One has to start into one's job straight away, you know. I am not a guest."

"I couldn't possibly imagine that you were," said Vanessa. She leaned against the door-jamb and drew a packet of cigarettes and a box of matches from the pocket of her chocolate-silk blouse.

Jill could not help noticing that though the blouse had a shirt collar it was very low cut in front; and by some wizardry of design its loose draped effect had been made to suggest and not hide Vanessa's beautiful form.

" Look . . ." Vanessa said slowly, taking out a cigarette and lighting it. She blew smoke in the air and lowered her lids as if it was the smoke and not Jill that was bothering her. " Take a piece of advice from me, will you ? Don't try to become one of the family. You can't, you know. It never works." She inhaled again, then exhaled at length, no longer looking at Jill but rather at the long shaft of smoke that rose in a diagonal line to the ceiling. " You understand what clannishness means, I suppose ? Old families stick together."

She brought her eyes back to Jill who stood speechless with anger.

How, Jill wondered, *does one answer a Bal-Annie guest for that ?*

Vanessa smiled—with charm.

"A word of friendly advice in time saves the best of us from making mistakes. Don't you think ? "

" Thank you," Jill said. She hoped her voice was steady.

" If you're on the point of leaving, I'm just going to knock Kim up. We usually have a drink together at this hour." Vanessa elevated her shoulders from the door-jamb and walked carelessly, yet gracefully, across the room and tapped—with a familiar rat-a-tap-tap on Kim's door.

" I'm just going now," said Jill. Hastily she fled.

On the back veranda near the tennis-table Don's punch ball hung on a leather strap from the roof beam. Jill on the way to the kitchen with an offer of help pulled up short and looked at it. Then drawing back her closed hand she gave it a forthright punch.

Tuffy, seeing her through the doorway, pursed up her lips and wagged her head.

" Letting off steam ! " was all she said to herself.

CHAPTER SEVEN

THE NEXT MORNING Jill was in the office before seven o'clock. She was determined to be on duty in case Kim had instructions for her.

He looked up in some surprise as she tapped at the open door. He had two men in with him, both dressed, ready for work on the great outside. They looked at Jill curiously but said, " G'morning," drawling in their soft flat-toned voices.

" Good morning, Mr. Baxter," Jill said politely. " Is there anything I can do before you go out ? The correspondence . . ."

" Damn the correspondence ! " said Kim, and both the men grinned. Evidently they knew how much his paper-work was a tie on his time.

" You've got yourself an off-sider, Kim," one of them said with a laugh. " Give the stuff to the young lady."

" The young lady's time is taken up with Don and his mates," Kim said shortly. Evidently he realised his words were not just. The first instruction he had given Jill had been to take Don and the boys off his hands.

" I beg your pardon, Miss Dawson," he said more kindly. " I haven't returned your greeting, have I ? Good morning ! "

" I'm sorry I interrupted you," Jill said, backing from the doorway. Instead of her good intentions rebounding to her credit it looked as if Kim wished her anywhere else on earth but in the office.

" Don't go," he said. " I've nearly finished here. I

want to have a word with you about the horses the boys are to round up."

Jill stood in the passage by the wall, opposite the open door so that Kim would know she was there : but far enough away to be out of earshot while he went on out-lining a whole list of activities to the men for the day's work.

Presently the men picked up their hats and went out, thundering with their heavy boots and smiling sheepishly at Jill as they passed her.

" Your turn next," the second one said with a grin as he passed her. " The boss is in no mood this fine and early morning."

" Come in, please, Miss Dawson," Kim said. His dark blue eyes had a touch of apology in them. " It was rather a welter last night, wasn't it ? I'm afraid my three days at the bushfire put me so far behind here at Bal-Annie I wasn't very civil company for our friends from the town ! "

Jill remained silent. Intuitively she knew this was not the time again to offer to help. The things that were bothering Kim were the kind of things about which she knew nothing. Quite clearly he was not in the mood for correspondence.

He looked at her steadily for a moment. Jill realised he actually was collecting his thoughts, bringing them back from Bal-Annie to her.

It *had* been a welter last night. The townsmen, evident-ly liking being out at Bal-Annie, and obviously enjoying the hospitality, had not wanted to go home until the early hours. They had eaten, taken much whisky, argued at great length about all sorts of town projects for November; and indeed had not piled back into their cars, homeward bound, until Kim had invited them to do so. He had done it in no uncertain terms.

Jill, who had remained up to help Tuffy and Mrs. Baxter, had been amused, though a little taken aback when Kim, in the midst of a free-for-all argument had suddenly stood up and said:

" Okay chaps, let's wind it up. Bill ! Your car's nearest the gate, you go first, then the rest can get their cars out."

Evidently the townsmen knew Kim Baxter, for after a quick laugh and an even quicker one-for-the-road they had gone.

" Really, Kim darling," Mrs. Baxter had said, pouches of tiredness under her own eyes. " How those men take that sort of thing from you—I don't know."

" It was a meeting not a party, Mother. Now you follow suit, and off you go to bed. You look tired. Follow Vanessa's example to-morrow, and have your breakfast in your room."

Jill, wiping the last of the glasses for Tuffy in the kitchen, had heard these words and she and Tuffy had exchanged smiles.

" There's no mistaking what Kim means, when he's in that mood," said Tuffy. "And he's implacable. If he says come, he means *come*. If he says go . . . that's what he means."

" Yes," said Jill. " I'm beginning to find that out myself."

Vanessa had gone to bed early, bored by talk of local activities. Mrs. Baxter could now be heard retreating in the direction of her room. Kim went off down the passage o his own quarters.

Tuffy wiped the sinks clean and Jill put the glasses away in an overhead cupboard.

" I've known Kim twenty-eight years. He was four when I came to Bal-Annie," Tuffy said quietly, her own tired head nodding slowly. " He's been my boy and there isn't anything I don't know about him. He's resourceful—that's why the town is after him now they want to jack it up for the officials and tourists coming. They think they know him, but they don't know he'd put anything and everyone second place to running Bal-Annie efficiently." She sighed and she hung up the dish-cloth to dry.

" He can have my right hand, because he's the only child I've ever had," she went on. "And he loves me as much as he can love anybody." She turned round and wagged her head at Jill. " That Vanessa now ! " she said eagerly. "She's been after him for years and he likes her as much as he'll ever like any woman. I suppose one day he'll marry her. She just doesn't know she'll never be first. Bal-Annie will always be first. Mrs. Baxter, me, Vanessa— and you, Jill, if you stay here long enough to make this your home, you'll find we'll all come second if he wants to do something his own way about Bal-Annie; and we're in his road."

" Oh no, Tuffy," said Jill, full of an unexpected kindly sorrow for this otherwise very composed woman who regarded Kim Baxter as her son; and loved him as such. " He's kind. I've found that out already. And he loves you. I can tell by the way he looks at you when you're talking to him."

" He loves me all right," said Tuffy wiping her hands on the roller towel behind the door. " Now off to bed. It's early up, even though we've had a party, or a meeting, or whatever they call it."

As Jill came towards the door Tuffy patted her on the arm.

" Don't you worry, dear," she said. " There's a shortage of girls hereabouts and one of those up-and-coming young farmers will snap you up before you find out it can be cold outside where Kim is concerned—if he needs all the room *inside* for Bal-Annie."

She sighed and switched out the light.

" Inside his heart, I mean."

Now, this morning, looking at Kim in the dim early morning light across the office table Jill remembered Tuffy's advice. She could almost believe it of Kim in this mood. Yet she couldn't find it in her heart to be sorry for Vanessa, if she did come second. She didn't think Vanessa loved Kim. She *wanted* him. That was something quite different.

"About those horses," Kim was saying. " They're mostly brumbies we've caught out on the ranges from time to time. We've culled them out and the best and most promising are loose in the forest paddock. The boys can round them up and bring them in." He suddenly stopped and looked up from the papers on the table where he had again attached his attention while he was talking.

" Do you know what a brumby is ? " he asked.

Jill smiled.

" It's a wild horse, or the progeny of a wild horse," she said. " Caught out in the bush. Generally small, certainly tough . . ."

There was a glimmer in his eyes. He looked as if he really might smile in a minute.

" I see they trained you well at that riding school," he said.

" Mr. Jukes occasionally bought a brumby," Jill said. " They turn out quite good horses if properly broken and properly trained."

He looked amused.

" I'm very glad to hear it."

Was he being sarcastic ? He was again looking down at the pile of papers on the table.

As if *she* could tell the great Kim Baxter anything about horses. Jill flushed. She had not been trying to instruct him. She had wanted to let him know she knew something of brumbies and would be quite reliable out with the boys later in the morning.

With a sudden flash a thought that had been at the bottom of her mind ever since she had arrived in Darjalup darted upward into the light of consciousness. How had Kim Baxter known in the first place she had fair hair and was an " outdoor " girl ? He'd written that description of her on the paper for Shane. And now, this minute, how did he know she had worked, even though only after school hours and in holidays, at Jukes's Riding School ? He'd taken her on because she was a gym teacher, stranded and out of work.

One day, if she ever got to know him well enough to ask him personal questions, she must ask him that one.

He looked up.

" Well, that's about all," he said. " Except . . ." he paused and then went on. " If you are in early, and have some spare time, I would like you to help mother with her correspondence. She is rather jaded and I think would welcome help."

He had moved round the table, picking up his own hat as he did so.

"And back to the problem child," he said with a sudden touch of the schoolboy in his smile. He waved his hat at the pile of mail on the table. " You can open all of that if you will. I have no secrets from off-siders." His smile was real now. Almost friendly. " I'm sorry I was abrupt about your offer. The stuff greeted me like a headache when I came in this morning."

" Yes, certainly," said Jill, very serious, very professional. She mustn't take advantage of that smile. She went over to the table and picked up the mail and began to sort it dexterously. She did not look up as he went out. He looked back as he put his hat on his head and Jill would never know that what did cause the look of amusement on his face was the sight of her capable professional air as she began slitting envelopes as if she had been in an estate office all her life.

She had the letters sorted and the "yes-no" ones pencilled off when Don appeared in the doorway. He wore a much used pair of long khaki cotton pants and a jagged straw hat on his head.

"Aw come on, Jill ! " he said. " Tuffy said you haven't even had your breakfast yet. Kim and the men start clocking the racehorses in twenty minutes."

" But Don, we're not going to see the men *training* . . . ."

" Just aren't we," said Don. " Plenty of time for the brumbies afterwards. Come on and get your breakfast."

Jill stacked her letters with lightning speed.

" I'll have some tea and bread-and-butter," she said. " Never mind about the rest."

" It's all cooked," said Don airily. " I did it myself. And Harry's and Dick's too. They've had theirs but yours is in the oven."

" Oh *Don*," said Jill gratefully. " You are a darling."

" None of that Vanessa-stuff," said Don wearily. " *Kim-darling* this, and *Kim-darling* that ! Don't try it on me, Jill. I just don't dig it . . ."

They were hurrying down the passage towards the kitchen and Jill couldn't help laughing. Don really was amusing and this " dig " business and the worse-than-sloppy clothes were all a pose. He could dress like a real beat, and she wouldn't mind, if he could cook breakfast for four at this hour of the morning, and make it sound as if it were a trifle.

Besides, late night or no late night, she suddenly felt marvellous.

The day might be going to be hot but at this moment the morning was heavenly. The night dews were still on the vines; the smell of stubble paddocks was a sweetness in the air . . . and in a few minutes she would be watching men training horses. Perhaps half an hour, or even an hour later, she would be astride and hunting brumbies in the forest herself.

Oh, what a lovely life ! Oh, what a wonderful job !

To-night she would write to Mum and Dad and tell them about it. What luck it had been for Jill that seven years ago her parents had migrated to Australia.

" It's always the second generation that benefits," her father had been prone to say before that good year came to the business. Now, if things went well, and Jill kept her job, they would never regret coming to this land of wide spaces and sunshine, for their own sakes.

But she must work hard for that taskmaster Kim Baxter, and keep her job ! That was number one priority in the list of the affairs of her life. *And forget Vanessa first giving her advice then knocking on Kim's door last evening.*

The boys, impatient for Jill, were in the stables, when she came hurrying down to join them. Four horses were saddled up, rattling their bridles and tonguing their bits. They too were impatient.

" Here's your mount, Jill," Don said. " Can't think what's gone mad with Kim, but he's given you one of the Edens. Oh no, not one of the racers but a good horse all the same. You didn't *Kim-darling* him the way Vanessa does, did you ? "

" Certainly not," said Jill primly. " Mr. Baxter is my boss, not my—well you said it ! He probably knew I learned to ride in a good riding-school. And you can take note, young Don. If ever I saw foot-loose riding that day I came to Bal-Annie . . ."

She swung herself up in the saddle with a professional grace that made Don whistle.

" That day you came to Bal-Annie ! " he said with heavy but youthful sarcasm. " Two days ago. The way you go on, Jill, anyone would think you were born here."

" Glad you're jealous of your heritage," Jill said airily. " Don't scramble up in a saddle, Don. Swing up . . . one leg over."

He was already up and the other two boys, mounted, were edging their horses through the stock gates.

" Look Jill," said Don, eyeing her so as to get some home truths well rammed in. " I can ride bare-back; and I've been riding that way since I was four. What's more I can ride the new foals before they're broken. And I won a prize in the rodeo last year."

"All right, all right ! " said Jill as she lifted her reins and touched the horse with her right heel. "All your points are taken, one at a time. It still doesn't hurt to look nice in a saddle. In fact it wins points at a show— not a rodeo. Think of that when we get some of those brumbies trained for ourselves." She glanced sideways at him and smiled. Don had taken that point too, she saw.

They were through the rails and through the stockyard and before them lay the long sweep of track, a mile down to the training ring.

They started to break from a trot to a canter.

" What do I call my Eden bay gelding ?" she called.

" *Gem*," Don shouted back. " Let her go ! *Whoopee— ee—ee !* "

They were full gallop, flat out down the track, the horse stretching under Jill as only a good horse can stretch.

Oh lovely, lovely ! she cried to herself. The air streamed through her hair. At the bottom of the home paddock —a long jump over the stock trap—and dancing shadows from the trees on either side were making a checker-board of the track. Startled birds flew off among the branches and Don, way out in front, was thundering away from Dick and Harry. Yes, he could ride, Jill thought. And he sat well when he wanted to. He had taken her point.

It seemed no time when they arrived at the training

ground. As they approached, one of the men had jumped
out from the trees and held up his hand.

" Steady on, Don ! " he roared. " Don't race in by the
fences. The horses are out on the track ready to start.
You'll shy them all over the place with that racket."

They pulled up, the horses panting but having loved
every minute of it.

Jill swung down first and handed her reins to the waiting man. The boys preferred to roll off on to the ground,
but Jill refused to notice this. Not too much advice in
one day, she thought.

" Give us your reins, you boys," the bow-legged
weather-beaten man was saying, less wrathfully. " I'll
hitch 'em up over by the pump. You don't want to
miss that try-out. They've got the best of the Edens
running."

Nobody said anything but all, including Jill, ran for the
white fence. There was a row of bent backs as a dozen
men sat on the top rail, their legs wound in amongst the
lower ones. Jill and the boys scrambled up beside them
and fell into the same tense absorbed silence.

Away round the other side of the ring were four
mounted horses. The very expectation in the air meant
that these horses were something special, and something
special was demanded of them.

No one stirred, not even to light a cigarette. The man
on the fence next to Jill looked at his stop-watch.

The morning air was like balm over the land and in the
distance the smoke from the starting pistol rose slowly
and gently like a fairy whip dissolving into a miniature
cloud, then into nothing. The horses were away !

Never had Jill seen anything so lovely, so breathtaking
as that race. One horse, and its rider, was outstanding.
She had no idea who the rider was. He wore a peaked
cap pulled well down on his forehead. He didn't stretch
forward on the horse's neck as did the other three men.

His back was curved, his stirrups short, but he seemed one with the animal; part of its make-up.

The gallery on the rails were no longer silent now. Their hats were off and they were egging the riders on as they swept round the circuit. Don stood up, his boot heels hooked in the rail, and shouted. The other two boys, less adept, fell off the fence and had to scramble back unaided. No one was watching them, everyone had eyes only for the glorious brown horse stretching out in front, his lovely white hocks flashing past like a Morse-code of horse-speed.

It was only minutes and the race was over. The man beside Jill had pressed his stop-watch as the horses passed the second time and swung himself down to the ground on the inside of the rails. He ran towards the riders, who were pulling up a hundred yards away.

They turned the horses and slowly trotted back along the fence.

" Oh that lovely horse ! " thought Jill. " That lovely, lovely horse ! " She was watching it, her heart in her eyes, when its rider pulled up.

" Whacko, Kim ! " The men were calling. " Whacko! You clocked under the three and a half ! "

The rider had pulled off the peaked cap, and it was Kim.

Jill blinked and swallowed.

How wonderfully he rode. She had never dreamed she would see horses ridden like that, and men riding them like that. Kim wasn't a man, he was almost a hero . . . because in his own training paddock he had magnificently ridden a horse to a time that meant that horse was destined for a great future.

He was leaning forward now, patting the animal's neck. As he came up level with the bunch of excited men on the fence rails he swung off, holding the horse by the cheek strap and rubbing its nose with his free hand.

" He loves that horse," Jill thought. " No wonder the town meetings and the office paper-work drive him mad. I must help him. I *must*! He wasn't meant to be shut up in an office. To take chairs at town meetings. He was meant to be out here with these lovely horses, with his men, with wonderful, wonderful Bal-Annie. No wonder he puts everyone including Vanessa in second place ! "

Kim glanced at the group that consisted of Jill and the boys.

" Hallo, young fellers," he said. " How about that brumby hunt ? "

" It's on," said Don carelessly. " We thought we'd take a look in and see how you were running those Eden nags."

Eden nags ! Kim's eyebrows shot up. He turned away to speak to some of the men and Don clambered down from the fence.

" Come on, you crowd," he said over his shoulder to Jill and the other two boys, as he walked away. " If we stick around here we'll give that brother of mine a swelled head."

Jill laughed to herself as she followed in Don's wake. Pride in his brother's achievement was sticking out all over Don's thin bony body, but he wasn't going to let his school friends see it. Showing off about relations was the one unforgivable sin of his age group.

CHAPTER EIGHT

THEY HAD AN exciting two hours hunting half a dozen of the brumbies out of the forest paddock, rounding them up and then drafting them into the road paddock. The forest had been fun because Jill had soon seen that all the boys were fearless riders. They simply didn't know what fear was. Their mounts went over logs, grazed through between narrow lanes of tree trunks, and pig-rooted occasionally in the dense undergrowth. Jill rode more carefully, not from nervousness but because she was aware that she rode an Eden horse, and that Gem was valuable. She didn't know the terrain as well as the boys and she couldn't afford to risk a broken leg for Gem.

Once out in the open road paddock it was different. She could ride as fearlessly as the boys. And did.

" You're not too bad on a horse," Don conceded when they were back in the stables. " I suppose you can afford to lecture."

" Lecture time's over," said Jill. " We've got to rub the horses down now."

" Where did you learn all this know-how," said Don presently as he watched the professional way Jill got to work first unsaddling and then rubbing down.

" Like I said," said Jill, speaking in the boys' own language. It made her one with them she thought. "At a riding-school. I was taught *properly*."

" Guess I'll have a look at that riding-school one day. Mostly riding-schools only turn out prissies."

" Not the good ones," said Jill.

Harry and Dick were up on the stalls riding imaginary horses in their idea of prissiness.

" Come down off there," commanded Don, who alone

was allowed to make jokes. "Any minute now I'll pull you down. It's lunch-time."

They loosed the horses out in the home paddock, watched them a minute as they raced away to the far side ; and then went up to the homestead.

They came in a bevy, talking earnestly, round the side of the house to the front veranda.

Three cane lounge chairs were drawn up in a half-circle round a small cane table. Mrs. Baxter, Kim and Vanessa were having a before-lunch drink.

Kim, his long legs stretched out before him in his riding pants and elastic-sided boots, watched the quartette approaching, their heads bent, the talk important.

" What a godsend it is that that girl gets on with the boys," Mrs. Baxter said. " This is the first morning I've had peace from worry about what they're up to, since the holidays began."

Vanessa glanced at the intent way Kim, from the depths of his cane chair, watched Jill and the boys approach.

" Well, they're all very young," she said with a laugh. This brought no reaction from Kim and Vanessa said . . . " Darling, a cigarette please."

Kim, lifting his shoulders from the back of his chair, offered her a cigarette from the box on the table. He lit it for her. Vanessa drew in deeply then puffed out the smoke, catching Kim's eyes with her own as she did so.

Jill and the boys came up the steps, Jill looking at Kim a little anxiously. She had been enjoying herself so much she could hardly regard the morning's occupation as work. She wondered if she should have been in earlier.

" Oh, Miss Dawson ! " Vanessa said, smiling brightly. " Your boy friend rang up. Did anyone tell you ? Of course, how foolish I can be ! You've only just come in. It was Shane Evans." She laughed in as friendly a manner as she could achieve.

" I asked if I could take a message, but he all but scorched me through the telephone. He said it was most frightfully private."

" Thank you," Jill said, looking at Vanessa but wishing more to look at Kim. After all, he was her boss and she wanted to know if he needed some service of her now. Vaguely she wanted to know if she stood well with him in spite of a morning chasing brumbies and telephone messages that being personal might not be welcome in the homestead.

Kim was looking out through the creepers at the rose-garden, and to the paddocks shining with gold stubble beyond them. His eyes were narrow, but that was probably because he was thinking of something miles away, not what Vanessa was saying to Jill. At least, Jill hoped so.

" It was very kind of you to take the message," Jill said, moving, a little unhappily, towards the door into the house.

"Any time ! " said Vanessa with an air, part of boredom, part of amusement. " You seem to have made such a hit with Shane I expect that telephone will ring *ad lib* from now on."

" I hope *not*," said Mrs. Baxter with some spirit. " The thing is nuisance enough as it is. Don, take your friends to the bathroom and brush up for lunch."

Shane Evans rang Jill again later in the afternoon when she was sitting at a side table in the front lounge doing Mrs. Baxter's correspondence for her. Mrs. Baxter was sitting in an arm-chair working out an agenda for her next meeting and as Jill read aloud to her the received letter, Mrs. Baxter gave her the gist of an answer.

The telephone rang in the hall alcove. Tuffy, from the homestead switchboard, just outside the kitchen door, made the connection.

" The fourth call since lunch," Mrs. Baxter said. " What a good job I've now got a pair of young legs to run and answer it. I simply won't have a connection put in this room to confound me when I have visitors."

Jill did not close the lounge door as she went to answer the call because she expected it to be another for Mrs. Baxter.

" Hallo, Piece-of-cake," said Shane. " So I've caught you at last. Where's that chip of ice Vanessa gone that she's not hooking into my conversations ? "

" Out in the car somewhere with Kim," Jill said. " I think he's gone to some place called the back-block where they're making a new dam."

" Good luck to them. I don't want either of them. I want you. Listen Jill everybody comes into Darjalup on Saturday. That's shopping day and the Shire office and shops are open all day. Are you coming in ? If so, stay in. We'll go to the cinema. There's supposed to be something good on."

Jill felt uncomfortable at having this private call in the middle of doing some work for Mrs. Baxter, and she was uncomfortably aware that Mrs. Baxter could hear everything.

" Shane—I'm a working girl," Jill said. " You shouldn't ring me up now. Oh, that sounds horrid of me. I didn't mean it . . . I'm sorry."

" Well, say yes quickly and I'll hang up and spare your blushes. *I* don't have to be afraid of Kim."

" I can't answer you, Shane. I don't know what the family is doing on Saturday. I'll probably be doing something with the boys."

" Well, ask someone what they're doing. And ask for a day off, girl. You're not a slave."

" Please, Shane," Jill pleaded. " I can't possibly answer you now. Mr. Baxter isn't even in at the moment."

" Oh, you mean Kim ? Well, I'll ask him myself . . .

all right, don't sound so hot-footed. I suppose Mrs. B is breathing down your neck. I'll ring you to-morrow. So long, Cake."

Jill put the receiver down and drew in a breath. She went back into the lounge, feeling guilty and trying not to catch Mrs. Baxter's questing eye. Mrs. Baxter hated that phone and she wouldn't want extra calls coming in to the household.

" Was that Shane Evans ? " Mrs. Baxter asked, looking at Jill with interest. " Well, I can't say you're going to be cut off from social life out here at Bal-Annie. What did he want ? "

Jill was back in her chair, her head bent over her writing-pad.

" I think he was wondering if the family was going into Darjalup on Saturday. It seems as if it is quite a practice on Saturdays."

" It's the one day we don't go in," Mrs. Baxter said firmly. " Too many people doing nothing but stand in gossip groups up and down the main street. As soon as the weather is cooler we go to the golf club on Saturdays and Sundays. I'll tell Kim to tell Shane so next time he rings the Shire office. By the way, do you play golf, Jill ? It's almost a ' must ' in a country district, you know."

Jill was relieved to find the subject of conversation changed.

" Yes, I play golf," she said, " I was very lucky at home. We were only half a mile from the Perth public golf course. I played often. I could never afford to belong to a private club."

" Good. Then we must have some golf in the winter. I'll take you. Now what were we up to ? "

The rest of the day passed with Jill being very busy first with Mrs. Baxter's affairs, and then Kim's. All was finished by the time the others were in for dinner that night.

The next few days passed very quickly, for each morning Jill went out with the boys and they really got to work grooming, riding and training the forest-frisky brumbies. The old stables began to take on a new look, the boys having done in the afternoons much carpentry, some professional, some amateurish, and brandished paint brushes. The old stables were going to be worthy of their new inmates.

On Saturday, instead of there being any talk of the family as a whole going into Darjalup, Kim drove Vanessa in to catch the bus-train down to Albany. There she was to be picked up in a car and driven to her own home for some kind of a family gathering amongst the Althrop clans. Vanessa, rather bored about it, felt compelled to go.

Jill had a sense of relief that Vanessa's visit was over. No one, Jill thought, likes to live in the same house as someone who doesn't like her. Besides, she knew Kim was desperate for time and Jill thought Vanessa took up too much of it. But who knows ? Kim might really like having some of that precious time wasted with Vanessa !

That sundown knocking on his door ! Had he opened it ?

Vanessa's farewells on the front steps of the homestead had been almost ecstatic about the lovely time she had had. She promised to be back the following month in time for the opening of the golf club. She would stay at least a fortnight then.

When she had gone Mrs. Baxter sighed.

" Well," she said, as she and Jill went back into the lounge. " Now we'll have another pot of hot tea. It's always an anticlimax when a guest goes away, isn't it ? "

Jill went out and made the tea because at that moment Tuffy was in her own room having her " constitutional " ... as she called her daily afternoon rest.

When Jill brought the tea in, had poured it and taken a cup to Mrs. Baxter with the little silver milk and sugar basket, Mrs. Baxter looked up at her and said with an air of disappointment :

" Well . . . I don't think they came to any decision. Do you ? "

" Decision ? I beg your pardon ? " said Jill puzzled.

" Kim and Vanessa. I did really hope it would come off this time. I wonder who is not making up whose mind. Of course, I could never *ask.*"

" You're quite different from some mothers," Jill said gently, pouring her own tea. " Some mothers don't want to see their sons married. They want to keep them."

" Not me," said Mrs. Baxter firmly. " I think Kim ought to get married. For his own sake. And Vanessa is really the only likely one. There isn't a girl round this district I care about at all. There aren't very many anyway."

Jill sipped her tea in silence. She hadn't anything to add to these remarks of Mrs. Baxter's. Vanessa might be the only " likely " girl about, but Jill still felt she didn't deserve anyone as good as Kim. Then she felt mean. She put her feelings down to the fact that Vanessa so obviously disliked her, that Jill could hardly be expected to return that enmity with love and hope.

She hadn't thought very much about Shane Evans's invitation to go to the cinema and presumed that either Kim, or Mrs. Baxter in one of their many telephone conversations with the Shire offices, had told Shane they were not going into Darjalup on Saturday. Shane had not rung again, and Jill hoped, rather forlornly, that he wasn't hurt.

The next week passed like the former one: the boys madly busy in a constructive way; Mrs. Baxter driving in to Darjalup twice to meetings; Jill going in with Mrs. Baxter on one day to take the Junior Farmers' meeting, with Shane in the chair—to spare Kim's time.

Jill had been greatly relieved that Shane hadn't been hurt by her defection on the former Saturday.

"Just as well," he said. "I had an unexpected duty call to the far fringe of the jarrah forest. A two hundred and fifty foot karri tree had fallen across the through road, smashing up a culvert and drain, not to mention blocking up the road and causing general motor hazards for hundreds of yards. You ought to have heard the Shire engineer. Really, the language some of these professionals learn at university!"

They agreed they couldn't do anything about the following Saturday because on that day the boys were catching the night bus back to the city and their boarding-school.

The Saturday of the boys' departure was like living in the middle of a domestic tornado, until finally, noisily and with many injunctions from the boys to "take care of the brumbies" until Easter and the May holidays, they were at last got on to the bus and waved away.

Two cars had had to be taken to drive the boys into Darjalup. Mrs. Baxter took her own Buick with Jill and Don's two friends. Kim took Tuffy and Don with him in his station-waggon.

Once the boys were away Mrs. Baxter turned to Kim and said:

"At what time are you going home, Kim? Tuffy and I want to go and see Mrs. Sykes. She's out of hospital now, and she'll give us late tea there. Three's too many for that tiny sitting-room of hers and I'm sure Jill would be bored."

" That's all right," said Kim, looking as if his mind was on something else which he would have to fix up before he left town. " Miss Dawson can come with me."

He turned his head and looked at her. Once again there was his slow, intent, oblique but charming smile that had a tendency to turn Jill's heart to water.

" Can you add cooking to your many other capabilities, Miss Dawson ? It looks as if we might starve otherwise." That smile, faintly teasing, was directed at Tuffy now. " I'm sure Tuffy's larder is empty."

Tuffy, used to her beloved Kim's jokes, remained unruffled.

" There's cold beef in the refrigerator and pickles on the shelf, Kim," she said. " If you're really energetic there's a loin in the meat-house and you could do some grilling to keep your hand in practice."

" What about it, Miss Dawson ? " Kim said, looking at Jill again.

" I can grill chops with the best of them," said Jill with a smile. She didn't know whether the thought of driving that thirty miles home with Kim and supping with him bumped the pace of her heart-beats up to celestial levels, or flattened it out.

True, her heart had leapt. Then dropped. It behaved very strangely.

She knew she had already developed a kind of absorbed devotion to Kim and Kim's interests. But thirty miles alone with him ? It wasn't easy for a girl to drive and cook and eat along with her boss. The conversation might be forced, even a strain.

Perhaps he was feeling that way too ?

Ah well, neither of them could do anything about it. Someone had to take Jill that thirty miles home and at least Kim was looking, and sounding, pleasant about it.

" If you would just come across and get in my waggon,"
he said easily, " I'll drive round to the Shire office. I
want to go in there for a few minutes. Then we'll take
the forest road straight away."

Walking across the road to the pepper trees where the
cars were parked, Jill felt as if she had dwindled in height.
She was taller than medium height for girls but she
noticed that her eye-level seemed to be Kim's chin.

He opened the door for her and stood back.

" Get in and make yourself comfortable," he said. Jill
noticed that, once away from Bal-Annie, his manner was
easier. There was nothing personal in the way he opened
the door for her—it was just the pleasant way of a man
putting a girl . . . any girl, she supposed, into his car.

He walked round the bonnet, got in and started up
the car. He backed out and ran the car a little farther
along the road and stopped outside the Shire office.

" I will be five minutes," he explained.

There had been no conversation in this few minutes'
drive and Jill expected this might be the way of it all
the drive home. Perhaps it would be easier.

Kim had no sooner disappeared in the main door of
the Shire office than Shane came out. He crossed the
gravel footpath and leaned in the drive window, talking
across the steering wheel to Jill.

" So he's stealing my girl, is he ? " he said teasingly.

" It's just one of those things, Shane. After all, he is
my boss and I do have to do what I'm told. Mrs. Baxter
fixed it all up to-day because of the boys. I could hardly
say ' please leave me in Darjalup and if I can find Shane
Evans he might take me home.' "

" Well, do it next time," said Shane severely. " Whatever I've got on, will be off, if you come with that par-
ticularly beguiling look in those eyes of yours and say
you're stranded.

" By the way," he looked at her severely. " You don't look at Kim Baxter that way, do you ? "

" No," Jill laughed. " That's Vanessa's prerogative. Anyhow, how do I look ? "

" Nice." Shane straightened up to take out a cigarette and light it. He threw the match down and put his foot on it.

" Vanessa didn't pull it off this time ? " he said, leaning once again on the car, his head and shoulders in the window. " Bet she tried ! "

" I wouldn't know," said Jill. " I wasn't looking."

" Better luck next time, huh ? Vanessa'll wear even Kim Baxter out of solitude. And that says something."

It was Jill's turn to be severe.

" I hate to be frank . . . but you're being unkind, Shane. Kim likes her."

Shane raised his eyebrows.

" I didn't say he didn't," he said. " He also likes Bal-Annie and being his own master. One day he'll have to toss a coin. Kim never did anything he didn't want to do, young Jill. When he wants to marry, he'll marry, and it won't necessarily be for love. It'll be because he wants it that way—for Bal-Annie."

Here we go again, thought Jill. *First Tuffy, now Shane. I don't believe Kim is really like that.*

At that moment Kim came out of the Shire office, down the three stone steps and across the path.

" Hallo, Shane," he said, not looking pleased. " Do you mind abstracting yourself from that window. I want to get in. Thanks a lot."

Shane had withdrawn his shoulders and stood aside so that Kim could open the door and get into the driver's seat. Shane turned up the collar of his shirt as if in a sudden cold draught. Jill tried hard not to catch his eye for fear she might laugh. Kim did not look like approving of laughter just now. Something must have happened in the Shire office, Jill thought. He was annoyed.

" 'Bye, Shane," Kim said as he moved the car forward. Jill gave a slight wave of her hand. She wanted to say good-bye to Shane but there was, indeed, something of a cold draught of air in the car and Jill thought discretion was the better part of valour.

Kim swung the car to the right, down a short street past some minor shops, and timber dwellings, then out along a road running into the forest, but in the opposite direction to the road to Bal-Annie.

"Are we not going home straight away ? " Jill asked tentatively, trying to thaw out that set look on Kim's face.

He made a visible effort to relax.

" I'm going to run out to the area where we had the bushfire over two weeks ago," he said. " I want to look at the damage. They're thinking of creating a town oval there."

He turned his head and looked at Jill.

" Have you seen the karri forest yet ? "

" No," said Jill. " But I've heard of the karri trees."

" In that case we'll make top speed through the burnt-out parts and take a short run into the karris. We might see something of them before nightfall."

Jill was thrilled. It was a lovely drive. The brown ribbon of road ran between wide pastures, then into the jarrah country. When they came to the burnt-out part Kim said an unexpected thing . . . considering he was supposed to be a man of action, not of sensitivity.

" Close your eyes. Then you won't break your heart." He was right. The burnt-out forest was a tragedy of black desolation. Jill did not close her eyes, and she noticed that Kim sat grimly silent.

When they had run through it the road, now bitumen, wound its way through taller trees, with shining trunks. Gone were the red-black barks of the jarrahs and their thick leafy crowns. The crowns of these tall trees were somewhere up in heaven.

"These are young karri trees," Kim explained. "We'll be in the big stuff in a minute."

Jill thought she would never see anything again so wonderful as that karri forest. Mile upon mile of giants stood in the thick undergrowth on either side of the narrow road. The dying sun was gold in the leafy arms but over two hundred feet below those crowns, near the earth, there was darkness and the quiet mystery of a forest at night.

Kim swung the car right on round a timber-truck overtake, and began the drive back.

"I'm glad you didn't have anything to say," he said after a long silence.

"There isn't anything one can say," said Jill. "There are no words . . ."

"No words and no paint brushes," said Kim.

He looked at her and again there was that quiet smile.

"You know why I let myself be pushed on to those progressive district associations?" he said. "To police that forest. It's a good thing to improve the facilities of the town, and the general tourist interest of the district." He paused, then said slowly, almost grimly: "But not a karri shall be felled; not a limb, not a strip of bark— not one inch of the forest land . . . while I'm alive."

Jill, who suddenly found she had been holding her breath, expelled it.

"I'm so glad I came to work for you," she said quietly. "I feel like that too."

They were silent for quite a long time. They drove back through the pasture lands, across the main street of Darjalup and out on to the gravel road leading to Bal-Annie.

"Don't get too involved with Shane Evans," Kim said unexpectedly. "He's a nice lad . . . as young men go. But he has no respect for trees. Anything that's in the way of a road or a drain can come down as far as the Shire Secretary is concerned."

He glanced at Jill, and softened his voice.

"From the way you seemed to feel about that forest," he said quietly, "I don't think you'd be too happy with a heart-loose Shire official, pleasant and all though he is in other respects."

Jill felt a touch of dismay.

She liked Shane. They had agreed to be friends—till they quarrelled, as Shane had put it. And she didn't want to quarrel. She had a feeling Kim Baxter would be on guard every time Shane rang her up, or any time if she did go out with Shane.

She supposed she could become very busy, and not be available. She was only a human girl, so she let a small sigh escape her.

"Perhaps you are right," she said soberly.

It was sundown now—on the road to Bal-Annie.

Without moving her head, Jill knew Kim looked at her. What had he been expecting to find in her face?

He couldn't possibly guess her thoughts because the sundown hour made her think of Vanessa, in that lovely soft chocolate silk blouse, knocking at *his* door. Now he minded Shane Evans knocking at *her* door.

Not very fair: but then the boss, and not the customer, is always right—to his off-sider!

CHAPTER NINE

FOR THE NEXT few weeks Kim Baxter proved almost a tyrant. He was always pleasant, but so busy and pre-occupied with affairs on Bal-Annie as well as in the town— that he gave Jill endless instructions without seeming to notice her as a *person*.

He had discovered that Jill was willing and able and he used her services in every conceivable way. She went down to the stables with instructions to the men; she looked after and helped train the brumbies for the boys; she took the minutes for Kim's meetings when he had them at the homestead. She went out and inspected the Junior Farmers' projects and reported back to Kim. On one occasion he went with her, driving Jill himself instead of sending her in the smaller saloon with one of the drivers from the property.

She did his telephoning for him, his ordering for him and she not only opened all his letters, she wrote return letters for him.

When the men went out to the back-block where the dam building was going on she helped Tuffy make their lunches and on one occasion when they were forgotten she took the lunches out to the men by horse-back.

Kim had probably forgotten he had ever been dubious about what a girl off-sider could do for him. She was there and she worked; and he worked her.

Jill began to think she really was his right arm, and occasionally wondered, when he asked her to do extra piled upon extra, just what he would do without her.

Once she had read that there was always, somewhere in the world, someone else to do your job.

So, not to worry. She loved every minute of it, and loved every patch of grass; every animal and every tree, noble or ignoble, on Bal-Annie. She could not think of a time when she could ever leave it. No wonder Tuffy was an institution on the place.

The weather cooled off, making riding a joy: but suddenly there was another burst of ferocious heatwave— summer's last kick.

Then came the day of the second bushfire.

Jill learned that in the forest land there were three calls for controlling bushfire.

The first call was for the bushfire-roster plus any additional volunteers. The second call was for every farm, shop and office to send its quota of help. The third call demanded every able-bodied man in the district—if over seventeen years of age—must help.

The undergrowth was tinder, and the dried out leaves in the trees were near-combustible. The last heatwave of the season lay on the land and the jarrah forest, fifteen miles south of Darjalup, broke into fire.

It was nine o'clock in the morning when Tuffy picked up the first call on the homestead switchboard. Kim didn't go out on the run but stayed in the office, waiting for a further report. At ten o'clock it came. It was a three-call fire. Every able-bodied man out !

Kim moved quicker than Jill had thought possible.

" Go down to the stables, Jill, and tell Watson it's a three-call fire. He'll know what to do. Find Jason and have him fill every car and truck on the place." He'd forgotten to call her " Miss Dawson."

He went out to the front garden where Mrs. Baxter was trying to save her roses from the intense heat by keeping up a constant spraying of water.

" Help Tuffy get food and water in the backs of the

cars, Mother. Take plenty for yourself. You'll fall in with the town auxiliary to cope with feeding fire-fighters, and any injured ? "

" Of course. I'll take the Buick." She stopped.

" Kim," she said. " Bal-Annie ? Can we leave it without a man ? The heat shimmering in the trees looks dangerous."

" We have to do that, I'm afraid. You know the rules. Every farmer has to take that risk. We'll leave Jill and Tuffy to keep watch. They can ring through if anything happens this way."

He smiled at her. She also had not noticed, in her anxiety, that Kim had used Jill's Christian name.

" The fire is over forty miles away," he said briefly.

There were more men employed on Bal-Annie than Jill had noticed. She wondered where they all came from, some riding up to the homestead on horses, others pulling in in old utility trucks, and jalopy cars.

Kim, standing on the veranda to give instructions, looked as if he was the head of the most rag-tag and bob-tail army that ever set out to fight. Every man had on his oldest clothes, oldest hat and stoutest boots, and carried spades, hoes and sacking.

"All right, fellers," Kim said. " It's a three-call fire. You know what to do. Every man take his shovel and water-bag. The usual drivers take the homestead cars. Go straight through Darjalup and out along the Fersdown Track. At the moment the fire is in the forest directly behind the sawmills."

That was all. Within a minute the men were rapidly dispersing and ten minutes later a stream of cars, new and old, was working its way in a snake-like cloud of dust down the main drive of Bal-Annie to the through road.

Kim was the last to leave.

" Tuffy," he said. " Watch the sky. If it gets storm

black and the cinders come over, telephone through to the Shire office. They'll get a message through to me." He turned to Jill. He looked as if he wanted to say something special to Jill, but couldn't do it.

"I'm sorry to put so much responsibility on your shoulders, Jill," he said at length.

Jill, she thought. He has called me Jill!

She had been disappointed at not being allowed to go with Mrs. Baxter to help feed and attend the fire-fighters.

Kim looked out over Bal-Annie for a moment, his eyes half-closed. Then he looked back at Jill.

"The stock are all in their feed paddocks," he said. "We keep them this way in this weather. If fire strikes at Bal-Annie open every gate. Have you got that, Jill? *Open every gate.* On my way out I'll throw planks across the stock trap at the main entrance so the stock can get through."

"You mean let everything out?" Jill asked wide-eyed, wanting to be certain. "Even the Edens? Your race-horses . . . ?"

"Everything," Kim said evenly. Then he smiled and said very quietly: "You wouldn't want my Edens to be burned to death, would you, Jill?"

"*No!*"

"Then do as I say. Open every gate on Bal-Annie. But don't worry. That fire is forty miles away and the sky is not yet darkening. I don't think it's coming this way."

He put his hat on at that absurdly abstracted angle and turned away. At the top of the steps he turned round.

"Tuffy," he said, "I wouldn't leave you and Jill if I didn't have to. You know that? Every farmer's wife in the district is in the same boat. Those who can't go out to help with water and food have to stay home and mind the place."

Tuffy nodded.

" Go on with you, Kim," she said. " There is nothing to worry about here. We'll keep a watch. See you don't make a funeral pyre of yourself."

" There are two horses saddled in the stable, Tuffy. Right ? "

Again the elderly woman nodded.

" I understand, Kim," she said.

He came back across the veranda. Pushed Tuffy's grey hair back from her forehead and kissed her on the brow.

" So long, mate," he said with a grin.

Jill felt like saying—" One for me too ! " But of course didn't dare. To-day was different. To-morrow he would be the boss again.

" So long, Jill ! " he said.

" So long, Kim," she answered.

She put her hand to her mouth. She had called him *Kim.*

Oh well, to-morrow the fire would be over, God willing, and they'd be back to " Miss Dawson " and " Mr. Baxter."

She watched him get in his car and drive off at terrific speed.

When the last of his dust cloud disappeared in the trees she turned to Tuffy, puzzled.

" Why did he leave two horses saddled in the stables ? " she asked.

" *You'll* need a horse to go and open all those gates, if it's necessary," Tuffy said.

" Yes. One horse but not *two.*"

Tuffy looked at Jill, straight in the eyes.

" You're grown up and responsible, Jill," she said. " I think you ought to know the facts of life. Those two horses are for you and me, if the fire strikes Bal-Annie. We can't *walk* away, you know. Not when the forest is ablaze. And neither of us can drive a car. Now come

on and let's have a cup of tea. Nothing's going to happen,
but Kim would be wanting in something if he wasn't
prepared."

It was a terrible day. The heat shrivelled the land and
the veranda temperature rose to one hundred and fifteen
by ten o'clock. The sky in the south west darkened and
the dark pall gradually spread. It was as if there was no
sun, only impenetrable grey cloud. Tuffy put a white
cloth out on the veranda path to see what cinder, if
any, fell. The cloth, over the space of an hour, gradually
became grey but no cinders that could be seen by the
human eye could be found.

" Why is it so dark ? " asked Jill.

" Minute cinders and smoke. But it's high up. Nothing
to worry about."

" I can't help worrying about the men," said Jill.

" There's nothing coming through on the switch-
board," said Tuffy. " They're all out. Don't you worry,
Jill. Kim's always come home again after a fire fight.
He's an old soldier at that kind of war."

" People's homes, perhaps . . ." Jill began, thoughtfully.

" And farms," said Tuffy. " Don't think about it,
Jill. Thinking never did anybody good at this stage.
It's only *doing* that matters."

" But I'm not doing anything. I'm sitting here on the
edge of the veranda drinking intermittent cups of tea;
wishing I could help."

Tuffy was, once again, on the searing-hot path below,
spreading a fresh white cloth.

" You know what the Bible says," Tuffy said. "They
also serve who only stand and wait."

She came back to the veranda, wiping her damp face
with a cloth. She sat down beside Jill and poured herself
another cup of tea. Then over the teacup she stared at

the cloth on the path. There was a small dark blot on it. A minute later there was another. Tuffy looked up at Jill and with her finger ran a line down Jill's face. Her finger-tip was grey. Tuffy looked at the cloth with which she had wiped her own face. It was a dirty grey.

" What is it, Tuffy ? "

" Cinders in the air. It's thick with it. Now's the time we've got to watch, Jill. You take the back side of the house and I'll take the front. Keep moving from west to east and don't take your eyes off the tree tops in the distance. It's fire in the tops of the trees that matters. And keep your hat on."

It was half an hour later that Tuffy said:
" Quick, Jill. Down in the far west corner. That yellow glow on top of the trees. Watch it."

As they watched, the yellow glow licked up then died down.

" You go and open those gates, Jill," Tuffy said steadily. " That's the jarrah on the other side of the through road. A cinder coal flying through the air has caught them."

" But the Edens, Tuffy . . ."

" Round them into the home paddock with the brumbies. We'll leave the outside gate till the last. The rest of the stock will find their own outlet if the smoke drives them to it."

Tuffy had said *smoke*, but she had meant fire. Jill knew it as she pulled her hat well down on her forehead. Commonsense told her not to leave her hair flying.

She took one of the horses and within five minutes was galloping down the track to the training yards.

She released the Edens first. They were intelligent animals and it didn't take her long to round them through the gate into the home paddock. Tuffy would look after the gate at the other end, if necessary. But it was an hour and a half's hard riding in exhausting heat before she had opened all the inside gates of the Bal-Annie paddocks. The white bullocks, prize stud animals, were already waiting to get through.

"Intelligence does pay," Jill thought. "Even in animals."

When she was back to the stables she longed to take off Gem's saddle and release him too, but she dared not. Poor darling, he had to stay there and sweat and wait too.

She gave both horses a drink and some chaff. As she put away the bucket she looked up. There was a yellow spurt of flame in the trees at the bottom of the rise.

"Oh *no*!" her heart cried. "Not Bal-Annie too! Not lovely Bal-Annie!"

She turned through the stables and raced for the homestead, but Tuffy, ever vigilant, had seen.

She was coming towards Jill, hat wedged on her grey head; carrying a saw and dragging a shovel.

"Don't worry," she said composedly. "It's only a flying cinder caught but we'll deal with it before it starts damage in real earnest."

"The home-paddock gate?" Jill cried.

"Like you, I'm not going to see those Edens, or the white bullocks for that matter, lost," Tuffy snorted. "There's no real fire for miles around. We'll put this little fellow out ourselves."

Jill took the shovel from Tuffy and half running, half walking, the two went on down the hill to where the verge of the forest infringed on the stubble oat paddock.

"But *Kim* said . . ." Jill panted.

"One of us will go back if necessary and open the gate," Tuffy said. "Meantime we've work to do."

The sky was leaden black. It was hard to believe this was cinders and smoke from a terrible bushfire miles away, and not an imminent storm. The outside temperature must have been in the hundred and twenties.

The tree that had caught fire in one branch, had dropped its load of fiery cinders. Flame was licking through the stubble and the near undergrowth.

" I'll shovel, you beat with a branch. There's a good one there," said Tuffy, throwing down the saw. " Then we'll change over."

They worked madly, side by side, their mouths dry like brown paper. The fire was not getting away in the undergrowth, but it wasn't being conquered either. It kept pace with the sand-thrower and the bush-beater.

Tuffy called a halt for a minute.

" I'll have to go back, Jill," she said quietly. " I don't like leaving you, but it's necessary. Without water one or other of us will collapse and that won't help anyone. I might have to open the home gate if the fire gets out of hand."

" Please go," Jill said. " But Tuffy, don't open the gate yet. Look, it must be getting late and fire always dies down at night, doesn't it ? The men will be home soon. Or some of them. If we can just hang on . . . just keep it from getting out of hand . . ."

Tuffy nodded.

" It's gone six o'clock. Kim'll send someone back to do the milking. I can hear the poor cows bellowing from here."

" Tuffy darling . . . you milk them. I can hold it here till the men get back."

" I might have to relieve them," Tuffy agreed, seriously.

" Thank God, if you do," said Jill. " I can't bear to think of the poor things in pain. There's no danger here so long as I watch it: and beat it where the fire starts to spread."

True, it wasn't as yet a big fire, but it would easily

have become out of hand since there was a touch of movement in the air, if it hadn't been for Jill's hard work and vigilance.

Tuffy was a long time in coming back, Jill thought. She guessed what had happened. The cows with their distended udders would have to have some of the milk taken away; and without bales or chaff bins this wouldn't be quick or simple.

The fire licked away into an old dried-out fallen log and Jill chased it with her beating branch. The movement in the air drove the flames under the log and this took time and assiduous care to stamp out. One small coal left alive under that log would set fire to it in the night. Later, the early morning wind would release the flame over the entire timbered part of Bal-Annie.

At last Jill was certain all was out. She turned round. Flames had crept into the undergrowth behind a very old jarrah tree and were licking up the trunk. A waft of air sent a thin tongue of fire straight up and along one bough into the dried-out leaves at the limit. This was the worst thing that could have happened. Wind, if it rose, would send the fire racing over the tops of the trees.

The saw was lying on the ground thirty yards away. Jill ran for it. Tuffy had brought it down against such an eventuality. Then she looked at the jarrah. How could she climb such a straight-trunked tree, one part of which had its bark already glowing with coal?

To the right of the jarrah was a banksia—not very straight and not very tall. Jill thought she could reach the burning bough from one of its crabbed arms. Mercifully this was the kind of tree with many forks, the first beginning within two feet of the ground.

As long as that upper branch would hold her! As long as the burning jarrah branch didn't drop on to her!

It wasn't a hard climb but it had to be a quick one. It was slowed down by the saw, which Jill had to fix in the forks above or to the side, before she could climb farther herself.

" No good to drop the saw," she thought anxiously.

It seemed an aeon but it was really less than four minutes before Jill was out on the banksia limb, clinging with her legs and one hand while she wielded the saw at a difficult distance to cut through the blazing branch. Fate was on her side for mercifully the oncoming night had put its own blanket over flame; and in addition, the tree branch was rotten. It didn't take very much help from Jill to cause the fiery branch to snap off and fall to the ground, a shower of sparks and glowing coals.

Then, for the first time she realised she was not alone. There were half a dozen men around and about.

As she dropped the saw, and started clambering down the tree she saw the figures darting about stamping and beating out coals and flames all over the area.

"Are you all right, Miss Dawson ? " a voice said, and one of the men gave her a helping hand to drop to the ground.

" Yes," she said. " I'm glad you've come." She looked at the men. They were black. Smoke cinder and burnt bush had left their marks all over them. They looked as if they'd been *in* a fire, not at a fire.

" What happened ? " Jill asked. " Is the big fire out ?"

"All but," the man said. " It's burnt out Redwood. Not a house standing. The forest is an aftermath. Couldn't call it anything else. Trees are down along the new roads. Wreckage everywhere."

" Oh ! "

Jill was too weary to absorb the shock. Redwood was the new town the Shire had built for the timber workers out near the sawmills. It had been the pride of the district. One by one old jarrah dwellings had been ripped down and replaced with fine new timber bungalows. Roads had been built with a shopping area around a wide circle of grassed oval. Beautiful gardens had been made ! A sports ground fenced.

This had been the first and proudest venture to bring the Darjalup district up to the standard suddenly imposed upon them by the new idea of country town-planning.

" Oh ! " said Jill again, conscious of the tragedy to the district as well as the loss of homes to all the timber workers.

" Go up to the homestead, Miss Dawson. We'll clear up here. Kim should be in at any minute. He was bringing the water-truck out."

" You did a good job, Miss Dawson," said another man, black with soot, as she passed him.

Darkness was falling on the smoke-hazed forest and land. Jill wiped the back of her hand over her face as she trudged up the long stubble rise to the homestead. Her mouth craved a long drink of water. Even in the poor light she could see the back of her hand was sooty black. The front of her blouse and slacks was quite black, her shoes were beyond redemption.

It was God's grace, she thought, that she couldn't see the sides and back of herself.

Through the shadows she saw a man coming down the hill towards her. He too was a fire-wrack. It was Kim.

He pulled up in front of Jill. She was tired, and dry of mouth, so didn't speak. She simply looked at Kim, and he looked back at her. They were like the last two people on a burnt-out planet : sick at heart for all that had happened to other people, other farms.

It was Kim who broke the silence. He did not speak of the ardours of the day, or how things had gone with either of them. He simply said, "I'll come up to the homestead with you, Jill. The men will look after the bottom paddock." His voice was quiet, tired, yet concerned for her.

He turned round and they trudged on, both weary, in a kind of speaking silence where everything was being said and none of it need be put into words.

It was dark but Kim's broad-brimmed hat was still on his head. When they reached the homestead he opened the side gate for her and said:

" Go and get yourself a bath, Jill. We're on picnic rations for dinner to-night. Go straight to bed, if you wish."

Jill lifted up her head quickly.

" I'm not as tired as you are," she said. "And I'm younger than Tuffy. I'll help. Are the cows milked, Kim ? "

" Two of the boys are stripping them now. Tuffy took off some of the milk to relieve them."

" Is it all right to leave all the stock, including the horses, in the home paddock to-night ? "

" Quite."

As Jill went on, up to the veranda and into the house, she wanted foolishly to laugh.

She'd been checking on Kim's management. He was home, to manage his own Bal-Annie property and she, Jill, had actually checked with him that the cows would be stripped and the stock safe. She had forgotten the day was over and that Bal-Annie's fate was no longer her responsibility ! Kim was home.

Yet that silent meeting in the smoke fall-out from the distant fires had been some kind of special meeting. They hadn't spoken but in their weariness and sense of bushfire tragedy something had reached out, each from the other, and touched.

Jill was too tired, too sad for the terrible losses out by

the sawmills, to try and puzzle it out. Time enough, another day! Maybe Kim felt that way too. Maybe he was beyond feeling at all.

Yet he had looked at her—those intelligent intent dark blue eyes, asking something: and saying something.

Perhaps he was asking no more than—how goes it with Bal Annie? Perhaps he was saying no more than—You did well!

Why dream foolish dreams?

CHAPTER TEN

The following day mercy fell, like the gentle dew, from above.

Temperatures dropped and a fine but general rain watered the land.

Some of the men were sent back to the sawmills to help with cleaning up. Mrs. Baxter once again took the Buick and went to Darjalup to organise a committee for the succouring of the women and children who were left not only homeless, but without clothes, money or supplies.

Kim stayed in the homestead because he knew he could do most, at the top level, and that by telephone.

It rang on and off all day. When he wasn't speaking on the telephone himself he was making notes. There was so much to do that Jill hardly left his side, and as the day wore on she took to answering the phone for him: presently to giving his answers for him without referring to him.

" Yes, Mrs. Buxton . . . Bal-Annie is quite safe . . . If your men are delayed at the sawmills Mr. Baxter will send one of his men over to do your milking. About sundown? That all right?"

Then it was the Shire President, followed by the Town

Planning Committee.   Then   the   Darjalup Retailers'
Association.

" Yes . . ." Jill said to each of them.   " What day and
hour ? Yes, Mr. Baxter will chair the meeting for you."

It became a repetitive Yes, yes, yes—all day. Yes, he
would do everything that mortal man could do to help the
town and district in its hour of tragedy. Three men were
dead in the fire and two hundred and thirty people were
without homes. The new creek bridges were burnt out,
culverts on through roads were smashed by falling trees.
The railway line was damaged.

Yes, Mr. Baxter would do this. Yes, Mr. Baxter would
do that.

Jill put the phone down and there came a moment of
respite.   Kim was standing behind his table, leafing
through a correspondence file.

"We'll have to get the main roads engineer down
again, and that town-planning fellow the Government's
brought in," he said, without looking up. Then he raised
his head thoughtfully. " We'll have to put them up at
Bal-Annie. We've the largest homestead in the district,
with more accommodation. They'll have a bevy of sub-
officials with them who'll fill up the hotel."

"At once ? " asked Jill, dismayed.

He looked at her.

"At once," he said. " We've six months in which to
rebuild what has taken us two years to do. In addition,
there are all the projects we had planned to be completed
by November."

Jill drew in a breath.

" But is it possible ? "

Kim smiled grimly.

" It's possible, and it will be done. Darjalup might
have to start again from scratch but it will still measure
up by November."

The telephone hadn't rung for five minutes so Jill sat down on the spare bentwood chair.

" Can't some other town be the centre of attention ? " she asked. " Must it be Darjalup ? "

Kim smiled sardonically.

" Darjalup, as a town, has the karri forest," he said. " That's what they're coming to see. Not the people. The tallest trees in the world . . ." he added, "Along with the Victorian mountain ash and the Californian redwoods."

He looked back at the papers on his table and went on leafing through them.

" We can't move the karri forest," he said, with irony. " So I'm afraid the tourists and all officialdom will come to us."

The telephone rang again and Jill answered it, committing Kim to this and that, suggesting alternative dates, and making notes as she listened. When she hung up she handed the paper to Kim who, still without looking up, put it on a file.

" You're looking after me very well," he said— " taking my time and my person and almost my immortal soul into your keeping, and committing them to God knows whom. I won't be able to do without you. You'd better marry me, Jill."

Jill stood perfectly still and stared at him, expecting him to lift his head and make one of his rare wry jokes.

His hands were quite still on the papers a minute, then he did lift his head. His blue eyes were dark, quite serious, though not expressive.

" I meant that," he said. " There's something insidious about your capacity to help. You've taken over my own will to manage the detail of my affairs."

There was a silence.

He smiled, with a touch of momentary shyness.

" I believe I can't do without you," he repeated.

Jill took the receiver from the telephone hook so it wouldn't ring and walked over to the window and stared out at the paddocks. They were a brittle blue-green now under the thin fine veil of rain.

Bal-Annie!

Who, or what had she been fighting for, almost with her life, yesterday?

Could she ever leave it, or *would* she ever leave it?

Beautiful, beautiful Bal-Annie!

That was how Kim felt too. And he needed help. Not a decoration, but *help*.

He went over to the window and putting his hand on her shoulder turned her round to face him.

" Is it such a bad idea ? " he asked, looking into her eyes.

" No," Jill said, her eyes serious. " It is a very good idea. What do you expect me to answer, Kim ? " She turned and waved her hand to take in that great expanse of paddock, the forest fringe which she had saved yesterday the rose-garden in the foreground—the stock— the buildings—the men who lived and worked on the estate.

" You are a very nice person, Kim," she said, not looking at him. "And there's all Bal-Annie ! There's the horses . . . the early morning rides . . . the round-ups . . . the stock-yards, not to mention Don's new lift to the old stables. You offer me all that and yourself on a plate. Do you expect me to refuse ? "

Bal-Annie, in exchange for *love* ?

" I need you, Jill. Bal-Annie needs you. I think you saved it yesterday. One careless coal married to a puff of wind and the fire would have been out of control. You didn't let it happen."

It was his turn to pause. He went back to the table and took a cigarette from the box, and lit it. Then he came back to Jill by the window. She was staring out of it again, seeing only the ribbon of track tapering away into the timber ... down towards those training grounds, the outer paddocks where the stock grazed, remembering the sun and the wind in her hair when Gem had taken her full pelt after Don and the boys that day the men were training the horses.

"You've just thought of it," Jill said gravely. "Out of thin air you thought of marrying *me* ? "

"I've thought all last night and all the morning that I'm married to you already. Married in the sense that you're my right hand, as much as a man hopes that is what his wife will be."

He paused, and drew on the cigarette. They were both, standing side by side, looking out of the window.

"Please go on," Jill said.

"I've thought about marrying for a long time. I wanted, in my conceit—and we've all got it—the right person. You're the right person for me, and for Bal-Annie, Jill. So, if you wish it, I ask you again. Will you marry me ? "

Jill half turned and leaned back against the window frame. She was facing him but she did not look at him. She leaned her head back so that it touched the woodwork, and she closed her eyes.

"Kim ... I am a poor girl. I come from a family that was poor but is not so poor now. My parents were immigrants and they landed in Australia with twenty pounds. They had a hard time but they're winning through. I think you should know all this. They want the best for me because I am their only child. *It's always the next generation that benefits*, they said about changing countries. I'm the next generation, and *I* want the best for *them*."

She lifted her head and opened her eyes and looked straight at him.

" Then you offer me this ! " she finished, half in anger, half in despair. " What do you expect me to say, Kim ? Do you expect me to refuse ? "

Suddenly he was smiling, as if he was amused.

" No," he said simply.

" I don't think I have the courage," said Jill. " But give me *time* . . . weeks, even months . . ."

" No," said Kim. " I need you. *Now*. Together there is much to be done ! Much to accomplish in so short a time."

" But marriage is *everything*," Jill said, her eyes almost imploring him for time—or was it for something more than Bal-Annie, more than the man himself standing there ? Perhaps a little of his heart ?

Kim walked over to the table and stubbed out his cigarette. He came back to the window, slowly, thoughtfully.

"All my life I've had to make decisions," he said. " I've been *given* much. This inheritance, for instance. But I have had to say ' no ' to many things because they were not compatible with what I needed to do ; and with what I must do in the district. A man with a big property has a responsibility to the whole community. I've always said ' *no* ' to the things that would prevent me playing the role I have to play. Now I want to say ' yes' to something that is wise and good."

Jill closed her eyes again.

Of course, he was saying " no " to someone like Vanessa !—some decorative Sybarite with whom the heart of any man is so often wedded in his dreams. The hard-working Kim, with his overwhelming sense of duty, was still human enough to have idle pipe dreams about the Vanessas of this world ! But he had both feet planted on the earth and knew the value, and the quick dissipation, of the stuff of which pipe dreams were made.

In a way Jill liked him better for this human frailty; opposed as it was by his real sense and strength. All men, she surmised, had occasional thoughts of the beautiful and idle women of the world who were pleasurably decorative; lilies that were gilded, but toiled not.

Kim's ability to say *no* to those pipe dreams was also the secret of his ability flatly to choose the opposite type. Someone who could share his work.

Cold-hearted? Yes.

Sensible? Yes to that, too!

"Are you all for the love-in-the-cottage type of thing, Jill?" Kim asked unexpectedly, a little sceptically.

Jill looked at him quickly. He was smiling again, not without irony yet not unkindly.

"It has its virtues," Jill found herself saying sadly.

"What is marriage? Isn't it companionship, admiration, respect? I have all those feelings for you, Jill."

Jill flushed, slowly and painfully. So nearly a declaration, yet so clearly a reservation.

What a speech was that! she thought, not without an unexpected heart-warming pride and not without a touch of the sorrowful anger with which she had a few minutes ago said:

"Do you expect me to refuse," and he had said *No.*

Yet she found it hard to utter the word "Yes," though she knew in the bottom of her heart she was going to say it eventually. She hadn't the pride, or the integrity, she thought, to say anything otherwise to Kim Baxter-plus-beautiful Bal-Annie.

To have all this, as her own, for ever and ever!

There were tears . . . not far away, as she said:

"Yes, of course I will marry you, Kim." She looked at him very seriously. "There, I have said it. I haven't any courage in me when you ask me a question like that—and offer so much."

He looked puzzled.

" Courage ? " he said. " I would have thought it took courage to marry someone like me and take on a load like Bal-Annie ? "

Jill shook her head slowly. Why didn't he look in the mirror ? Why didn't he look at Bal-Annie, not for its beauty but through eyes like her own that had first seen the light of day in a built-up area in a dark Midlands town ?

What did he expect her to say ?

As if she hadn't been in love with him since she had seen him race that horse down at the trials that day !

This—she mustn't even admit to herself ! Not yet !

" You thought of it on the spur of the moment," she said, anxious that he too should know that she understood how this had happened, and he not regret it. " You were looking at your papers and I was saving you time on that telephone. You thought I was being your right-hand. You realised you needed me—that way. Then on the spur of the moment . . . ."

" Rot ! " he said, quietly. " I thought of it last night when I saw you toiling up the hill after climbing the tree to save the flames spreading through the tops; and possibly spreading through Bal-Annie. I said to myself—I need someone like this; someone who loves Bal-Annie. I've looked for the right girl, and here she is bang under my nose. She's covered in fire smuts, like the rest of us. In fact, to my eyes this fire-stained face, and this drooping figure, has a very special charm."

He put out his hand and took Jill's arm. She could feel the gentle way he touched her flesh yet the sense of powerful strength that was in his finger-tips.

He drew her towards him and, irrevocably drawn, Jill went to him. He put one arm round her shoulders, holding her lightly as if not to oppress her. Her cheek rested against his and with a soft brushing movement his free hand stroked her arm.

Kim had talked about his immortal soul being in her keeping, but now she would have given her own immortal soul to have thrown her arms around him. This she could not do. Something, his own careful gentleness perhaps, stayed her.

And of course there had been no *foolish* talk of love. Intuitively, even if he had thought of it, he would have been too honourable and too aware of her own sensitivity at this moment to have acted such a lie.

Sufficient that he liked her; that he wanted her. Ah well!

"You have such a soft skin, Jill," he said, drawing away from her, speaking once again in that odd, almost uncharacteristic half-shy way. He looked into her eyes. "Skin like a child's," he added. Then he smiled. "Or is it like an angel's. *Non angle sed angeli?*"

Time to laugh, Jill thought.

"Not like last night," she said with a touch of gaiety. "Then it was very black."

"Weren't we all!" Kim said.

The time had come to be sensible, now that a bargain had been struck and a certain kind of sweet tenderness exchanged in token.

"The receiver has been off that telephone hook for at least twenty minutes, Kim," Jill said more gravely. "At least half a dozen people will have wanted to get in touch with you, and Tuffy out there at the switchboard will wonder if we've dropped dead, or something."

"We'll let Tuffy be the first to know that we've made certain momentous decisions," he said. "I'll speak to her."

Jill felt a real tenderness towards him as he walked across the room and after tapping the phone rest lifted the receiver. Tuffy had been his mother, having brought

him up through all the important years. He was going to
tell her first.

He half turned and smiled at Jill as Tuffy's voice came
through.

" Yes . . . yes, Tuffy. Stay calm," he said. " Nothing
disastrous has happened except that Jill and I have been
making arrangements to get married. We thought you
would like to know . . ."

He held the receiver away from his ear, a little towards
Jill, so that she, across the room, could hear Tuffy's
exclamation.

" *What did you say, Kim ? Come straight out here to the
kitchen and tell me what has happened.*"

The telephone clicked because Tuffy, in her state of
shock—or was it alarm—had put her own receiver down
with a bang.

Kim's smile was wry. He came back to the table and
took another cigarette from the box. He lit it as he went
to the door. Jill had not moved from her place by the
window and some extra sense of awareness in Kim made
him realise that there, for the moment, was where she
wanted to stay.

" To Philippi'." There was an ironic kindness in his
eyes as he looked across the room at Jill. " By the time I
get to Tuffy in the kitchen she will be glad. You'll be
kind to Tuffy, won't you, Jill ? "

" Of course," Jill said. She returned his smile, unwaveringly. Then he went out.

Jill turned back to the window.

The rain had stopped, perhaps minutes ago. The
air was full of a pure clear light, the sky was a washed
blue.

The stubble, brittle bright, shone with diamonds of
moisture and far down the hill the forest stood newly
dressed because the rain had taken away the dust as
well as the languor from the trees.

It was very lovely.

" Beautiful Bal-Annie ! " Jill said. Though she saw it, in this new dress, and loved it—it was of Kim she thought.

She rested her head against the window frame.

" If he would learn to *love* me . . . " she thought. It was more like a prayer.

Tuffy, because she herself had now momentous matters to consider, switched the main telephone line to the homestead through to the office. While she talked to Kim, Jill could get on with some work. Perhaps it was as well, for within minutes of Kim having gone outside the rings began coming through. Jill was called back into action by the compelling, not-to-be-denied repetitive ringing of the main-line telephone.

As she picked up the receiver she knew why Mrs. Baxter hated it. That ring was so commanding. And it interrupted that most sacred pastime of all—reverie.

CHAPTER ELEVEN

THAT FATEFUL DAY Jill had flung herself into all the work at hand, and all the demands made of her.

The telephone had continued to ring incessantly.

Half the time she wondered why everyone else seemed so helpless ! then she wondered why so many foolish persons cluttered up the world. There were any number of calls from people far, far distant from the fire-razed district who simply rang up *socially*, to get the news of what had happened; and in any event how was dear Mrs. Baxter ? They hadn't rung for weeks ! How had she stood up to the heat ?

Journalists and even radio news-hounds rang to know if there was any " human angle " to the story. What about the three men who had lost their lives in the fire, for instance ?

Why ring Kim ? Jill wondered desperately, flat-out answering legitimate calls and arranging for succour or help to those who had a claim.

He was the big man of the district, was the obvious answer. The Shire officials were all out at the scene of the fire, as were the policeman and other major officials in Darjalup.

So ring Kim Baxter—he'll know! That had been the psychology behind all those calls.

Kim had not only done as much top-level planning for the immediate alleviation of hardship from his office in the homestead but inevitably had to go out on to his own property and help maintain some kind of a skeleton routine there. He'd sent as many men as he could spare to other people's aid. He now had to do something about keeping everything on Bal-Annie from becoming chaos.

He and Jill had worked shoulder to shoulder in the office, then Kim had gone out, brought in Gem and his own horse, saddled them, and later they had begun the business of quietly drafting the Edens and stud bullocks back into their grazing paddocks.

When Kim went down to the saddling paddock to bring the horses in, Tuffy came into the office to see Jill.

She had put on a fresh dark-coloured alpaca dress with a neat white collar, and done her very pretty silvery white hair. She had obviously got *ready* for the occasion. She came in, very composed but just a little buttoned up about the lips, her round smooth face—anxious.

Jill almost expected her to fold her hands and say: " Well now, young miss ! Explain yourself."

Instead Tuffy stood in the doorway and looked at Jill. Jill rose from behind the chair and looked at Tuffy.

In that moment's silence the older woman read the plea in Jill's face.

Unexpectedly her own face creased; then she held out her hands.

It was as simple as that.

Jill went straight round the table and took both the hands in her own then suddenly her forehead was pressed against Tuffy's shoulder.

She straightened up quickly. Tuffy wouldn't like anyone *soft*. That hadn't been the way they had done things together yesterday.

Tuffy smiled and nodded her head sagaciously.

" What you want, Jill," she said with a certain sombre precision, " is a good cup of tea."

" Oh Tuffy ! " Jill laughed. " If only you knew— that is just what I do want."

She would never ask Kim what had passed between him and Tuffy in the kitchen. She didn't want to know. That clean alpaca dress and the white collar spoke volumes, but as soon as she and Tuffy had looked into one another's eyes nothing that had been said or thought, earlier, mattered any more. Each very simply remembered how each had acted for Bal-Annie, and yes, for Kim . . . yesterday. It had forged a bond, never to be broken.

They sat in the kitchen and drank tea; Tuffy told Jill a few things about Kim as a boy and a young man. She had also explained to Jill some of the paradoxes of Mrs. Baxter's character.

" Mrs. Baxter never was a farmer's wife," Tuffy explained. " She hated farms. She was a doctor's daughter, and used to town life. City life. But she fell in love with Mr. Baxter, and he with her. What were they to do ? "

" Like Ruth in the Bible, I suppose," said Jill. " *Whither thou goest, I will go* . . . ."

" That's easy enough for you to say, Jill," said Tuffy

severely. "You like country life. You love Bal-Annie. Oh yes, I can see it sticking out a mile. But it's not all Bal-Annie, is it?" Here the plea was in Tuffy's face this time. "It's Kim too, isn't it? You haven't got an empty heart where Kim is concerned, have you, Jill?"

Jill shook her head. There was nothing but truth in her eyes for Tuffy.

"I fell in love with him. I don't quite know when, but almost at once. Certainly the day he rode that beautiful horse, in the try-out. But how does one know it is love and not infatuation? I thought it might be that. I even hoped it might be that. Then the last few days—yesterday —to-day. I just *know*."

Tuffy nodded her head.

"Good," she said. "I'd never forgive anyone who married Kim and didn't love him."

Jill wanted to ask—"What about Vanessa?" More imperatively she wanted to ask—"What about *me*? Isn't it important that Kim should love me too?"

Instead she asked quite a different question.

"When Mrs. Baxter married Mr. Baxter did they come to live here on the property at once? Didn't she like farming then?"

"No. She loved Mr. Baxter but she never loved Bal-Annie. It was like a prison to her. But she never let him know. *I* knew, but Mr. Baxter? *Never*. She took up all that town work as an escape. Though mind you, she's a good woman and has a mind for helping people. That's the doctor's daughter in her."

"But then—when he died?" Jill asked tentatively.

"She had Don. Bal-Annie is Don's home and along with Kim is his heritage too. No, she's a good woman. She's stayed on to keep it a home for Don."

"Tuffy," Jill asked soberly. "Do you think she will like my being here—permanently, I mean? I ask you because I know that deep in Kim's heart it is *you*, more than his stepmother . . ."

But she couldn't finish. She had no right to be thinking things like this.

" She'll be downright glad he's going to marry someone," Tuffy said, getting up and refilling the teapot with hot water. She came back to the table. " I think she felt Kim marrying was her only chance of escape, before it was too late. She wants a home of her own, with plenty of large rose-gardens . . . not just somebody else's inheritance."

" Oh dear ! " said Jill, wishing she knew what to think, let alone what to say. Then she had another thought.

" I think she would have liked Kim to marry Vanessa," she said, half probing, half anxious about the reply that might come.

" Well . . ." said Tuffy judiciously, stalling that one off, perhaps for Kim's or his stepmother's sakes. " She's very beautiful. And it would have been a great society wedding. I think all the landed families down here in the south kind-of expected it. At all events they expected a grand hoo-ha in the district and that makes for visits to Perth and new wardrobes; and talk about who is invited and who is not. With that sort of wedding there are grand week-end parties with everybody's relatives coming south and staying in the big property homesteads. It's a proper going-on I can tell you. Sometimes it lasts a week or more; long after the bride and bridegroom are out of it."

Tuffy had not answered the original question and Jill now found she did not want to ask it again. She didn't want to *know* the answer. This was one of the things Kim had turned away from in the interests of his future life, and Bal-Annie.

Even Tuffy had said, when Jill had first arrived, that

Kim would never put Vanessa first. Bal-Annie would always be first. Now it was Jill, and not Vanessa who was in second place.

Well, somebody had to be second!

Jill wondered what sort of a wedding she would have. Certainly not a big district one. Her mother and father were not landed people. They were simple people. She was their only daughter, and she would be married from their home.

She hoped Kim wouldn't make a *hoo-ha* about that. Oddly enough she didn't expect him to make any kind of a fuss, either way. She had a feeling he wanted peace, quiet and the thing over and done with.

Then *work* could go forward.

Kim came up to the homestead after he had brought the horses in and saddled them. Not finding Jill in the office he rang through to the switchboard to ask Tuffy where she was.

" She's coming," Tuffy answered adroitly. She wasn't going to let Kim know *yet*, that she had swallowed whatever were the words she had uttered earlier on this sub-ject of this marriage.

Jill dashed water over her cup and saucer from the hot faucet above the sink and put them up on the draining rack.

As she hurried through the door, she passed Tuffy coming in from the switchboard. Like quicksilver she pressed a kiss on Tuffy's cheek; then looking back gave her a gay smile. She didn't wait to see how Tuffy took it. Somehow she knew Tuffy would be her ally. Tuffy would never let Kim, or Kim's possessions, down.

"And that's about what I'll be," thought Jill, hastening down the passage to the office. " One more possession." Yet incomprehensibly her spirits were lifting. Her heart beat faster. In a minute she would see him again. The half-hour he had been down at the saddling paddock had been half a lifetime.

Perhaps he would put his arm around her again. Perhaps he would put his cheek against her cheek again. This time she wouldn't be stiff, afraid.

As she reached the door the telephone rang.

Kim looked up, smiled at Jill, as he went to the phone. " Yes . . . . It's trunk-line again, is it, Tuffy ? Put it through."

This putting through took several minutes, as Jill well knew, and Kim turned away from the wall phone back to her.

" The horses are in, Jill," he said quietly. " Do you think you'd better get your hat ? The sun looks as if it's staying out and it's got the wrath of God in it again."

" Yes. I'll get it on my way out. I left it hanging on the side veranda. I just want to put these loose appointment slips in order. I might forget later . . ."

She had worked side by side with Kim all the morning and it didn't occur to her, by this time, that he had *private* telephone calls. It was he who had said she had all but taken his immortal soul into her keeping.

A voice came through on the telephone and Kim turned back to it. There was no more than his back, and a little of his profile, presented to the rest of the office now.

" Yes, this is Bal-Annie, exchange. Put Mount Sterling through . . . . Yes, it will be the Althrops calling."

The name didn't quite click with Jill. She wasn't listening. She was concentrating on the order of those slips and placing them between the leaves of Kim's table diary.

It was Kim's voice, the quality of it, that brought her eyes up. It was deeper, softer; there was the unmistakable intimacy in it of someone talking to someone else well-known and . . .

" Yes, Vanessa ! " he said. " Kim here . . . No, I'm afraid Redwood was wiped out . . . Yes. We lost three men. Bal-Annie missed trouble except for a scrub fire they managed to control down at the bottom of the stubble paddock . . ." he gave a laugh. A friendly easy laugh. " I'm all right, thank you, and Mother's flat-out serving tea and new clothes to the Redwood people . . ."

Jill closed Kim's diary and quietly went out of the room.

Perhaps, in a minute, he would tell Vanessa—about Jill. Or would he ? Was that why he had that nearly intimate, half-tender note in his voice ? Did he know he was about to hurt someone he liked well ?

Or . . . .

Or what ?

Jill realised, for the first time, the full impact of that pain, so peculiar to those who marry a man who has had half his heart in a pipe-dream girl.

She knew in advance that when the time came, and she was to feel his heart against her heart, it would be to wonder if it was all of his heart.

He needs me. I am right for him, she said to herself as she took her hat from the veranda peg. *He is mine, by his choice.*

Out there in the paddocks, as formerly in the office, they worked together. They worked impersonally, as only two people intent and concentrated on work can and must work, forgetting all personal relationships ! Relegating them to their proper time and place.

They ate a quick sandwich lunch, with hot billy tea, down at the stables with the two men left on the property to look after the horses.

Even over that brew of billy tea, they were impersonal. Or so it seemed to Jill who found all this an effort but thought there was no such effort on Kim's part. He simply was the man of action. He didn't have to try.

Yet he'd been very nice to her in the office over that proposal.

She remembered the way he had smiled at her ; the amused way he had said " *no*," when she had asked him did he really expect her to refuse his offer and his proposal.

Her spirits lifted. Of course he had to be nice about this marriage-to-be to Vanessa. He had to let Vanessa down lightly. He would have been less than what he was if he *hadn't* let her down lightly.

A feeling of tenderness crept back and warmed Jill's heart. Looking at him made her feel a little dizzy.

He was more than kind. He was a wonderful person.

In the evening Mrs. Baxter came home exhausted; too tired really to comprehend Kim's words when, sitting drinking their coffee in the front room after dinner, Kim picked up his coffee cup, looked across the space to his mother with those dark intent blue eyes and said:

" Mother, Jill and I are going to marry. We think it's a good idea, and hope you do."

Jill looked anxiously at Mrs. Baxter. The latter was sitting on the sofa looking almost too tired to hold her coffee cup. How would she take this stark announcement ?

Mrs. Baxter evidently knew Kim. She was not perturbed by the abrupt manner of his delivery.

She put her empty coffee cup and saucer on the low table in front of her and leaned back against the cushions. She closed her eyes.

" Really, Kim ! " she said. "All your life—or all the part of your life I've known you—you've picked the strangest times to do inconvenient things. Why, when I'm so devastatingly tired do you pick this minute to give me that kind of a shot in the arm ? "

Then she opened her eyes wide and looked at Jill. Unexpectedly she laughed.

" My dear girl," she said. " If you knew the doubts he had about having you foisted on him as an off-sider—I think that was the word you all used—you would realise just how funny it is to me that Kim now wants to marry you. Really, you can never tell about men. No matter how well you think you know them."

" I hope you will approve, Mrs. Baxter," Jill said anxiously.

"Approve, my dear girl ? I'm delighted Kim's going to marry. I thought he'd never take the plunge. Now I'm so unspeakably tired I can't quite take it in."

She began to pick herself up from the sofa. Kim stood up and moved round to help her.

" Do you have to go into Darjalup to-morrow ? " he asked. " I think you are knocked-up."

She had his arm now. She stood, slim and well-dressed in a very simple way, and looked at him.

" My dear Kim," she said. " Why can't you tell me something else in addition to the fact you're going to get married, to make sure of my being knocked-up ? I wish I could feel glad. I expect in the morning I will. Now if you don't mind I'm going to bed . . ."

She took a few steps towards the door, her hand still on Kim's arm. She bent over, as she passed Jill's chair and patted her shoulder.

" See if you can make a good job of Bal-Annie, my dear. It'll be a hopeless marriage if you can't do that——"

" Please, Mrs. Baxter," Jill said, getting up. " Please let me come into Darjalup and help you to-morrow." Her eyes pleaded, past the older woman, to Kim. " Could you spare me, Kim ? " she asked.

He looked at her thoughtfully for a minute.

" Of course," he said. " I think you had better go, Jill.

As a matter of fact I think I've done all I can do at the 'arranging' level here. I'll keep Bevin and Johns back on Bal-Annie to-morrow and come in to Darjalup myself. It's time I swung my effort there. I'm afraid it won't be till later in the morning."

"It will be chaotic," said Mrs. Baxter, having dropped Kim's arm and now on her way to the door. "The Red Cross and Country Women's Association have moved in. Also the Lord Mayor of Perth put in a television appeal for help from the citizens of Perth and truck loads of stuff are coming down. Look, my dears, I can't think about it any more, let alone *talk* about it."

Kim had reached the door first and he held it open for Mrs. Baxter.

"Good-night, both of you," she said. She touched Kim's arm as she went through. "What a bear Jill's got herself," she added with a laugh. "I hope she reforms you."

Jill had a feeling that when Mrs. Baxter was sufficiently through the hall to be out of earshot she would say . . . "To think he's going to marry that girl! Well, wonders will never cease and it will probably turn out all right. One never knows about these things."

Too tired, and just a little unhappy because of that tiredness, Mrs. Baxter didn't really care.

Kim watched her go, then he turned and came back to Jill. His eyes were serious but his mouth was framing a smile that was meant to be something kind and considerate for Jill.

He held out his hand to her.

"Come out on to the veranda," he said. "There is a moon shining and you must come and see your kingdom when it's silver."

Yes, he was doing all the right things, in the right order and in the right places. She must do likewise.

She took his hand, wondering with a delicate kind of

shock, at the little river of feeling that ran through her when she felt his hand touch and grasp hers.

They went through the french window and when they reached the balustrade he put her hand under his arm.

"There it is," he said quietly. His voice had the soft intimate quality with which he had spoken to Vanessa on the telephone. He was looking at something he loved.

Perhaps, one day, he would love her, Jill, just for loving Bal-Annie too.

The paddock stretched out, a silver sea, to the black rim of the forest.

In front of them the rose-garden was secretive and sweet-smelling, haunted with lovely scents; a hundred and fifty yards away the timbered fence of the home paddock made a black stick-pattern of shadows on the ground; the sky was moonwashed and serene.

" It is very lovely, Kim," Jill said. She let her hand curl, round his arm.

They were silent a minute. Then he said:

" Thank you for being kind to mother. She is very tired——"

"I hope she will approve of us," Jill said. " I couldn't bear anyone to be unhappy because . . . well, because . . ."

" Because we're getting married ? " said Kim. Again his voice was quiet, kind. She could almost mistake it for tenderness. " No one is ever unhappy when a marriage is a good one."

Jill longed to say . . . " But what would she have said if it had been Vanessa ? " But of course she couldn't ask this.

Kim moved his arm along her shoulder. Quietly he turned her towards him. Their faces were blue white in the moonlight but she could see his eyes—dark with the light just catching them. He bent his head and kissed her.

Jill closed her eyes and received the kiss, but something

in her wouldn't quite thaw out to return it. She wanted more, oh so much more ! How did she ask for it ? How did she *give* it ?

Why was it, longing to be in his arms, she stood shyly there and took his mouth on her mouth, yet did not move ?

Perhaps time will help me, she thought, wanting to cry aloud at her own frozen anxiety.

" Go to bed, Jill," Kim said quietly. " You too are tired and to-morrow you're taking on quite a load."

There was that soft, vibrating timbre in his voice ! It suddenly filled Jill with a wild kind of longing, for something intangible and perhaps for ever beyond reach.

" Kim . . . ? "

" Yes, Jill."

" I think if you put your arms around me . . . both of them . . ."

Both arms went round her and he drew her against him. She shivered then lay still, her head cradled against his breast, his arms warm and comforting around her. She felt the rough touch of his coat against her cheek; and the unexpected male strength of a man's arms.

He stroked the back of her head, then put her away from him.

" Time you went to bed," he said again; very firmly. He kissed her a second time on the lips and this time Jill considered that kiss with her head and not her heart. It was light and good, with perhaps an awakening touch of passion.

" How silly this will all be in ten years' time," she thought. " We have to teach one another love. Of course, it is not easy at first. There'll come a time . . ."

" Good night, Kim," she said, drawing away.

" Good night, Jill," he said. " See you in the morning."

" See you in the morning, Kim."

She went back through the french window into the lounge, leaving him alone on the veranda; alone with his silvered paddocks and dark night-shadows in the distant trees.

Oddly, the farther she went away from him, the more her heart rose, the more her love, real love, welled up in her.

Why, on the veranda, hadn't *she* been able to teach him something with that kiss?

Perhaps it was true—they had to learn together.

Perhaps it was because she was afraid that already she loved; but he did not. The saying flashed through her head—so true yet so banal—" *Man's love is of man's life a thing apart.*"

Several days passed quickly, borne on the wings of activity. Each day Jill went into Darjalup with Mrs. Baxter. As a result of the Lord Mayor's appeal, gifts poured by truck load into the town. Furniture, clothes, baby-sets, prams, kitchen and living-room utensils—they all had to be sorted and distributed. Money came in, in great sums and this the Shire Council set aside to build new homes immediately for those who had lost their former ones.

Jill thought it was wonderful, almost fantastic, how order came out of seeming chaos and how the generosity of people seemed limitless when it came to the sufferings of others from the holocaust of bushfire.

Working side by side with Mrs. Baxter, driving in and out from Bal-Annie each day, Jill learned that Mrs. Baxter did not mind in the least that Kim was marrying her, a virtually unknown girl. Mrs. Baxter was thankful Kim was marrying somebody; and actually her mind was on other things. What to do with the overflow of clothing that had arrived, how to take the opportunity, now arrived, to see that the Jones family did not live next door to the

Linton family because formerly, in their beautiful new houses in Redwood, they hadn't agreed—which particular house in Darjalup she would buy herself.

"Now I can have my own rose-garden," she said. "And never again have to drive thirty miles in and thirty miles out every time I have a meeting, or want to make a call."

Jill, at first, had been upset at this decision of Mrs. Baxter's to leave Bal-Annie, but it soon became clear the older lady was determined.

" I'll call on you at least once a week," she said. " My farming days are over, Jill." Then added a fervent . . . " Thank God."

Jill knew she meant it.

Only once did Jill get near the subject of Vanessa.

" You really wanted someone ' decorative ' for Kim," she said diffidently as they drove home on the third day after the fire.

" Yes . . . well . . ." said Mrs. Baxter reflectively. " But it was not to be, was it ? Not that you're not decorative, in your own way, Jill. You're a very pretty girl. Vanessa is a different type of course. Oh look . . . someone's left the Meechams' gate open."

She pulled up with a skid of tyres.

" Do get out and shut the gate like a good girl, will you ? City people who don't know that farm gates should be left closed shouldn't be allowed across the river."

Jill closed the gates and felt as she did so that she was closing the door on Mrs. Baxter's reflections about the differences in type between herself and Vanessa. She would probably never know how the district would react to this " engagement " nor what would be said for and against this marriage between the great Kim Baxter and the little girl from nowhere who had landed a job with him because she was out-of-work. And landed him as a marriage partner too. They would probably make plenty of their wry-humoured comments about that !

The only thing that Jill cared about was that Kim should love her.

CHAPTER TWELVE

IN ALL THAT week following the bushfire Jill did not see Shane Evans once. For the first few days he had been bivouacked out at the fire scene, helping organise the clearing of burnt-out debris from the blocks that once had been homes. At the latter end of the week he went to Perth with the Shire president interviewing government officials and assisting them organise relief for the homeless and plans for the immediate future.

Each time Jill passed the Shire offices in Mrs. Baxter's car she thought of Shane and her promise to be his " slice of cake " *until they quarrelled*. It had been a joke, and a happy one. She imagined Shane would have given a hearty chuckle at the news of her engagement to Kim Baxter.

For three of the nights of that week Kim himself had stayed with the temporary camp out at Redwood.

On the Saturday midday he came home.

" When do you want to get married, Kim ? " Mrs. Baxter asked over lunch. " Now the first of the worst is over we've got a breathing space. We'd better talk about our own affairs."

" Straight away, I think," Kim said. He looked across the table at Jill. " Yes ? " he asked her.

" I think so . . ." Jill said. She felt she couldn't much longer bear this sort of half-relationship with him. Marriage, she thought, would fix a pattern. After that everything would work itself out. It would all be so easy . . . she and Kim together, alone in some part of those days, anyway.

" I'm all for it," said Mrs. Baxter, without enthusiasm but quite firmly. " I can't stand this rushing in and out business and not knowing what's going to happen next. Long engagements are too, too trying on everybody's nerves. At least we'll cut out all the party racket ! Not that anybody is in the mood for parties with this bush-fire business."

" Go and get yourself a special licence, Kim," Tuffy said from her end of the table. " Mrs. Baxter and I'll go and take a breather in Perth and leave you to the home-stead for a few days."

Kim was watching first one face then the other as they spoke. Clearly he wanted their views and he didn't want to hurt anybody in the process of carrying out his own ideas.

" Please—no," Jill said. " I've written to my father and mother and I had a letter to-day. They haven't met Kim yet. They're very happy about . . . well, about us. But they want to meet Kim. And you, Mrs. Baxter."

" Of course," Mrs. Baxter said agreeably. " On Monday morning I shall take you to Perth. You need clothes anyway. Whoever heard of a girl getting married without some new clothes. Kim, what about it ? "

He crumbled bread thoughtfully then he looked up at Jill. His eyes, so serious yet always with a lurking hint of intent kindness at the back of them, were beginning to have a devastating effect on Jill. They made her heart lurch a little and her head say . . . " You're falling in love, Jill. You're in love, in fact."

" I'd like to get married on Monday and be done with it," Kim said. " But I guess we've other people to think about—mostly Jill's parents. I had a very nice letter from Mr. Dawson to-day, and the least I can do is go up to Perth and meet him."

" You'll come too ? On Monday ? " said Jill, her face
lighting up eagerly.

" I'm afraid not," said Kim more seriously. He turned
to Mrs. Baxter. " If you take Jill up to town on Monday
I'll come up at the end of the week. There's a temporary
lull in affairs here, at the moment, but I've neglected
Bal-Annie."

He looked at Jill again with that old half-ironic smile
that sometimes troubled her.

" I'll come up on Friday or Saturday, meet your
parents, and we'll get married on the following Monday.
How's that ? "

" Really, Kim," Tuffy interposed, pursing her mouth
and wagging her head as she must have done through the
years when she had " mothered " him. " You're not
the only one getting married. Jill's getting married too.
And her parents are marrying off their daughter . . ."

" Please," said Jill, looking at Tuffy, wanting to per-
suade her. " I'd like that too. I'm like Kim. I hate
long-drawn-out planning. Besides, there is only a ' lull '
here in Darjalup. We both need to be here. There is so
much to do."

" Good," said Kim, pushing back his chair and standing
up. His smile for Tuffy was a little wry. " Defeated again,
Tuffy," he said. "Never mind. Think how much you'll
enjoy yourself with one whole week of Bal-Annie homestead to ourselves. Only you and me, Tuffy. You can
do all the spoiling and scolding you like. No one to hear,
and I'll promise you I shan't be listening."

As he passed round behind her chair he put his hands
behind her head and brushed her hair up into its top-
knot. He took out a hair-pin, fixed in a wisp of hair and
replaced the pin. Tuffy, sitting upright in her chair,
under his ministering hands, had her lips pursed and her
hands folded in her lap.

" That'll do, Kim," she said quietly. " I know all your

tricks about getting your own way. I'm not convinced, but it's many a long day since I won a battle with you."

Mrs. Baxter lit a cigarette and with her free hand was making a pattern of the silver peppers and salts on the table.

" Where are you going to live in the homestead when you are married ? " she asked without looking up.

" In my own hideout, of course," said Kim over Tuffy's head. " You're not thinking of moving out, Mother ? Not till you've got the right house and all done up as you want it. And then only in the face of our stern disapproval, isn't that so, Jill ? "

He looked at Jill over the top of Tuffy's silvery hair.

" Of course," Jill said emphatically.

" In that case," said Mrs. Baxter, re-arranging the peppers and salts back to their original order, " Kim goes about his affairs, Tuffy does something about those rooms in the side passage, and Jill and I go to Perth. Am I right ? "

For the first time she looked up and around the faces.

"Absolutely right," said Kim. He tilted Tuffy's head back so that he could look into her face, upside-down though it was. " Tuffy, can you manage ? Things like fresh curtains . . . and some beds or something. We haven't got a double bed in the house anywhere, Mother, have we ? "

Jill tried valiantly not to blush. Double beds seemed to be something one took for granted after marriage, but as a public topic of conversation—well, only Kim seemed to think it was all right.

" We have not," said Mrs. Baxter. " Of course you could always order a suite of furniture when you do come to Perth."

" That's just what we'll do," said Kim. He released Tuffy and walked round the table to the door.

" I've to go and see what goes on at the back paddock dam," he said. " See you all later."

He smiled at Jill and for one startled moment she had the feeling Kim knew he had shocked her and Tuffy, possibly his mother. He had done it on purpose . . . and was somewhere, deep inside him, laughing.

She wondered why it suddenly lifted her spirits to soaring heights. He was *human*, and in such a subtle gorgeous way. It was going to be wonderful to be married to him !

Without any hitches in their planning Jill and Mrs. Baxter caught the north-bound bus outside the hotel in Darjalup on the Saturday morning. Kim drove them in, with Tuffy sitting in the corner of the back seat, bound for a day's shopping for that set of rooms in the side passage and not to be done out of the excitement of seeing the travellers off.

There wasn't much opportunity for Kim and Jill to take more than a speeding farewell of one another. A bus was a public place, for one thing. For another thing, half the country world seemed to be congregated in the main street, even at that early hour.

Kim simply took off his hat, kissed first his mother and then Jill. As he did so he smiled into Jill's eyes.

" So long, Jill ! " he said.

" So long, Kim ! " She thought perhaps her heart was in her eyes but now that didn't seem to matter any more. In the last few days she and Kim had come closer to one another. He was still remote as if there remained something of the stranger in him—for Jill ; and for herself to Kim, there was something of the girl who had to be led gently along the paths that led to his idea of love in marriage.

Just as the bus was pulling out Shane Evans came along the main street. He saw Kim first, and then when Kim explained who he was seeing off in the bus, Shane stood in the road, raising both hands clasped above his head as some kind of a hail-and-farewell greeting to Jill. He was grinning widely all over his face but the last Jill saw of the two men was Shane arguing with mock belligerence at Kim, and Kim standing, tall, unperturbed, but listening with head a little on one side, his hat forward over his brow, his shadow casting itself on Shane and at length on to the bitumen road.

What Shane was saying Jill would never know but what she did know was that he was play-acting in his own inimical way. Kim too, she hoped, would know that. After all, Kim had known Shane Evans for years and years.

The little scene, with Tuffy on the footpath in the background, made Jill smile. Then she turned her face forwards, looking up the long, long road through the town and then the forest and so on to the wheatlands and finally home.

For the first time in weeks she thought she couldn't bear to wait the necessary time to see her mother and father, and the charming green and white, red-tiled bungalow they had built themselves in a treeland garden suburb between Perth and the ocean.

Then when Kim came !

In her mind's eye she could see already the bursting pride with which she would produce Kim, less than a week away, when he would knock at the Dawson door.

All this was enough to lift any girl's heart and Mrs. Baxter, seeing the expectancy and the light in Jill's face, suddenly furrowed her own brow and looked out of the window.

What, she wondered, was Kim doing to this girl ? She was certain he wasn't in love with Jill. She doubted if Kim would ever be in love with anybody. Too many girls had tried without any reaction from Kim. Vanessa alone had won something from him but that, Mrs. Baxter guessed, was admiration and a possible desire for Vanessa's sheer physical beauty.

Nothing wrong with that, she thought. That's the prerogative of any man when a beautiful woman is around who knows how to look inviting. That was just one of the facts of life every woman had to face.

She hoped Jill knew about the facts of life.

It was a wonderful week. Mrs. Baxter and Jill's parents took to one another at once, all on account of the rose-garden. The varieties that Mr. Dawson didn't have Mrs. Baxter did have. And vice versa. They spent hours discussing them and promising exchanges.

Mrs. Baxter was staying at a good hotel in the city and each day Jill met her. They did shopping together, some for Jill herself and some, with Mrs. Baxter's guidance and foreknowledge, for the homestead. Mrs. Baxter also had an eye on bargain hunting for her own projected home. She, it soon became clear to Jill, loved a bargain. But she never bought rubbish.

Then they had lunch together at the hotel. Each day at lunch-time Tuffy rang up on the long-distance line from Bal-Annie with news of progress with that set of rooms and for any requests she had for things to be sent down by freight bus. She also gave the news of Bal-Annie and as far as news of Kim was concerned it consisted of saying :

" Kim's busy, but well."

Each time that telephone call came through Jill wished it was from Kim for herself, but it never was.

At last Saturday, the day Kim was to come to Perth, arrived.

He was driving himself up and Jill had no idea when he would arrive. Not before late afternoon, she was sure of that.

Quite early after the midday meal she found herself going again and again to the window of the front room and looking out. The minutes, the half-hours, and indeed the hours crept by. Jill thought she would never live through them.

She knew now she didn't want anything else in the world but the sight of Kim's tall figure walking up the curving path from the gate.

A hundred times a big heavy car, the over-landing type, turned the corner but swept on past the bungalow. " When will he come " turned into " what if he doesn't come ? "

Jill's father had gone to attend to his business, for Saturday afternoon was a busy day with the news-agency and book-store he kept ; but Mrs. Dawson hovered about in the kitchen, cooking the party-like evening meal that was to serve as Kim Baxter's welcome. She tried not to notice and not let her heart ache for her daughter's long wait.

" This is something every girl goes through," she thought. " Jill the same as anyone else. When he comes it won't matter any more."

In one way her heart rejoiced. Clearly Jill was in love with this man. She wasn't marrying him for what he had to offer in that great big property of his down in the south. No girl who didn't love a man ever had that waiting look in her eyes.

At last half past five came, and with it came Kim.

It was one of those moments when Jill had gone out to the kitchen to find something to do to help her mother. Mrs. Dawson had gone into the front room to make sure the roses looked well in their vases and that everything was perfect, ready for this momentous visit.

It was she who heard the car pull up, and she went to the window.

She watched the tall bronzed man get out of the car,

walk round it, then look back at it, as if making sure all was well. Then he looked up at the house, as he came through the gate, and Mrs. Dawson could see his face.

Her own heart fluttered.

" Goodness me ! " she thought. " What a fine man he is ! "

She liked his clothes, casual tweeds; she liked his hat — that broad-brimmed station-owner's hat; she liked the expression on his face which was strong, assured, yet human.

" Jill ! " she called. " He's here. He's coming up the path now."

Jill flew into the front room and mother and daughter stood side by side and through the fine veiling of lace curtain watched Kim Baxter come up the three stone steps that led to the bungalow veranda.

Jill stood so still that Mrs. Dawson looked at her.

Her daughter's eyes had tears in them.

" There, there ! " said Mrs. Dawson. " Blink those silly things back. Every man wants his girl to greet him with a smile."

Jill blinked. As the door bell rang she glanced at herself in the wall mirror before she went to open the front door. Mrs. Dawson shook her head, puzzled, for it was a very circumspect Jill who went into the hall.

Jill drew in a deep breath and opened the door. All that circumspection didn't go for much when there was no door between herself and Kim. He took off his hat, put one arm round her and kissed her.

" Still going to marry me ? " he asked, looking at her. He was joking, yet there was a look of real inquiry in his eyes.

" Of course," said Jill. " I've got a beautiful dress. No, not white satin and a veil, but a *dress*. Mrs. Baxter loves it, and so does Mother."

Mrs. Dawson, having given them a moment or two in the hall, came towards them.

" Mother," Jill said. " This is Kim."

They stood and looked at one another, quite gravely. Then Mrs. Dawson put out her hand and Kim's went out to meet hers.

" I . . . I don't really know quite what to say . . ." Mrs. Dawson faltered.

" Nothing, Mother," said Jill, with a laugh.

Mrs. Dawson's eyes, like Jill's, said everything for her. She was bowled over.

The next two days went like lightning. Kim stayed in the hotel with Mrs. Baxter but they both spent a good deal of their time at the Dawson bungalow. Kim had to meet all Mr. and Mrs. Dawson's friends: and both families had to have dinner in the hotel with Kim and his mother.

Jill felt madly grateful to Kim for the way he took everyone seriously, listening, his head a little on the side, with that concentrated look in his dark blue eyes, as the neighbours and friends called.

His manners were impeccable and Jill could see he had that one great but rare facility of making each person feel that, for the moment, he or she were of great interest to him.

Jill was a little strung up herself but both Mrs. Baxter and Mrs. Dawson reassured one another that this was very usual in brides.

" It's a big strain," they agreed. " She'd be a funny girl if she wasn't strung up."

But why was Kim so calm?

Jill looked at him with envy and admiration; sometimes with a tiny query at the back of her mind.

" But he's doing this logically," she told herself. " He's worked it all out, step by step, and now he's putting it into operation."

For Kim, she thought, it wasn't a love match, it was a sensible match. He didn't have to be wrought up about it.

Yet he loved her in a little way. She knew that already. He held her in his arms and kissed her so tenderly. He smiled at her, ruffled her hair and when he left her each evening he said . . .

" So long, Jill ! "

" So long, Kim ! "

It was their love call. Not passionate, but very sweet.

On Monday afternoon they were married. Jill looked lovely in her white chiffon dress with a panel floating away at the back, and a large wide-brimmed straw hat on her head. For a bouquet she carried her father's prize roses. Don, released from school for the day, looked a young replica of his older brother.

It was the first time Jill had seen Kim in a tailored suit. He looked suddenly remote and dignified, something of a stranger. Mrs. Baxter was chic in a pink lace dress and Mrs. Dawson looked charming in a blue silk one.

The wedding ceremony in the parish church a quarter of a mile away from Jill's home was soon over, and they were back in the bungalow, now massed with flowers and champagne corks were popping. Mrs. Dawson shed a private tear because she thought she had lost a daughter; Mr. Dawson, not a tall man, grew in stature and exuded pride because he considered he had got a son.

Tuffy, who had come up from Darjalup late the night before, sat on the sofa, not in alpaca this time, but in a steel grey silk dress and a new hat.

She watched Jill and Kim with pursed lips and nodded her head.

" They're happy," she said to herself. " It'll work out all right."

Like Mrs. Baxter she had her doubts as to how much Kim, that reserved Bal-Annie addicted man, loved anybody with all his heart and soul.

There was no doubt in Tuffy's mind about Jill. One look at that radiant face was enough. Tuffy, in her wisdom, smiled.

" She'd soften a heart of stone," she whispered to Mrs. Baxter when that lady was freed from the official duty of helping to receive the few friends of the Dawsons who had been invited to the wedding.

Mrs. Baxter furrowed her brow and looked at Tuffy through half-closed eyes, an expression she affected when she was about to dispute something.

" You're not suggesting Kim's not in love with her, Tuffy ? " she asked, a trifle askance.

" What do you think yourself ? " said Tuffy, not in the least put out, and not wanting an answer.

Mrs. Baxter decided it was time to reach for a cigarette on the nearby table.

" I hope those rooms look nice," she said. " What did you do for beds, Tuffy ? "

" Two of those three-quarter beds that used to be in the guest room. They've been in the attic this last five years. Burns polished them up for me and I must say that being antique they now look valuable and dressy. Of course I put the divan bed in Kim's own room. He's got to have somewhere to sleep when it's shearing and all-night sowing time. Only a month or two off, you know."

" Yes, I suppose so," said Mrs. Baxter. " Jill will find out with a vengeance what life is like on a big property when the May rains come, and we start sowing."

At last it was time for Jill and Kim to go. Jill had slipped into a light tan linen suit and a small head-fitting hat with chrysanthemum petals around it.

" She certainly looks lovely," said Tuffy, still sitting

on the sofa, fixed there as if for ever; the matriarch of
the party. She felt a sudden pricking behind her eyes
as Kim came over to her, bent and kissed her on the
cheek.

"So long, *Maman*," he said quietly. No one but Tuffy
heard him. It was what he had called her in the long
ago before Mr. Baxter had married the second time. He
straightened up and looked down at her, his eyes inviting,
just a little mischievous. "Do you like my girl, Tuffy?"
he said.

"Be good to her, Kim," Tuffy said. "You've got
more than you deserve considering the hard-headed way
you went into this thing."

"I'll let you into a secret," he said, smiling down at
her. "She's softened me up."

He turned away and went across the room to Mrs.
Baxter.

"Come and see us off, Mother," he said, holding out
his hand.

Jill, in the midst of all her farewells, had seen those
little by-plays. He was really very wonderful, she thought.
He'd had two mothers all these years in Bal-Annie and
he'd never let either know if, or how much, the other was
in his heart. He'd kept the peace.

Don raced after the car until it had turned the corner.
The last thing Jill saw looking back through the rear
window was Don jumping in the air, both hands held
in a loop high above his head—so like a very young
edition of Shane, she thought.

Kim had turned-in his car, a Chrysler Royal, for a
new one. It was to be sent down to Darjalup by rail.
He and Jill were taking the plane down to the south coast
where they were to have a two-day honeymoon. One of
the other Bal-Annie cars was to be left at the Southern
Ocean Hotel, and they would drive back on Wednesday
afternoon.

Jill was still too keyed up to feel completely natural with Kim, but he was calmly competent to cope with everything including their air-tickets, their luggage and even a cup of coffee in the lounge of the airport while waiting for their flight to be called.

The plane was a small single-engined mail plane and would take less than two hours to drop them down at King George's Sound, a beautiful harbour and town facing the Southern Ocean.

The plane was like a tiny mosquito beside the big trans-continental planes on the tarmac. Its main duty was to drop the newspapers and mail at country towns on the southern route.

Inside the plane's body were single seats on either side of a minute aisle. Kim and Jill could not sit together but they were near enough for Kim to talk to Jill, asking her questions about her parents, their home, and their friends. Jill began to have an awed feeling that Kim did everything right. She couldn't bring herself to believe he was really so interested in the Dawson friends.

She was tired now, and she wished she didn't have that awed feeling. She wanted to make herself feel more natural with him; more his equal.

How strange it was when a girl married! She wasn't herself any more. She was someone else, with a different name.

Almost as if Kim sensed this feeling of strangeness and uncertainty about Jill he put out his hand, across the tiny aisle, and took hers in it.

Jill smiled as her own hand clasped his. She rested her head back on the head-rest and closed her eyes. She was happy. That was all she wanted—reassurance; and he had given it to her.

It was half past eleven, late at night, when they arrived at the Southern Ocean Hotel. Jill was sleepy in a happy way; the luxury of the hotel warmed her heart.

The great vast lounge with its glass front wall looked out over the ocean, now a dark canvas under the stars. In the morning it would look wonderful. The sun would be shining and the sea would be a brilliant blue under a blue dome of sky.

In the morning everything would be different!

Kim put Jill in a comfortable chair in the semi-darkened lounge while he crossed over to the desk to register, and ask for his room keys.

" The bridal suite for you, sir," the clerk said, trying to look bland.

" Thank you," Kim said, not looking up as he drew the register towards him. He picked up a ball-point pen on the desk. " Will you ask the lift boy to take up the cases, please."

He glanced up now.

" I would be glad if you would see that some tea is sent up to my wife." He said it evenly, his eyes uncommunicative and unconcerned that now the clerk doubted that this was indeed a bridal couple.

Some of these rich farmers ordered that suite because it not only cost more but was more comfortable.

" Certainly, sir," the clerk said. " Shall I get someone to take Mrs. Baxter up ? "

" Yes please, if you will," Kim said, still unperturbed.

He wanted to go round to the hotel garages at the side and see whether the Bal-Annie car was there. His young eighteen-year-old stable boy was to bring it down. Kim always liked to check everything.

The clerk moved round the desk to call a porter and Kim glanced down the register. He stood looking at it, his pen ready to write; but not writing. The name above the space for his own name was one that stuck out as if it had sign-posts on it.

Vanessa Althrop—Mount Sterling.

For a long moment Kim stared at it. Then he bent his head and wrote " Mr. and Mrs. Kim Baxter—Bal-Annie " in a large bold signature.

He put the pen down and swung the register round so that it now faced about.

In the mirror, half the size of the room and which hung on the wall behind the desk, Kim saw a steward taking Jill across the lounge to the lift. He stood quite still and watched her.

When she was in the lift, the door closed and the button pressed, he watched the flicker of red lights on the check-board as the lift ascended to the right floor.

Then he turned and walked across the lounge to a chair facing the far wall and what view of the ocean the night would reveal.

" Bring me a large whisky and soda," he told the steward.

He sat, his elbow on the arm-rest, his chin resting in his hand. His hat which he had long since discarded was lying on a table near the reception desk. For the moment he had forgotten about that car.

Outside the ocean was dark but the stars above it were very bright. An ocean-going liner passed, a necklace of lights.

The steward came back and after placing a mat beside Kim, put the whisky and a small jug of iced water on the mat.

" Did you arrange for some tea to go up to my wife ? " Kim said without looking up.

" Yes sir." The steward stood very upright while Kim dug in his pocket. " She'll be having it served now, sir. Thank you, sir. Is there anything else ? "

" No thank you. I think I shall wait here a little while. Good night."

" Good night, sir."

Kim did not touch his drink. He sat looking out where

the stars became dancing yellow diamonds on the dark ocean below. There in the light and shadows of those moving waves were two faces . . . one so fair, so radiant, so young. The other, petulant but beautiful, with eyes that offered everything ; and insolent promise of pleasure in store.

Kim picked up his drink and sipped it. Then he, too, put back his head against the chair rest, and closed his eyes.

The desk clerk was turning down the lights and there was a shrill ringing of the phone beside him. He picked it up with a gesture of irritation.

" Yes ? . . . What's that ? . . . Yes, he's here in the lounge now. I'll call him."

In a modified tone he called across the room to Kim.

" Were you expecting a call, Mr. Baxter ? This is the switchboard from a relay line below the southern hills. They're asking for you."

Kim lifted his head sharply, then stood up and came across the floor quickly. He took the phone from the clerk.

" Yes ? Baxter here."

He listened for a few minutes and his eyes lifted and met the inquiring ones of the clerk. It was an odd time for a telephone call from a relay line. Generally such lines closed down at six in the evening.

" Who was driving it ? Is the boy all right ? . . . You don't know ? . . . the car was empty ? . . . Can you get a message through to other relay stations for me ? . . . There's no one answering at Mount Sterling or Bardup ? . . . Well, thank you very much for letting me know . . . Yes, I'll do something about it at once."

He slammed the phone down on the rest and stood looking at the clerk, hardly seeing him. He was lost in worried thought.

" Can I do anything for you, sir ? "

Kim pulled himself together.

" They've found one of my cars turned on its side on the Darjalup-Mount Sterling track through the foothills. I was expecting it to be brought in here this afternoon."

" You can borrow or hire a car round King George's Sound, Mr. Baxter. For a few days anyway "

" That's not the point. Phillips, my young stable-boy, was driving it. He could be wandering about the bush injured; perhaps with concussion." Kim frowned. " Ordinarily he would have stayed with the car until picked up." He looked hard at the clerk again. " Isn't that what you would do ? "

The clerk scratched his head.

" I guess it is," he said. " You can't tell what anyone'll do if they get a crack on the head though——"

Kim drew in his mouth as he stood thinking. For a moment he closed his eyes as if some very painful thought crossed his mind and now he had to make a painful decision.

" Do something for me, please," he said suddenly. " Get me a car. Try the hire-service people round the town. Get them out of bed, if necessary. If you can't raise anyone, then damn-all borrow a car for me round the hotel. I'm going out to look for that boy."

He turned away towards the lift then stopped with a second thought.

" You'd better let the police know. They'll probably want to send someone with me."

He walked quickly over to the lift and pressed the button.

Upstairs, Jill had had a bath and changed into a new soft silk nightgown. She brushed her hair and cold creamed her face. Then looking in the mirror at herself, she picked up the lipstick and made a tiny pink outline with it on her mouth.

She went over to the bed and climbed in. She did not look at the tea-tray. She would wait for Kim.

She stretched her arms out, hands downwards on top of the beautiful soft surface of the lovely candlewick bed-cover.

" Kim's double bed," she said to herself, a tiny smile curving round her mouth as she remembered Tuffy's face when Kim mentioned such a subject.

She let the lids droop over her tired eyes. In a minute he would come.

CHAPTER THIRTEEN

JILL WAS TIRED; tired and at peace. Her world would be a golden world . . . Sleep stole over her so insidiously she did not know it was there.

Kim tapped at the door and then came in. The room was in a soft glow for the only light was from the shaded bedside lamp on the table. Jill lay in the bed, her head in the shadow, as if asleep. Kim walked quietly across the carpeted floor and stood looking down at her. Her lashes lay quite still on her cheek.

He sat down on the side of the bed and touched her hand where it lay palm down on the coverlet.

" Jill," he said softly, leaning over her; not really wanting to waken her and frighten her.

Her eyelids fluttered up and she looked at him out of a drowsy nowhere.

" Jill. I'm so sorry, dear. I have to go out. I must go to Mount Sterling to pick someone up. There may have been an accident."

" You mean someone is hurt? " She was really waking up now.

" I don't know, but it's possible. I must go though——"

" Couldn't someone else go ? "

" No, Jill. There's such a thing as duty to one's own people. You understand that, don't you ? I must go."

" Is it far ? "

"A goodish way, but I'll be back as soon as possible. Will you go to sleep ? Look, I'll turn out the light. Then when you wake I'll be back."

He leaned across the bed and turned out the light. Only the street lights now lit the room with their reflections, and shadows from the funiture cast themselves longways across the floor and the foot of the bed.

He bent and kissed her, then drew back quickly.

Not now. Not *now*.

He said something under his breath that Jill did not catch; was not meant to catch.

Jill tried to gather her wits. Someone might be hurt ... someone who belonged to Kim . . . a goodish way . . .

" Don't be long, Kim," was all she could bring herself to say.

He smiled down at her.

" I won't," he said gently.

He drew in his breath as he went to the door. Fifty miles in a fast car might not take all that time, but the track through the foothills was a rough one and only God knew where young Phillips was.

It was early morning and the light was breaking across the land and over sea when Kim came in.

He had found the stable boy bedding down on the veranda of a small farm neighbouring on Mount Sterling property after a long farm-house to farm-house hunt through the night. The boy was unharmed but was one very scared person after Kim had stood him off and told him what he thought of him.

" Damn turning over the car ! " Kim had said wrathfully. " That's only half of it. You should have stayed with it. First principle of a road accident—if unharmed, don't leave the vehicle."

" I was trying to find some place to ring up," the boy said uneasily.

Kim felt he couldn't himself explain other things like leaving a young wife on her wedding day. He remained grimly silent on the drive back to the Southern Ocean Hotel.

When he got out of the car he relented. After all Phillips was very young and had probably received a good shaking-up.

He took the boy round by the back way to the hotel kitchen where the early morning staff was now stirring.

" Can you give this lad something to eat and find a bed for him ? " he asked. The drowsy kitchen maid took one look at the handsome but ruffled stable boy and her heart softened.

" Leave him to me, sir," she said. " I'll fix him up." Kim allowed himself half of a weary smile. He had an idea that was just what she would do.

He left a note on the reception desk in the main hall asking whoever came on duty to have a brake-van sent out to bring back the car. From examination by torch-light Kim had thought it was, like Phillips, unharmed except for a few scratches. The boy had skidded on the gravel road and the car had turned over. That was all there was to it.

Except it happened to be Kim's wedding night.

Jill, after a restless half-hour after Kim had left her, slept deeply. For days she had shopped and walked and helped her mother, and gone through every kind of daze getting her clothes and herself ready for the wedding. Then had come the long exciting wedding day. Youth and a certain sense of happy reaction came to her aid, and when at last she again fell asleep it was to a dreamless one and the belief that Kim would come—soon.

Vaguely in the light of the early morning she heard quiet movements in the room. Then Kim was lying on the bed beside her. She sighed and turned up her face towards his face. He kissed her gently. His arms tightened round her.

Outside he could hear the tea-cups rattling as the maids brought round the early morning tea.

He ran his fingers through her hair and said:

"Don't get up, dear. I'll go and shave."

"Was everything all right?" she asked, not opening her eyes, not wanting to let him go.

"Yes. Only time-consuming, and a lost night."

If he didn't go and shave now, he would stay here for ever.

He stood over her, bent down and kissed her quickly then went towards the bathroom.

Jill, opening her eyes very wide, saw the light streaming in through the windows and that, except for his coat, Kim was still fully clothed.

She lay and watched the light turn to sunshine, and listened to the sounds of Kim's electric razor coming from the bathroom.

"Poor Kim!" was all she thought. "Poor Kim!"

The maid brought in the tea and Jill sat upright and took the tray from her.

"Kim," she called. "Shall I pour a cup of tea for you?"

He put his head out of the bathroom door. His razor was in one hand still working over his chin in small circular sweeps.

He looked at her over the razor.

"Good morning, Mrs. Baxter," he said. "You seem to have slept well."

" Oh I did, Kim. I did. It was the loveliest sleep in all my life except that now I feel guilty. I should have come with you."

She put the tea-tray on the side table, swung her feet over the bed and reached for her gown. She slipped it on as she came across the floor to him. " It must have been because I was so happy, and now I feel mean. Kim dear," she said gravely. " Why didn't you shake me up, and take me with you ? "

He smiled at her over the swirling razor.

" I was in too big a hurry," he said quietly. " It was one of those things. Someone might have been wandering about in the bush—injured."

She tied the sash of her gown as she watched his face anxiously.

" How far did you go ? What happened ? "

"As far as Mount Sterling," he said. "A car turned over but nothing happened and no one was injured. Such a waste, wasn't it ? " He didn't want to bother her with details. She might make for that kitchen and start mothering the wretched Phillips. Out at Bal-Annie she had had a very soft spot in her heart for the stable boy. He switched off the razor and kissed her on the brow.

" Don't worry, Jill," he said. " It's not even worth talking about. Someone who ought to know better driving too fast on a gravel road . . . and not even a scratch to show for it." He smiled a little wryly. " Only a lost night for you and me."

" I am so sorry," she said, and she leaned her head against his shoulder.

There was so much sincerity in her voice his eyes darkened for a minute. He put his free arm around her and kissed the top of her head.

She looked up at him. "A wedding night won't ever come again. Will it ? Only once in a lifetime," she said shyly. Her eyes were clinging to his.

"What's to worry?" he said with a grin. "There's all the rest of our lives. And Jill, your tea is getting cold."

"Yours too," she said. "Come and have it now. You must be dying for it."

She turned and ran with a skipping step back to the bedside. She was being sorry for herself when she ought to be ministering to her husband. Anyhow, lost night or not, she felt oh, so happy! The way he had said— *Good morning, Mrs. Baxter!*

She was Mrs. Baxter and he was Mr. Baxter, and they were *married*.

She didn't give another thought to who had turned over what car and where and how; only to that lovely moment when he had held her in his arms when he had come in and lain down on the bed beside her.

"Have you got your swimming things?" Kim asked her, watching her expressive face as he sat down on the bed beside her and took the tea she had poured for him.

"Oh yes. I love swimming. I was even going to teach it . . . if . . ."

"If you hadn't turned off-sider instead. Well, hurry up and let's breakfast. Then I'll take you swimming. After lunch I'll get a boat from the yacht club and take you sailing."

"But Kim! You must be tired!"

"Not in the least. I've lost many a night with a new foal or out at a bushfire. I'm used to it. We've only one day, Jill. Let us make the most of it."

"Oh yes," said Jill eagerly. "You go and have a shower and get dressed then I'll take my turn in the bathroom."

Half an hour later they went down to breakfast.

In the dining-room Vanessa Althrop watched them come in, pass behind the centre stand which was loaded with cannas and other tall brilliant flowers, to a table by the window.

Kim and Jill had their heads turned and were looking out at the sea. They had not seen Vanessa. She watched them over her steaming cup of coffee.

She had smiled a little cynically when she had seen Jill's face.

" That fresh, young-girl look ! " she thought. Eyes like that weren't the eyes of an awakened woman. There was nothing of the self-conscious bride and bridegroom about Kim and Jill this early morning. They were more like friends. She had heard from the hall porter before breakfast that during the night Kim had gone as far out as her own home, Mount Sterling, to rescue his stable boy who had turned over one of the Bal-Annie cars.

Vanessa put down her coffee, then carefully buttered another piece of toast. She scraped most of the butter away, and withstood the temptation to add marmalade.

" Time to look after one's figure," she thought. " When a mere nobody of a girl like that can win Kim Baxter in the marriage stakes."

How had it happened ?

No love overtures from Kim. Of that she was certain. If she herself—someone who knew all the moves in the game—couldn't break through his shell of iron-coated self-protection she was certain that girl over there had not done it.

And hadn't even kept him by her side last night.

" Something to do with that damn' bushfire," Vanessa thought. Something to do with Jill and that stuffy Tuffy looking after and saving Bal-Annie ! Gratitude on Kim's part ?

No. He wasn't as soft-headed as that. In plain fact Kim Baxter was the most hard-headed man she had ever known.

Well, she would find out before the day was much older. She poured herself another cup of coffee and looked over towards the window table again. Jill was leaning forward talking to Kim.

She was too eager, Vanessa decided. Kim, as usual, had that polite listening attitude of his, his eyes unwaveringly on Jill's face, but his mouth without expression.

Vanessa laughed to herself.

The girl was in love, but he was not. Vanessa had seen that situation too often round the ocean-going liners of the world and in the clubs of Sydney and Rome.

Then she looked at Kim's profile, not Jill's.

Frankly and candidly, anywhere in her travels, she had not found anyone who quite measured up to Kim; who had quite so much challenge for a woman like herself.

That was it . . . *challenge.*

Vanessa finished her breakfast. Presently, when she was sure Jill and Kim Baxter were not addressing their attentions to the window and the view, she pushed back her chair and began to walk slowly down the length of the dining-room.

She stopped at the huge vase of cannas and touched them, first one then another, as if admiring their gorgeous blooms. She bent and smelled them, knowing well they had no scent.

She also knew that Kim, if he was watching her, would know she knew they had no scent. He would know just exactly what she was doing, and why.

Kim was much more worldly than that soft-eyed girl he had married even dreamed.

Vanessa moved on towards the double swing doors. She knew she looked wonderful. She always arranged it so in the early mornings when people least expected it. She wore a straight, perfectly cut linen dress. No sleeves, only straps for shoulders, and under and around those straps her skin was tanned beautifully to a golden brown.

Her dark hair set off her tanned skin as well as the white, nearly skin-tight linen dress.

Her shoes were high-heeled and strapped, and the beautiful golden brown calves of her legs were bare. Nothing, Vanessa knew, was warmer than real flesh and she had plenty of it showing to-day.

Arms, shoulders, legs! Well, Kim who was looking, could get on with *that* !

Vanessa glanced up at the mirror beside the swing doors and saw Kim's eyes following her progress out of the dining-room.

The ball was in his court, she thought. Next move from Kim.

Jill had her back to the door.

" But she doesn't matter ! " Vanessa said aloud, as she let the swing door fall behind her.

It wasn't till they were down on the beach that Jill began to think that all was not well with Kim. He was silent, and his eyes, slitted against the reflection of the brilliant sun on the water, were thoughtful. He was thinking of something else, not of what she was saying. He must be tired after all.

Jill too fell silent. She had wanted to tell Kim everything, pour out her whole life history to him.

She had bored him ? No, she was being childish ! After all Kim had said nothing about his own school days and early life.

He put out his hand.

" Let's go swimming," he said. " Sun-baking is only for the lie-abouts," he stood up and pulled her with him. He was wonderful in swimming trunks. His brown shining torso dominated even the white sands and the blue sea.

He was smiling at her, regretfully, as if sorry for his long silence.

" Race you into the water," he said.

" Yoicks ! " said Jill. She threw down her towel and ran, beautifully long-limbed and fleet-footed across the sands. He passed her and she heard his splash as he dived in ahead of her.

They came up, shaking the hair and water from their eyes. Now Kim was really with her. His eyes were the colour of the sea and they were looking at her, really smiling.

" I can swim," she called gaily. " I mentioned it, didn't I ? Race you to the buoy."

They raced but of course Kim beat her to the buoy. He beat her at everything they tried, but she was glad. He was a man, and she was married to him. She wanted him to be better at everything in the world.

Presently, tired out, they swam back to the shore, waded through the shallows to the wet edge of the sand. Jill looked up and shook her hair back.

Then, beside her own beach bag and the towels, she saw Vanessa, sitting—no, lolling back—smoking a cigarette !

It seemed to Jill as if a shadow had crossed the face of the sun.

It wasn't that it was Vanessa; it was the way she was half-lying, half-sitting, and the fact she was sitting by their things. Vanessa had seen them and she had come to join them.

Instinctively Jill knew, as one woman knows another, that this was not meant to be kind, nor even friendly.

Vanessa watched Jill and Kim come slowly across the beach, their feet stepping high because of the burying effect of the fine sand.

Her lazy eyes were on Kim. She didn't even bother to look at Jill.

" Hallo, you two ! " she said when they came up. " Is the water wet ? "

She still lolled back on one elbow, her lovely shoulders

and legs a magnificent tan against the white sand and her
own dead-white strapless swimsuit.

" You ought to try it, Vanessa," Kim said.

Why has this happened to me? thought Jill. *How long
before she will go away? Soon . . . make it soon . . . !* She
hadn't any idea to whom she uttered this prayer.

She stooped down and picked up her towel and began
wiping her face and arms free of salt and water. Then
she saw how Vanessa was watching Kim. And Kim
was looking at Vanessa !

Some message was passing between them. Their eyes
were saying something to one another. Kim's had no
expression in them, yet they said something. There was
no question about Vanessa's eyes. They were a straight
invitation to conspiracy.

Mount Sterling. Last night.

No, thought Jill. *No!*

Bewildered she sat down on the sand. It was the worst
thing she could have done at that moment because
Vanessa, sitting up, now patted the sand beside her with
her hand.

" Sit down, Kim," she said. "And give me another
cigarette. I lost that one in the sand. Tell me about the
wedding ? Was it just too-too ? Or was it not ? " Was
Vanessa play-acting ?

Jill did not understand this language, but evidently
Kim did. He sat down beside Vanessa and leaned forward to fish in the pocket of his reefer jacket beside Jill's
beach bag. He brought out a cigarette case and opening
it offered it to Vanessa.

" Very nicely too-too ! " he said.

Jill had to do something. Neither of them had said a
word to her. They were three and she, Kim's wife, was
the one who was *de trop*.

She was being mad, of course. Just stark staring silly !
She must break in.

" It wasn't a big wedding, Vanessa," she said, trying to sound gay; careful not to sound brittle because she was trying very hard. " Just my parents' immediate neighbours and one or two girls who were in college with me. Kim and his mother and Tuffy and Don."

Why did she have to explain herself; excuse her wedding to Vanessa ?

Jill laughed again. It was a splendid try at being gay.

" If Kim had had his way there would only have been Kim and me," she said.

Vanessa, bending her head over Kim's cupped hand as he lit her cigarette, did not even look at Jill as she spoke.

" How clever of me to come to the honeymoon," she said. " Makes up for not being at the confetti-throwing."

" There was no confetti," Kim said.

" Don't be so serious about it, old thing," Vanessa said. " It's over now; and time to laugh."

She turned her head and looked at Jill who was sitting, knees drawn up and her arms around them. Jill was watching the sea, trying desperately to keep her face relaxed, her manner natural.

Vanessa's eyes roved over her, and Jill knew it. With an enormous effort at self-discipline she turned and smiled at Vanessa.

" I hope I may come and see Mount Sterling someday," she said pleasantly. Anything to change the conversation.

" Oh you shall," said Vanessa lightly. " You'll be showered with invitations from the entire southern districts." Again her eyes slid over Jill. " Tell me," she said. " How did you manage to snare Kim ? "

Jill dared not glance past Vanessa to Kim. He was smoking a cigarette, his profile turned away, his eyes narrowed. Once again his eyes were on the sea.

The frightening thought reared itself again in Jill's mind. " He has seen Vanessa before. Last night . . . Why would he not have told me ? "

She felt sick with fear for what this sophisticated Vanessa might do to them; and sick with horror at herself because she feared she herself was no more than jealous. At all costs she had to hide this last.

Kim *had* seen Vanessa before. He had not been in the least bit surprised when he had seen Vanessa sitting on the beach. He had known she would be there. That wordless exchange with their eyes when they had come across the sands and Vanessa had looked up at Kim! They had said something to one another with their eyes. Perhaps it wasn't Kim's fault, but why didn't he come and sit next to her, Jill? She was his wife, not Vanessa.

It had been a long time since Vanessa had asked that question. How had she snared Kim?

"A leg-rope and halter, I suppose," said Jill, being gay. She must never, never let them see! "You know how it is with women," she added. "We're dangerous with lethal weapons such as fire-arms and ropes."

Not to mention eyes, and an awful lot of bare flesh, she thought, trying not to see these things so much on display by Vanessa.

It was Kim who turned. Clearly he was about to say something. With a flood of relief Jill thought he was going to save her. But Vanessa was too quick for either of them.

She brought herself up to the kneeling position with a jerk and reached for her own towel.

"Let's go up to the hotel and have a drink to celebrate," she said. "Mine's a martini, Kim. Remember?" She put out her hand for Kim to pull her to her feet. It was a gesture he could hardly refuse. Jill scrambled up herself and began to collect her beach bag, towel and sandals. She put on her sun glasses as a shield—not from the sun but from Vanessa and Kim.

Vanessa leaned on Kim's arm to steady herself while she stooped to put on her gilt-thonged sandals. For all the world they might have been the married couple.

How strangely silent Kim was!

"We'll sit on the patio," Vanessa said. "We're allowed there in swimsuits."

She talked to Kim eagerly, ardently, as they walked up towards the road and the hotel. As Kim walked between them he could not keep his face turned to both of them. He had to keep his head and ear inclined to Vanessa. She didn't stop. She kept up a running, laughing commentary on everything. The beach, the hotel, the people and then, really to pin Kim's attention, she went on about the bushfire in Darjalup.

To defeat her, or even share Kim, Jill would have had to cut in on the conversation. This she could not bring herself to do. Some deep current of pride refused to let her compete for her own husband.

At this thought she remembered last night.

Jill was horrified at the ideas taking root in her mind and horrified at herself.

Was this what jealousy was like? Something so mean she could not bear to ascribe it to herself? Something that bred ideas that her better self rejected?

They reached the road and had to wait for the passing traffic before they could cross.

"There's the patio!" Vanessa said, pointing to a creeper-hidden part of the lookout veranda. "They dance there at night. Let's dance to-night, shall we? You and me for the cha-cha, Kim! Yes?"

She turned to Jill now, speaking across Kim. Vanessa was too much a stage hand at this game to overplay it.

"I'm sure you've got at least one gorgeous dance frock in your trousseau. You must bring it out. I'd love to see you dressed up, Jill."

"Would you like to dance to-night, Jill?" Kim asked. Was he saving her, or was this just a formal way of saying he would like to dance? Again Jill knew, with a kind of desperation of pride, that she must not let either of them know how she felt.

"I love dancing," she said. "Is there another man to join us, do you think?"

"Oh . . . if there's one about," Vanessa said carelessly. "If not, then we'll share Kim." She looked up into his face and laughed. "You really are in a most enviable position, Kim," she said. "Two fair ladies, one beating time at a table waiting for you to finish dancing with the other. What fun to be a man!"

"If you two ladies must dance," said Kim carefully, "then I suppose I am in an enviable position."

He sounded as if he was about to say something more but at that moment the traffic eased.

"Quick!" said Vanessa, grasping his arm. "We can get across now."

Kim took Jill's arm with his spare hand and the three of them crossed the road.

Jill felt she had to have a respite.

"I'm going up to change," she said. "You and Vanessa order the drinks, will you, Kim? I'll be right down." She sought his eyes, hoping for something, though not knowing what.

"It's not necessary, is it?" he said, puzzled; smiling to reassure her.

"Of course it is," said Vanessa lightly. "She's been swimming, and the salt's in her hair. Be fair, Kim. Every lady likes to be her best. Take a look at me. I make darn certain I won't get tousled. I stay out of the water."

She laughed.

"Come on, let's get a table," she said. "The crowd will be coming up any moment now."

Jill reached the bedroom and shut the door behind her and leaned against it.

She put the back of her hand across her eyes.

"A fool would see what she's doing," she cried to herself. " Why does he let her do it ? Is he, too, beguiled ? Perhaps a man, even a strong man like Kim, can't help himself when a woman looks at him like that." Was it Vanessa who turned over the car ?

Why hadn't Kim told her ?

Jill walked over to the dressing-table and stared at herself in the mirror.

" Why am I afraid of her ? " she asked her image. " It is she, not Kim, who is doing this."

Kim hadn't wanted to marry Vanessa. He had wanted to marry her, Jill. She was useful, reliable and loved Bal-Annie. Vanessa had none of these qualities, she had something else, and Kim was very much aware of it. Vanessa was seeing to that in so blatant a way, Jill was sure that any other woman in the world would forgive her, the legal wife, for feeling the way she did at this moment.

Jill went into the bathroom, stripped off her swimsuit and had a shower. She let the water pour over her head . . .

" To cool my brain," she said. " If I keep it cool I will think of something—anything, not to share Kim to-night."

CHAPTER FOURTEEN

IT WAS WHILE they were having lunch that Jill thought of something. A man and a woman, newly arrived, had come in and were shown to a table farther down the dining-room. Kim had not seen them but Jill had recognised them. They came from Darjalup, and the woman, a pleasant but plain person, had helped with Jill and Mrs. Baxter in sorting out school clothes for the children after the fire. The man, middle-aged and bald-headed, was something in the town. Jill couldn't remember what.

Very desperately she didn't want to go to that dance to-night. Pride and a cold heart wouldn't let her tell Kim this. Even trying to get out of it was a victory for Vanessa and whatever Kim might say they were doing as an alternative, Vanessa would invite herself.

Kim's good manners, and their old friendship, would never have permitted him to brush Vanessa off.

Already, in advance, Jill knew what that dance would be like. When it wasn't her turn to dance with Kim she would sit, a wallflower, trying desperately to look graceful and without a care while Vanessa wrapped herself in Kim's arms and gazed up at him with those eloquent, suggestive eyes.

Jill couldn't bear the thought of it. Vanessa wouldn't be a wallflower in between dances. She would use that technique on some other man . . . any other man around . . . simply to get up on the floor.

Alas, Jill thought sadly. If only she herself could be that type too. Just for one evening.

Now Mrs. Elberton and her husband had come in, and to Jill they were like saviours.

When she and Kim had finished lunch she made an excuse to leave him.

" I must go and speak to Mrs. Elberton," she said. " Please go on to the lounge, Kim. Vanessa is waiting for us to have coffee together."

Kim had looked at her in momentary surprise. The Elbertons were townspeople he knew only slightly. He was half pleased that Jill was going to be friendly with the Darjalup people, half annoyed for fear the Elbertons too would turn this one-day honeymoon into a general free-for-all party.

" If you must . . ." he said looking at Jill gravely. He had thought she was pale at lunch-time. They had scarcely talked. The strain of arranging a wedding, even a small one, must be very great on a girl he surmised. He had wondered and been even a little awed by that deep abandoned sleep in which he had found Jill last night when he came in.

Jill walked down the length of the dining-room. Mr. Elberton rose from his seat and they all shook hands. Kim had joined Vanessa and gone through the swing doors into the lounge.

" It's mighty nice of you, Miss . . . I mean Mrs. Baxter . . ." Mr. Elberton smiled, delighted but embarrassed that the First Lady of Darjalup had come over to speak to them like this. On her honeymoon too.

" Oh please," Jill said sitting down. " It's just ordinary of me. Mrs. Elberton and I worked so hard together after that fire. We're friends for life."

Mrs. Elberton beamed.

" It's things like that bring us all together, isn't it ? " she said.

" Yes, and now all of us have a day or two to recover in the same hotel." Jill smiled at them. " Of course for Kim and me, it's more than that. It's our honeymoon."

" Yes . . . yes indeed," Mr. Elberton said, nearly blushing himself. " When I looked up and saw you both sitting down there I felt almost an intruder."

" You mustn't feel like that," said Jill, smiling at him with what he thought was a very lovely pair of grey-green eyes. For a moment they seemed to cloud. " Will you and your wife ask us to come and have a drink with you after dinner to-night ? " Jill asked. " Perhaps about nine o'clock ? There's such a nice small drawing-room upstairs. We could be all by ourselves . . ."

She was hurrying on, desperate for the Elbertons to say yes, and save her; totally unable to explain to them now or ever, why she had asked them to be the hosts and had not offered to be hostess herself.

She looked at Mrs. Elberton and the older lady saw the flush and the plea in Jill's eyes.

" Why . . . why, of course," Mr. Elberton said. " Do you think Kim . . . er . . . but, of course." He turned to his wife. " What about it, Mary ? " he asked. " We'd feel downright honoured. Wouldn't we ? "

" Of course," said Mrs. Elberton. " What a lovely idea. There's a little drawing-room upstairs, you said ? "

" Yes," Jill said. " Along the centre passage. It's so pretty."

There were nearly tears in her eyes and Mrs. Elberton saw them. She nodded her head sagely.

Girls on their honeymoons were often like this, that nod seemed to say. *Suddenly they want home and mother for no sensible reason at all. They have to get used to being married . . . sharing a room with a man, and his ways.*

Privately Jill asked God and the kind heart in Mrs. Elberton to forgive her for plot-making. Suddenly she felt better, not because she was saved, but because she had known by the kindness, even compassion, in both the Elbertons' eyes that had she told them the truth they would have forgiven her; and upheld her.

The sprite of mischief that was not quite dead in Jill told her that Mrs. Elberton would have taken a broom to Vanessa and not made any bones about it. She was that kind of person. She would heartily approve of Jill's way of winning a round of mental fisticuffs with a predatory woman.

Jill stood up and smiled cheerfully.

" Thank you so much. We'll look forward to to-night."

"*And how!* " she thought as she walked away. Was it the sheer indignity of doing this that made her feel shaky inside herself as she went to join Kim and Vanessa in the lounge?

The long day came to an end. In the afternoon Kim had taken Jill sailing but as this was an art hitherto unknown to her the whole time had been taken up with the business of Jill learning and Kim teaching. A breeze had sprung up and the water in the sound, though not rough, had not been easy. It had been quite a task, albeit an enthralling one, keeping the small yacht on course and learning to jibe at the right moment, and in the right way.

Jill had been nearly happy again. Kim had been patient though a little stern. When they had finally brought the boat in, dropped the sails and stowed away the gear Kim jumped ashore and held out his hand to Jill.

She leapt over the gunwales and stood on the wooden planking of the jetty beside him. She was wind-blown and salt-caked, but for a moment wonderfully happy again as she looked up laughing into Kim's eyes and he bent his head and kissed her. He ought to have been tired, but he wasn't. Not in the least.

" There's something of the sailor in you, after all," he said. He looked down at her. " Did you like that, Jill ? "

" Oh yes, Kim," she said fervently, turning with him

and holding his arm, walking back towards the yacht club with him.

Now there was no Vanessa she had no doubts. She even began to think she was mistaken about the morning and that everything had been in her own imagination.

Perhaps she was going to turn out to be that awful thing—God forbid—a possessive wife.

She couldn't bring herself to ask who it was who had overturned the car last night. It had to come from Kim. Yes, even now she was still afraid of the answer.

When she saw Vanessa all dressed up for dinner her heart misgave her again. Vanessa looked gorgeous, of course, but too, too cosmopolitan-society for the Southern Ocean Hotel in King George's Sound.

Everyone turned his head and looked at Vanessa as she came into the dining-room. Kim's eyes, steadily on the menu, were so concentrated that Jill knew this was an effort on his part *not* to look. He was aware of Vanessa, which was, after all, the thing that Vanessa wanted. Perhaps this was her punishment to Jill, who had said, after they had finished their coffee in the lounge at lunch-time . . .

" I'm so sorry about the dance to-night, Vanessa. I'm afraid we can't join in after all. Mr. and Mrs. Elberton have asked us to have drinks with them. It's a sort of private party in a separate drawing-room . . ."

It would have been too embarrassing to add—"And Kim was up all night. He must be very tired."

She had let her words drift away into nothing, too nervous to look at Kim; a little sick at stooping to Vanessa's game and feeling with a kind of last ditch of desperation that even Vanessa couldn't say anything contra to such an arrangement . . .

She couldn't say—" I'll come too." It was, after all, the Elbertons' party.

In fact Vanessa had coolly looked Jill up and down and then laughed.

" My God, the Elbertons ! " she said. " You are in for an evening. Kim darling, have you turned local squire so much that this is your new life—partying with the locals as a religious duty ? "

" They are rather nice people, Vanessa," Kim said.

The only thing Kim had said about the evening with the Elbertons was:

" Wouldn't you like to do something gay, Jill ? Dance . . . or even go to the cabaret along the beach ? "

He had looked at her quizzically as if thinking her decision to spend the evening with the Elbertons a strange one.

Of course he thought it was strange ! They only had one day and one evening for a honeymoon. She couldn't tell him that anything else they did Vanessa would somehow manage to get to it too. Vanessa would mono-polise him and he would wear that faraway troubled look that meant he was torn between two women. The one he *needed*, the one he *desired*.

The evening with the Elbertons came to an end and irrespective of its cause Jill was glad it had happened. They were good kind people and Kim had found a lot to talk to Mr. Elberton about. Suddenly he was back to being a Darjalup farmer talking shop with another man, who though not a farmer, had the same interests.

Jill's spirits went up because she felt that unexpectedly, though not very honestly, she had given Kim something he had enjoyed.

He wasn't a dancing or a cabaret type of man at all. A quiet talk about Darjalup and Bal-Annie with someone he hadn't known well but who now turned out to be a mine of information in new farming methods . . . the use of trace elements: the sub-clover crops in poor country . . . was something that brought the best out in Kim.

Across the small room Jill watched him, her heart reaching out towards him.

In a minute she would forget about Vanessa for ever, and that Vanessa had nearly wrecked their one-day honeymoon.

It was eleven o'clock when Kim and Jill said good night to their hosts and went upstairs to their room.

" Jolly nice chap—Elberton," Kim said thoughtfully as he opened the door and stood aside for Jill to pass him. " I must see more of him when we get back to Darjalup. He can be quite helpful. Something to do with the Agricultural Department. An expert on crops."

If good had come out of it Jill felt her own motives would be forgiven.

She stood in the bedroom watching Kim absently putting the door key in his pocket.

" If you change your clothes in the morning, Kim, you'll forget where that key is," she said softly.

He looked up at her and laughed.

"A one-day wife, and how right you are ! " he said. He took the key out and put it on the mantelshelf.

He stood thoughtfully a moment. Jill wondered was it Mr. Elberton, sub-clover crops, or the key that was pre-occupying him. It wasn't herself, she felt with that old touch of unhappiness coming back. Now was the time for him to put his arms round her, and kiss her.

He looked up quickly. He seemed to guess her thoughts. He came across the room and took her in his arms. He bent his head and kissed her on the mouth.

Jill closed her eyes. Now she must forget everything, even Vanessa.

Kim lifted up his head.

" Would you like some tea sent up, Jill ? " he asked. " I'll go and have my half-hour constitutional while you get undressed." He shook his head, smiling teasingly at her. " But don't go to sleep and leave it to get cold this time. Nothing looks worse in my lady's boudoir than a tray of untouched tea things."

Jill smiled back at him. She was sorry about "that constitutional." It was nice of him to leave her to undress in privacy. That was his reason for going out, of course.

" I don't want any tea, thank you, Kim." A faint flush touched her cheeks as she added, " I won't go to sleep."

He dropped his arms, turned away and picked up the key from the mantelshelf and went to the door.

" I won't be long," he said, and a minute later he was gone.

Jill stood in the middle of the bedroom and stared at the closed door. Why had that nagging fear returned ? She was not afraid of Kim. She was afraid of Vanessa; and afraid of her own ignorance of men. She was afraid to ask a very simple question about an overturned car, because she feared the answer.

What did a man feel, or even think, when a woman like Vanessa looked at him that way and made a language not only with her eyes but with her whole body . . . every exposed inch of it ?

How could Kim help it if, when he took Jill and her slim athletic body in his arms, he thought of something that was just plain luscious.

What were men really like ?

I must stop this ! I'm torturing myself unnecessarily. I've been reading too many books. Vanessa will have found other occupations hours ago.

She slipped her pretty silk dress over her head and hung it in the wardrobe. She put on her bath robe and went over to the dressing-table. She had not pulled the blinds. It was blue-black night outside but their room was on an upper floor. No one could see in through the fine veil of lace curtain. There was only the roadway far below and beyond that the sandy beach under a parapet, and then the ocean.

Jill sat down to cream her face.

Perhaps she had better pull that curtain.

She stood up again and moved round the side of the table to the window and looked out at the ocean wistfully. It had been lovely swimming in it this morning. All heaven had been shining until they had walked back across those sands. Now the ocean wasn't blue; it was black, spattered with reflected star dust. Below, the street was softly lit by the standard lamps along the waterfront.

Jill leaned forward and looked down at it.

Kim must have come out through the hotel door immediately below the window for he was walking across the road.

Jill's eyes looked at his broad back and her heart softened. He was her husband, and she loved him. More painful, she was *in love with him*. She must take a pull on herself. Nothing in the world was worth losing that distant sense of loving everything about him as he walked across that road, then, first stopping to light a cigarette, leaned against the parapet railing and looked out over the sea.

She wondered that he wasn't aware of those waves of feeling that were going out to him, from her.

Jill dropped her eyes to the road again. Another figure had come out from the hotel and was crossing the road. It was Vanessa and because it was a warm late summer night she had every excuse to go out into it with nothing, literally nothing, not even straps, over her shoulders.

She walked straight up to Kim and leaned her arms on the railing so close to him she must have been touching his shoulder.

Kim turned his head and to Jill there were two white

profiles, Vanessa looking up and Kim looking down.

He put his hand in his pocket and drew out his cigarettes and gave her one. Then he lit it for her, Vanessa bent her head over his cupped hand in that curiously intimate way that had somehow so affronted Jill this morning. Her dark bent head was so close to Kim he would have only had to move an inch to touch it.

Jill pulled the blind and turned away. She sat down in front of the mirror again and put her head in her hands.

Apart from sheer pain she felt bewildered. This sort of thing just didn't happen. People didn't gate-crash in on honeymoons. A husband didn't stand in the moonlight and light cigarettes for other women.

But it had happened. It was happening. Out there . . .

Jill sat up, creamed her face and brushed her hair. Then she stood up and, taking off her clothes, went into the bathroom again. She had bathed so often to-day she couldn't imagine ever wanting to bath again. It was something to do . . . something to warm and comfort her, and pass the time. She mustn't look at her watch. She couldn't bear to know *how long* they were out there together.

Jill had her bath, creamed her face all over again without realising she had done it before; and in any case it wasn't necessary. Then she got into bed.

It was a warm night and the covers should be thrown off but Jill felt cold. She had even shivered when she had slid down between the sheets.

She closed her eyes. No, she wouldn't look at the clock.

She didn't know how long it was before Kim came in. Her eyes flew open as he came through the door.

He shut it behind him and came across the floor and sat down on the side of the bed. He put both hands on the pillow, one on each side of Jill's head.

He was looking at her, but his smile was contrived.

Jill was sure of it. He was doing the right thing for this was now his role.

"You were a long time," Jill said. Her voice was faint because there was a frog in her throat. She coughed to clear it.

Kim frowned.

"You haven't caught a cold, Jill?"

This was like a straw to a drowning man. Jill clutched it.

"I think so . . ."

"What bad luck . . ." he said, unexpectedly looking at her with a quick inquiring tenderness.

Don't look sorry for me, Jill thought. *That I couldn't bear.*

"Did you . . . did you have your walk?" she blurted out.

"Yes. Along the waterfront."

Not a word about Vanessa. If only he would tell her, or she had the courage to ask!

Jill closed her eyes as if she had a pain in her throat and it hurt her to speak.

"By yourself?" she said at length.

"Yes. By myself," he said. Jill's eyes flew open, and saw his, dark blue and intent; looking at her.

She turned her head on the pillow and closed her eyes again. Anything to escape that quiet, steady implacable inquiring expression in his face.

He leaned forward and putting his hand under her cheek, turned her head back.

"Jill," he said very quietly. "You've got an attack of 'nerves.' I can't call it anything else. Isn't that it? Something has happened?"

"Yes—nerves," she said, grasping at *this* straw. "I can't help it, Kim. I'm sorry . . . I just want to be *alone* . . ."

"You are afraid of me. Is that it, Jill?"

"Yes."

She turned her head away again. Sick at heart, feeling

she had crossed some special and dreadful Rubicon. It seemed an aeon that Kim sat on the bed, not moving, probably looking at her. Jill kept her eyes closed. She didn't want to see his tired, dark, enigmatical eyes.

At last he stood up.

" There's no need to be afraid of me," he said, looking down at her. " You have nothing to fear, Jill. I wouldn't hurt one hair of your head. You know that, don't you ? "

No, she didn't know it. He had hurt her. He had been with Vanessa.

All day she had told herself it was her own imagination. Now she *knew*. He had been out there, under that lovely sky, walking along the waterfront with Vanessa. And he had lied. True he had married her, Jill, because he needed her; even liked her. But Vanessa was the epitome of desire. How could he forget that if he took his new " needed " wife in his arms ? He had lied to Jill to spare her, of course. She knew that. In a way he was being kind.

She did not answer him.

She heard him turn away and walk across the room. At the door he turned round.

" Go to sleep, Jill," he said, his voice quiet and level. " I not only won't touch a hair of your head but I won't even touch the silk on your arm." Then he added, his voice suddenly weary, as if he too had had pain: " I suppose we've got the rest of our lives to work out what being married actually means."

He went out of the room and closed the door behind him.

The next morning they left for Darjalup soon after breakfast. Jill did not see Vanessa again. She supposed Vanessa was indulging her usual practice of breakfast in bed ; and wondered, a little bleakly, if the other girl knew that she and Kim were leaving before lunch.

At all events Vanessa had not appeared by the time Kim pulled out the Bal-Annie car—brought in and the scratches spray-painted over—and they swung round the corner of the hotel, down the waterfront road, then northwards. Kim had made arrangements for Phillips to get home and still felt it was unnecessary to concern Jill with what had happened to the stable boy and the car.

They both had worries enough of their own now, without Jill going off at a tangent to start worrying about Phillips.

It had been a strained two hours before they departed.

Kim had come in at some very late hour; had lain down on the side of the bed only partly undressed. In the morning he was first up and in and out of the bathroom before the housemaid brought in the early morning cup of tea.

He was standing in front of the wardrobe mirror knotting his tie as Jill sat up and took the tea-tray on her lap.

" I won't have any tea, Jill," he said, not turning round. " I'll go down and see if the car is serviced. I've packed my bag and I'll take it down now. I think we'll make for home as soon as possible."

His fingers stopped working on that tie as, in the mirror, he looked at Jill. She was sitting up, her hair ruffled and her face pale. She looked very young. She dropped her eyes when she saw he was watching her; and began to pour the tea.

Kim saw that her fingers trembled. She had passed the worst night in history. He himself had had four and a half hours, sleep in two nights.

To Jill he seemed to be passing judgment. His face was

set, his eyes very dark. If he had been a headmaster that was how he would have looked at a young delinquent.

Jill was too miserable to be indignant.

He turned away from the mirror, slipped on his jacket as he went to the door. He opened it and turned to speak to her.

"Breakfast in half an hour," he said. He relented a little. "Is there anything you want, Jill?" he asked more kindly. She shook her head and as she raised the teacup to her lips, her hand was so uncertain she almost spilled it.

She hadn't said a word to him yet. She couldn't speak because that frog was back in her throat.

At breakfast he talked about the weather and the fact it would be a good drive home. The weather was cooler and there had been one of those late summer showers in the night which would have laid the dust and watered, although very lightly, the bushland.

"It's very pretty, Jill," he said suddenly, looking at her again, trying to be more gentle. "I'll bring you down here again at the end of winter. Then all the wild flowers will be out . . ."

"I've always heard they're wonderful," Jill said. "Of course we see the wild flowers selling on the streets and in the florists in Perth . . ."

Such banal talk when her heart was aching and Kim's was flint cold!

He had said he would bring her down at the end of winter, and winter had not yet begun.

Jill tried to assess what this meant. It almost sounded as if he intended they should carry on. Not part, or something silly like that.

Irrespective of any infatuation he had for Vanessa he didn't want to marry Vanessa. He intended to stay married to Jill for a while, anyway.

To Jill, there was hope in that. Time, and Vanessa—absent, might bring them together.

It was mid-morning when the car turned on to the bitumen road, a main clear-way that would ordinarily take them two-thirds of their way home. They drove in a near silence for thirty miles. The grey scrublands had turned to light jarrah forest again, except where great areas had been cleared for grazing and farmlands. It was a beautiful morning and Jill couldn't help thinking with a kind of painful regret, " *if only yesterday had been different!* "

How much happiness had Vanessa Althrop wrecked by accidentally choosing the same hotel as they had, for her shopping visit to the southern port! Perhaps overturning her car on the way. What tricks on mere humans can Fate play!

At the thirty mile peg Kim suddenly turned west, off the main road, on to a brown gravel track. The car bumped a little unevenly as if he had made up his mind to change direction suddenly.

" I'll take you to see the Valley of the Giants, Jill," he said. " It's one of the wonders of the world." There was a sardonic note in his voice as he added, " it's one of the usual sight-seeing trips made by honeymoon couples down in this part of the world."

Jill remained silent. What reply could she make to a comment like that?

Yet she had to say something.

" Would you like a cigarette, Kim? " she said at length. " I'll light it for you."

" Yes, please," he said. " They're in my jacket pocket. The one nearest you."

Jill put her hand in his pocket. She was touching him. She could feel the hard muscle of his thigh under her hand.

With an effort she sought the packet and withdrew it.

She put a cigarette in Kim's mouth and lifted the lighter from its socket in the dashboard. He watched the road before him as the cigarette was lighted. Then holding the steering wheel with his left hand he moved the cigarette and blew a long long stream of smoke out of the window, almost as if expelling pent-up feeling.

" Light one for yourself, Jill," he said gently. "A minor vice sometimes makes human beings of us." He glanced at her. There was a touch of irony in his expression but it was no longer so cold. " The Giants are almost a thousand years old," he added. " When you see them you'll think how puny our troubles are compared with what they've lived through."

Yes *puny*, like anthills, but how did one get over them? Did one step over, jump over, or merely kick anthills away ?

How badly she wanted to break down and ask Kim to put his arm round her. Yet if she did, she knew she would be afraid the thought of Vanessa would come to his mind. There was ice in her heart too.

They swung down over a creek bridge then round a curve, out of the light timber into deep heavy forest. The trees were bigger and bigger. The undergrowth, thick and dank from last night's rain, smelt pungent and sweet. Silent birds whirred here and there from the bushes, and high up the great branches embraced above their head.

The road narrowed and they drove down into the valley. There was a Giant tree here and there in the heavy timber. Jill gazed through the windscreen. How vast and lonely was that silent bush. No wind reached it here. It was as moveless, silent and timeless as if human beings had never touched it.

Then they were in the bottom of the valley and all around them stood the great trees, huge boles of trunks, vast immovable arms and at the ends and above them the dense mat of dark green eucalypt-scented leaves.

Kim stopped the car. They sat in silence, Jill looking out at the forest of Giants.

It seemed as if she and Kim and the car weren't there. Nothing was there but this silence, this damp floor of dark green undergrowth; the mats of dried scented gum leaves, and the great red-brown charred trees, utterly still in their immensity, and incredible silence.

There was nothing for human beings to say. The trees were too aloof to listen.

Jill's hand lay in her lap and quietly Kim put out his hand and let it rest on hers.

Jill lifted her head and looked at him.

" Time enough when we're old to look sad, Jill," he said quietly. " You're young and I'm not yet hoary. We'll find a way to make a go of it—given time."

She nodded.

" Given time . . ." she said in a very small voice.

Kim turned on the engine and released the brake. He eased the car forward into a self-start.

" Time is a very inexpensive word down here, in this valley," he said. " Shall we go home now, Jill ? "

The way he said " home " had an undercurrent of warmth in it.

CHAPTER FIFTEEN

THEY DROVE up out of the valley into grey bushland country in a silence that was in the nature of peace between them. After a while Kim broke the silence. He told Jill some of the plans for opening up the forest to enable the people to see something of it. There were bitumen highways already across it but others were to be built.

" Somehow tourists and the forest don't seem quite to go together . . ." Jill said.

" Not tourists. People with whom you want to communicate," Kim said. " There's a difference. When you've got something like that and you have a depth of feeling for it, you want to communicate. You've got to make it possible for people to come and see for themselves."

Jill could see what he meant. It also explained to her Kim's willingness to take on all those responsibilities around Darjalup that took up so much of his time ; and deprived Bal-Annie of that same precious time.

They stopped once at a small farmhouse with the label *Teas* hanging on a veranda post in a nest of vine creepers. They had glorious Satsuma plums and cream followed by tea with fresh home-made bread.

Then they were on their way again, at top speed now for they were once again on the bitumen highway, heading for Darjalup. Kim meant to get there shortly after midday.

As they swung off the bitumen on to the now familiar brown road to Darjalup Kim said:

" I want to call at the Shire office. They may keep me a little while. Will you mind waiting ? "

" Oh no. Please do all you have to do, Kim."

They were passing through a ring-barked forest at that moment and the white graveyard of dead trees saddened her.

" I suppose it has to be," she said, meaning the sight of the white bark-stripped trees standing, some half fallen, some lying in a stricken and deathly silence waiting for the fires to destroy all trace of them.

" Man has to till and sow," Kim said gravely. " There is no other economic way of clearing the ground."

Jill knew that apart from being married to Kim, she loved him for the fine feelings he had for all around him.

No man can be perfect, she thought. If only he hadn't had that image of Vanessa and what Vanessa stood for ! It lay between herself and Kim, and she didn't know how to dispel it. " *Thy shadow—Cynara——*"

Time ! That inexpensive *time* of which the forest cared so little !

Perhaps it would help, someday.

They pulled up outside the Shire office.

" Would you like to go and do some shopping ? Or perhaps have another cup of tea," Kim asked as he opened the drive door. " We haven't had a real lunch and it's over an hour since we stopped at the farm ? "

He was getting out of the car, and over his shoulder Jill saw Shane Evans come through the main door of the Shire office and run down the steps into the road. He wore one very wide grin.

" Oh Shane ! " Jill said. He was too far away to hear her, but Kim looked at her quickly. Since he was already out in the street he shut the drive door and walked, quite slowly, round to Jill's door and opened it for her. For some stupid reason the sight of Shane had brought near tears to Jill's eyes. It was like coming home to a *friend,* after sailing alone in alien seas.

She remembered her mother one day walking along the main street in Perth, not very long after they had arrived as migrants and seeing someone she had known very slightly in the far off home country. The tears had run down her mother's face.

That wasn't going to happen to Jill now, for she blinked back the moisture and quickly got out of the car and held out her hand to Shane.

He had already slapped Kim on the shoulder and Kim had winced, not from the pain but from irritation. He liked Shane Evans well enough but did not feel on back-slapping terms with him. Few men in Darjalup district would actually have presumed to slap Kim Baxter's back. He just wasn't that kind of man.

Nothing, this bright day, deterred Shane.

" Glad to see you both," he said cheerfully. He grasped Jill's hand and drew her towards him and kissed her. " Best man's privilege," he said out of the corner of his mouth but meaning Kim as well as Jill to hear. " By which, of course, I meant next-best man."

" Oh Shane ! I'm so glad to see you," Jill said.

Then they both started to laugh. Each realised how absurd they were. It had only been ten days ago that Shane had stood in the road, his arms looped above his head signalling farewell as Jill's bus had pulled out from the footpath to make the long journey to her parents' home. Why were they both behaving as if it had been a lifetime ? And as if it *mattered* ? Jill hadn't any idea, and she doubted whether Shane had.

" I've to see Browning," Kim's voice cut in quietly. " Is he in, Shane ? "

" He's in," Shane said cheerfully. "And he has a file a foot deep for you. Most of the stuff came in yesterday and this morning. Seems as if the whole dashed Government's coming down to see the bushfire damage."

He wasn't looking at Kim as he spoke, but at Jill.

"Mind if I take your lady while you hoke-poke in there?" he asked. "She owes me a cup of tea, and I'm raring for one."

"Would you like that, Jill?" Kim asked. He sounded very remote. Jill thought his mind was already on Darjalup affairs and that foot-deep file waiting for him in the Shire office.

"Yes please, I would."

Again she smiled at Shane. Now she wouldn't feel self-conscious running the gamut of the main street for the first time since her wedding. She would have Shane as a protection.

Moreover, she had an unexpected feeling of happiness to be back on that old comradely footing with her first friend in Darjalup.

Shane slipped his hand under her elbow, looked at Kim over his shoulder and said . . .

"So long, Kim!"

Jill had a sudden wild longing to hear Kim say:

"*So long, Jill!*"

And hear her own voice answer:

"*So long, Kim!*"

But she knew it wouldn't happen. She turned away with Shane as Kim lifted his hand in a gesture, was it farewell or dismissal? It was something in place of, but not the same as, the intimate call of one to another that Jill had wanted so badly to exchange.

"Now let's hear all about it," Shane was saying, his hand still under Jill's elbow as they crossed the street at the corner and went on down the cement footpath towards the café. "Who was there and who threw confetti?"

Jill, smiling, told him of the smallness of the wedding, and that no confetti was thrown.

"Then were did you go next?" Shane wanted to hear all the news.

He was partly teasing, partly playing a game of comradeship.

" To King George's Sound."

" Good Heavens ! " said Shane as they entered the small shop and sat down at what he was now pleased to call—*our favourite table.*

" Good heavens ! " he repeated. " Half of Darjalup went down there for a breather after the worst of the chaos was straightened out. Who'd you see ? You didn't get off with *no one*, I'll swear to that."

" The Elbertons, who were darlings to me," Jill said. Then she looked into Shane's mocking eyes. There was a shadow in her own. She had to tell Shane. Perhaps in some obscure, even unwitting way, Shane might help her.

"And Vanessa . . ." she added.

" Oh *no* ! " groaned Shane. Then more hopefully, " But she was the other end of the town ? You pretended you didn't see her ? Now come, Jill . . ." he shook an admonitory finger at her. " You weren't close enough to let Vanessa see you and Kim ? "

" I'm afraid it was unavoidable. We were at the same hotel."

Shane was going to laugh, but he suddenly stopped, in mid-air. He was very thoughtful.

" Jill, you were in real trouble," he said.

" Why should you say that ? " Jill asked.

" Because that lady is no lady. You have to know that now, Jill, if you didn't know it then. Vanessa has never dreamed of any other finale to a high life of society, travel, and general good time than marrying Kim Baxter. Mind you . . ."

He looked at Jill to see that all was well with her and he wasn't digging some kind of nasty pit under her feet. Jill kept her face as nearly serene as possible. She must know. It would help her to know. She had to let Shane talk.

"Go on," Jill said smiling, aghast at her own capacity to deceive. First the nice Elbertons and now Shane! Surely if you touch pitch, then you are not untouched by pitch! She would never again be the naïve, guileless person who had got off that bus outside the hotel, to be met by Shane, and later to know Kim.

"Vanessa played one card wrong," said Shane with a worldly air that didn't quite suit him. "She kept Kim *waiting*. That gave him time to think; and time to breathe good clean healthy Bal-Annie air."

"I think you're guessing all this," Jill said with a laugh. "Who knows whatever goes on in anyone else's heart?"

"Well, I guessed the same as everyone else around for roughly ten thousand square miles. That's about the area where Kim Baxter is known—and known about."

"Yes, it's a vast country," Jill said thoughtfully.

"Anyhow, Vanessa gave Kim time to think *square*," Shane said. "He's a man who takes risks—often. But he's no fool. You've nothing to worry about, sweet Jill. His head told him not to waste the soft air of Bal-Annie on Vanessa. And when Kim listens, it's to his head."

"Thank you," said Jill. "You're trying to tell me, Shane, that Kim married me because I was good for Bal-Annie and Vanessa was not. Don't look so astonished. But please tell me. Why do you think I married Kim?"

Shane suddenly realised where this conversation that had begun in sophistication and fun-making was leading them.

"You're a true honeymoon girl, Jill," he said with a laugh, edging her away from the subject. "You can't stop talking about your brand-new husband. Why should we have to keep to the subject of Kim? Let's talk about me. I'm the neglected one. Now listen, little bell-bird, those Junior Farmers need us. You and me . . ."

Jill nodded.

" We'll talk about the Junior Farmers in a minute, Shane. But please answer me . . ." She leaned across the table and looked into his eyes. " I was your piece-of-cake, remember ? In some ways I'm still that, because you were my first friend and you are my best friend. So I want you to answer me. What *you* think, the rest of Darjalup will also be thinking. Why do you think I married Kim, Shane ? "

He leaned across the table to her. There was only three inches between their noses.

" For two reasons," he said.

" What are they, please ? "

" Bal-Annie is one reason. It won your heart. The second reason ? You fell flat-bang in love with Kim Baxter." There was a wry expression of amusement as he drew back and watched the effect of his words on Jill. Her face had suffused with colour and there was a real and touching happiness in her eyes.

So her name stood fair in Darjalup ! People would not think she had been a gold-digger. They would know the truth. As long as people *knew* . . . But would Kim know ? And how would she ever know about Kim ? Even Shane knew he had married her with his head and not his heart.

" Now please tell me about the Junior Farmers," Jill said.

" No more about Vanessa ? "

" No more about Vanessa. I don't even like her very much, Shane. It's a pity, but it's the truth. Please . . . about the Junior Farmers ? "

Shane began talking in earnest.

" Those boys have fair taken the wind out of our sails," he said. " To think I thought of them as a lot of overgrown kids ! Jill, they set to . . . the biggest five-day working-party I've ever even thought of. Between them they cleared the burnt-out debris from darn-all every burnt-out house-block in Redwood. The place is as clean as if the ants had been through it—except for the debris piled like black cairns around the outskirts. But they had to put the stuff somewhere . . ."

Jill's eyes were shining.

"They were always so earnest," she said. "I could see it. Those experimental plots . . ."

The waitress had come and set cold ham and salads before them, with giant helpings of red plums and cream in bowls at the side. Shane had insisted on eating properly. He was hungry if Jill was not, so she had to join him, willy-nilly.

Now as Shane began to talk he put large helpings of food in his mouth and chewed through his words. He was too enthusiastic to mind his manners or his digestion. Jill ate to keep him company.

"That's exactly it," Shane said. "Those experimental plots of theirs were their various kinds of religion, back a few weeks ago. They devoted every darn waking minute to them—when they weren't doing their ordinary day's slogging on their father's farms."

"I know," said Jill. "That's why . . ."

"What you don't know," said Shane interrupting her, levelling his fork at her, "is that in order to clean up Redwood as well as do their stint of the milking, feeding, and general rouseabout on the papas' properties, they had to let their plots go. No man, not even a Junior Farmer, can do five days' work in one. Every man jack of them sacrificed his own plot to do his whack at Redwood . . . as a *team*."

"Oh, what a shame!" Jill said sadly.

"You know, as I know and as that fine district-leader of a husband of yours knows, those boys had their plots up for competition. The winners here were open to compete in the state competitions. The three state winners were to go to Britain, the United States and Europe to meet Junior Farmers there."

Shane paused to swallow more food.

" So they wiped up those chances and cleaned up Redwood instead," he finished. " We had one day of rain after the fire, then two days of blistering heat. There's not a plot left worth looking at. All because their owners weren't there to water them."

" What can we do ? " begged Jill. " Isn't there something ? "

" You mean that ? You're with me, Jill ? "

She nodded her head vigorously.

" Please tell me what to do."

By this time Jill's mouth was full of red plums and cream, and she too was forgetting digestion, if not good manners.

" I'm staying as chairman of that group," Shane said. " Kim can have the final say-so and call me deputy-chairman if he likes; but he's too busy a man to do what you and I are going to do. You're staying as my secretary. Right ? "

Jill nodded.

" Of course."

" Good. Well ! Operation Number One is that we form that group into the same kind of working-party they formed themselves into to clean up Redwood. Then . . . as a working-party, *as one group*, we all put those plots back into order. Every man helping everyone else. We'll have working bees every Sunday until we've got every plot growing something, and showing something. Then each man can take over his own plot and finish the job off for competition. Got it ? "

" Oh yes I have, Shane. It's absolutely splendid."

" No letting Mrs. Baxter shoot you off to golf, or Kim have you running with those Edens of his ? "

" Not till the plots are in order," Jill promised stoutly. "And they wouldn't want to stop me."

" Let's hope ! "

They went on talking, planning, hoping—even plotting. Then Shane looked at his watch.

" Great Scott ! Look at the time. Kim'll think I've abducted you. He'll be raising dust all over the parish . . ."

" He knows where I am," laughed Jill. " There's only one tearoom in Darjalup."

Shane gulped half his tea and Jill left hers untouched. Then they eased themselves out from behind their corner table and began to make for the door. Shane was still talking, breathing ideas and instructions like a railway engine climbing a hill, as he paid the bill. Then grasping Jill's elbow he rushed her out into the street.

Jill was laughing, partly at Shane's enthusiasm and masterly manner of making their exit for them, and partly because her own sad troubles had an overlay of something important she could do to help the people of Darjalup. For a brief moment—almost a respite—she was happy.

Out on the footpath they pulled up with a jerk. No need to hurry off at top speed for the Shire offices ! Kim's car was drawn up near the café and Kim was sitting in it, his hat pulled forward over his brow as if looking out from under a brim was nearer his mood than looking out any other way. He was smoking a cigarette, leaning back behind the driving-wheel and watching a man edge a small flock of sheep down the dusty main street out of the way of a horse-drawn cart and an oversized luxury car. Kim looked as if he might have been there quite some time.

Shane opened the car door for Jill.

" I'm so sorry, Kim," Jill said penitently. " I wish you'd come in and hurried us. We were talking . . ."

Kim pushed his hat to the back of his head.

" Must have been a very important conversation," he said quietly. " You seemed so in earnest, almost nose to nose, when I looked in I thought it was a pity to interrupt you."

"Oh, it was earnest," said Jill, getting into the car. "Shane and I were making plans . . ." She turned to Shane as he shut the door, and smiled at him through the open window. "Thank you so much, Shane!" she said. "You've given me a wonderful fillip. Food for thought."

Kim started up the engine and was already easing the brake.

"'Bye," said Shane, holding up one hand in salute. "See you Tuesday, Jill. Twelve o'clock sharp. Bring your pencil and pad."

Jill leaned through the window and waved back to him. "Dear Shane!" she was thinking, loving his youthful exuberant figure as he stood on the edge of the footpath and waved the car off. "Dear Shane! He has saved me. He's given me something to think about; something to do!"

She turned to Kim. The coldness and strain of the morning had gone out of her face, indeed out of her whole bearing. The colour in her cheeks was young and lovely; her eyes were gay and bright.

"Oh Kim . . ." she said, looking at his profile as he watched the road in front, edging the car past those sheep. His expression was concentrated. Yet, having been away from him for over an hour, it made Jill feel she had been lost but now was found. Perhaps she had been wrong-headed, foolish, jealous. Was it Kim's fault that someone like Vanessa chased him to death! even gatecrashed his honeymoon? Perhaps he *had* married her, Jill, with his head, but it was a beautiful head. She loved him. And she had work to do.

A whole life of loving someone and having wonderful work to do streamed away into the future before Jill's inward eye.

"Kim," she said. "Shane and I have a wonderful

idea. At least it's Shane's idea. Yes, that was unfair of me to claim any of it as my own. Kim, do you think I can be spared from Bal-Annie on Sundays as well as Tuesdays? Shane and I are going to plot-build. I don't know what else to call it."

Kim had passed the sheep, he now rounded the corner, crossed the railway line and doubled back on the side track to come out on the Bal-Annie road south of the town.

His silence was so formidable that at last Jill, wrapped a little in the egotism of her own enthusiasm, was aware of it.

She looked at that profile again.

" Kim . . . you don't *mind* . . ." she said.

" Not if you're happy, Jill," he said quietly. He knew every inch of that road and could have driven safely home on it blindfolded yet now he watched it with a concentration not to be broken.

" You see, there is so much we can do for the Junior Farmers, *together*. Every chairman needs a secretary. Then I'm used to working outside. Remember ? I'm an out-door girl . . ."

Kim's head turned and his eyes took in Jill. They were dark, intent, yet oddly tired eyes.

" Since when has the Shire Secretary promoted himself ? " he asked. Again his voice was soft, drawling, his lips hardly moving. Jill had learned long since that this was the way all out-back men spoke when they were thinking . . . weighing up and considering.

" Please Kim, don't call him the ' Shire Secretary.' It sounds so distant, even unfriendly. He's just Shane. He hasn't promoted himself. He will ask you about it, and perhaps just be deputy-chairman to you. You see, you're so busy. And Shane is so full of ideas . . ."

" I would say he was very full of ideas," Kim said. Jill's heart dropped a little. Perhaps Kim didn't

mean it that way. After all, he hadn't been so terribly
enthusiastic about Shane at any time, now Jill came to
think of it. Kim had rather taken this " Shire Secretary "
attitude to Shane right from the beginning of Jill's
acquaintance with him. It was probably because Shane
was exuberant, a little bit casual and over friendly in
his manner; and Kim himself was so reticent.

There had been quite a silence, and it was Kim who
broke it.

" *Deputy* ! " he said. " That's rather a good word.
Quite the word that one imagines Shane could use for
the occasion."

Jill didn't know what to say to that. She wasn't sure
whether Kim was being ironic, or not.

Time to change the subject perhaps.

" Shall I light you a cigarette, Kim ? " she asked
gently.

" Yes, thank you."

Once again she fished in his pocket for the packet. She
felt this was a peculiarly intimate and wifely thing to be
doing and she longed for Kim to say some softening word.
Her barriers were no longer existent. She would forget
Vanessa. The sun was shining slantwise through the
big timber on either side of the winding road and making
a pattern of light and shade on the brown gravel. It was
beautiful, it smelt lovely; and she had her hand in Kim's
pocket. She would forget the disasters of Vanessa's
appearance at their one-day honeymoon.

" Light a cigarette for yourself," Kim said, still watching the road. He glanced at her; those dark blue eyes
were holding no light or warmth in them. " The little
weaknesses don't matter very much in life," he said,
" if they bring comfort. It's the big ones that destroy
happiness."

Jill withdrew her hand and with it, the cigarettes.
She hadn't the faintest idea what Kim meant. She only

knew that her hand in his pocket conveyed no living intimacy to him.

She put a cigarette in Kim's mouth and lifted the lighter from the dashboard and applied it to the tip of his cigarette. When she put the lighter back she noticed they were in the tall timber again and the sun was hidden behind them. The road was in shadow, still beautiful but somehow touched with the old inscrutable loneliness of the forest.

The shadow touched her too.

CHAPTER SIXTEEN

IT WAS AFTER four o'clock when they reached Bal-Annie for Kim had detoured from the through-road to look at the progress being made at the dam out at the back paddock. This meant they drove up to the homestead over an old track through the bush and light timbered paddocks. Kim couldn't go at his accustomed speed over that track.

They came into Bal-Annie homestead square from the east instead of by the main drive, but Kim drove round the house to the front entrance.

Once again he had that look in his eyes that said he meant to be kind but could only feel the irony of the situation.

" We can't bring the bride home by the back door," he said.

" It's fun to come home either way," Jill said. She had long ago given up talking about Shane Evans or the Junior Farmers. Her words had been dropping on unreceptive ears. She thought it was because Kim was angry because Shane had " promoted " himself. She wished she'd never mentioned it.

Jill walked up the steps of the veranda and to the front door, while Kim took the cases from the boot of the car. There could be no sentiment about this home-coming, she knew. She didn't think that Kim had ever heard of such silly practices as carrying the bride over the door-step, anyway.

The main door of the homestead stood wide open. She knew that neither Mrs. Baxter nor Tuffy were coming back until after she and Kim were home. They had arranged all that at the wedding. It had been their idea because they had thought it would be nice for Kim and Jill to have the house to themselves for the first two days.

One of the neighbouring farmers' wives had arranged to prepare the house for them.

Jill went into the hall. It was so still and quiet she knew no one was there. There was a great bowl of Mrs. Baxter's roses on the hall table and they filled the air with their lovely gentle scent.

The sun came through a portion of the glass roof on the west side and it lay splashed across the carpeted floor, turning everything it touched into gold.

Jill could see roses standing about in bowls through the open door of the front room too. Light and air and warmth flooded in through the open french door.

She looked around her. For the first time she realised she had come to her home. She felt as if she had never seen this hall, that living-room before.

Kim came through the front door, and put the cases down by the centre table. He tossed his hat on to a chair.

" Looking round your domain ? " he said. There was neither kindness nor an absence of it in Kim's voice.

" We'd better come and see the rest of it," he went on. " It's all yours now, Jill. Your homestead."

He walked to the door of the front room and made a gesture for Jill to go in. She stood in the doorway and looked around. It was a lovely room with the light flooding in and the roses standing everywhere. Yet it had the strange aspect of a room she had never seen before. It was waiting and ready for her. And Jill had not expected it.

" Now down this main passage is Mother's room, and of course her work study and bathroom beyond it," said Kim, walking towards the main passage. Jill took a few steps after him, then stopped.

" No, Kim," she said. " Those are your mother's rooms and this is her house . . . till she doesn't want it any more." She thought she sounded mutinous and hoped she sounded firm. " I'm not going to her rooms till she asks me."

" Very well. Perhaps you are right. The room at the bottom leading to the back veranda and the ping-pong table is Don's menagerie . . ."

" Please, Kim," Jill pleaded. " I've seen it often. I can smell something nice coming from the kitchen. Do you think Mrs. Parrish has left the dinner cooking for us in the oven ? "

" Possibly," Kim said. He was purposeful and impersonal. " Perhaps we had better go and see what Tuffy made of *our* rooms."

If there was the faintest inflection on the " our " it was an ironic one.

He walked down the cross passage and opened the office door. Jill went in slowly, feeling again she was entering a room she had never seen before. It was the same old office, only beautifully polished up, and very tidy. The pinewood table had been replaced by a cedar one and on it stood yet another bowl of roses.

" Flowers everywhere," said Kim. " It seems that you are very welcome home, Jill."

He was not looking at her. Jill thought he was going to usher her in and out of passages and rooms for the rest of his life and never look at her again.

"I don't feel it is home," Jill said slowly. "I feel strange . . ."

Now he did look at her, his eyebrows raised.

"But you know it all very well," he said.

Jill looked round the office and then at Kim's eyes.

"But not as your wife," she said. "I feel different. I am different."

Again the eyebrows moved.

"Not so very different," he said.

Suddenly, with a flash of insight, she realised what was wrong. She had fallen in love with him and that had altered everything. If she hadn't done that then Vanessa wouldn't have mattered. She and Kim would have fallen into the routine of ordinary married life in an effortless way. Time, and the shared interests, would have brought them closer together, even into a kind of loyalty of love.

But she, Jill, had wanted all of him; too much. And she hadn't played fair. She hadn't been prepared to take some but not most.

She must do and say something now to shake Kim from that distant impersonal attitude with which he was guarding himself, as well as keeping her at a distance—showing her the thing she had married—*Bal-Annie*.

With a great effort she smiled, right at him.

"It's nice to be home, Kim," she said. "Shall we look at those other rooms?"

If only Tuffy had found that "double bed" of which Kim had made the kind of joke that had shocked them all, including herself!

Kim stood aside so that Jill could go into the adjoining room. He had used it formerly as a personal sitting-room. Vanessa had called it his "sanctum."

It was like a new room. It had been painted in bright modern colours, there were new curtains, new cushions, two lovely chairs. This time there were no roses in the vases. Instead there were sprays of vine leaves and some early dahlias. This was Tuffy's gift, for while the rose-gardens in front and at the side of the house were Mrs. Baxter's, the dahlia beds at the bottom of the kitchen garden were Tuffy's.

" She must have told Mrs. Parrish . . ." Jill said, looking at the flowers.

" Tuffy would have left no stone unturned," Kim said evenly. " She was rather preoccupied with other people's rights to happiness."

" Yes, I know," Jill said.

Kim walked across the pretty room and opened the door into the room that had formerly been his own bedroom. It was a fairly big square room with double windows looking over the west paddock and the track down to the training grounds.

It too had been painted, and all the furniture changed. Where there had been Kim's severely masculine but wide single bed, there were two beds. They were too large for the room and somewhat old-fashioned with their carved headboards, scrolled legs and high mattresses. Covering them were two new candlewick covers.

" Good God," said Kim, looking at the beds. " Those things belonged to my grandparents."

Jill said nothing because she saw only the small square table carrying a reading-lamp, that stood against the wall, between the beds.

Like one sees in American films, Jill thought.

Funny, she didn't ever want to sleep by herself again. She wanted to sleep for ever and ever in Kim's arms.

What a fool she had been !

What did Vanessa matter ! Hadn't it been her job to take Kim on his own terms ? He needed her . . . and that should have been enough.

Now, even dear Tuffy had made it hard for Jill to make amends.

Kim appeared to take an impersonal view of this room too.

" How did she get it redecorated ? " Jill asked. She had to say something.

" We do have paints and paint brushes. We even have a man who can wield those things professionally," Kim said. He actually smiled. " In addition to my young half-brother, of course. You will remember his efforts with the old stables ? "

The mention of Don suddenly broke the ring of ice in which Jill felt she was standing.

" Yes . . . Don and the stables ! " she said, suddenly tilting her chin and beginning to feel the life of Bal-Annie surging around her after all. Everything was not lost.

" I must see how the brumbies are . . ."

" Perhaps we'd better look at the kitchen first," Kim said. He was easier too. " I have a feeling something is cooking in that oven, but meantime we could have some tea."

He had been looking round the room but his eyes came back to Jill, blue and inscrutable.

" Unless . . . in Shane's company, you've managed to get yourself tea-logged ? "

" We talked so hard I didn't have time to drink my tea," Jill said with a laugh. She was happier now. Something of the ice had been broken after she and Kim had thought of Don and his rapscallion school mates. It wasn't an empty homestead any more. First Mrs. Baxter and Tuffy would come home; then at Eastertime Don and his school mates would be back.

Bal-Annie wasn't just a lovely place of field and paddock and distant forest trees with the afternoon sunlight pouring over it in silence. Soon, it would be full of life. There were things to do.

Somehow she and Kim would find a way.

" You are very fond of Shane ? " Kim said.

" Of course," Jill said. "He was the first person I knew in Darjalup. And we get on so well together. You know . . . talk about the same things. Somehow we laugh easily . . ."

" Youth calling to youth, I suppose," said Kim.

He was not looking at Jill. He had walked to the end of the bedroom and opened the door into what had formerly been a small cubby hole of a workroom where he had kept his tools, and small personal mechanical things. Tuffy's hand had been on that room too. The tools on their wall brackets had been adroitly covered by a small wooden partition that opened like a door. The work bench looked respectable by having the vice fixed at the end instead of the side of it and a green baize cloth put over the whole. Against a wall was a narrow divan bed with a simple patterned covering.

Jill followed Kim to the door and stood beside him looking in.

" What is that for ? " she asked, gazing at the bed then at Kim. " That's supposed to be your workshop."

" That . . ." said Kim, not with amusement, " is where I am supposed to sleep when we quarrel, I expect. Tuffy leaves no stone unturned. Or should I say—no bed unprepared."

Tuffy had told Mrs. Baxter, but not Kim, she had put a special bed in for Kim when he was moonlight-seeding when the first winter rains came. Tuffy had exalted ideas about chivalry, and the unkindness of disturbing other people.

" No need for the whole household to lose a night's sleep," she had said.

Jill raised her eyes to Kim and they stood looking at one another.

" But we're not going to quarrel, Kim," Jill said soberly.

His eyes had that tired expression in them again.

"No," he said with irony. "We'll not even argue."

Jill looked round the room with unseeing eyes. How did she tell Kim she was sorry for what had happened?

How had other women—all through history—who had made marriages of convenience turn them into normal marriages?

She had had one chance. And lost it.

Kim turned abruptly away from the door. "Now if you'll excuse me, Jill, I'm going to work right now. I'll change into my outside clothes . . ."

"But that cup of tea?" pleaded Jill.

"We're home now. I've work to do. I'm sorry. That was the big idea, wasn't it? I'll have some tea with the men down at the stables, and if the telephone leaves you alone long enough, perhaps you'll be able to manage in the kitchen without Tuffy . . ."

Jill, rebuffed, went to the door. Kim was already taking off his jacket. As Jill reached the door he was unknotting his tie.

"Jill," he said, looking at her over his tie. "I'm glad you and Shane are going to do something about the Junior Farmers. You have my blessing. I won't obstruct you. You can tell Shane that."

Until that moment it hadn't occurred to Jill that Kim *would* obstruct them.

Somehow she got through the rest of that day. Kim went out and did not ask her if she wished to go, or even if she wanted to see the brumbies . . . her charge for Don.

Jill found it hard to stay in the homestead. She wanted to put on her slacks and blouse too . . . and run down to the saddling yard and find Gem there. Or better still, race in her light fleet-footed way across the home paddock to where the brumbies grazed. Day by day for days, she knew, she would have to go into that paddock and quieten them; get them used to her, then used to obedience when being ridden.

They had been broken long ago but left too long in the forest paddock and needed schooling again.

But sense as well as sensibility told her that for to-day her place was in the homestead and her role that of house-wife. Until Tuffy came home she had to " feed the man."

That was a good idea, she told herself as she unpacked her case, and changed into a house dress. She made sure this last was a pretty dress. Given time, given the will-power, and given sense she might forget Vanessa and win Kim. Now, in a queer kind of spiritual loneliness she would take him at his price—himself because he needed her—without his whole heart.

What a schoolgirl of a bride she had been !

She would work, for herself, for the Junior Farmers, for Bal-Annie. Perhaps need would turn to some kind of love.

Jill's spirits began to rise as she basted the roast of beef that had been set at the right regulo heat in the oven to be cooked by seven o'clock.

Shane and the Junior Farmers! Kim and Bal-Annie! She would win. It would take time, but she would win. One can't share a room for ever with a man without him one day looking at her, and seeing her as a woman and not only as a helpmate.

" Patience and keep your temper, Jill," she told herself.

Meantime . . . " feed the man." It would be a good dinner to-night, this their first night at home.

That day and night passed, and the next one too. Jill, though longing to go down to the training paddock and see Kim ride that horse again, denied herself. She con-fined herself to going only to the brumby paddock and walking round in it, getting the young frisky horses used to seeing her. When she walked to one side of the paddock they raced off in a bunch to the other side, but presently one of them . . . Snubby, came a few paces forward towards her as if wanting to investigate this strange intruder. Jill held out her hand and Snubby lengthened his neck and held out his nose, smelling the air, scenting her hand. Then changing his mind he turned and galloped round the paddock, his mane flying, back to the corner where his mates were standing restlessly, showing the whites of their eyes, their noses likewise distended.

Jill knew she had won the first round. Snubby wanted to find out about her. Another three days and he would come so near she would be able to touch his nose.

No rounding up those brumbies in one day and putting the hated halter on their necks for Jill. They were to come to *her*. Then they would be hers . . . bit, saddle and all; but her friends.

Don would have a real surprise waiting for him when he came home at Easter.

Meantime, as Kim had predicted, that telephone rang. Neighbours with kindly inquiries; town and Shire officials rang up with information as to how things were going forward about putting Darjalup to rights, and at top speed. And yes, most difficult of all, those government officials were coming down and would Bal-Annie put up the big nobs ? Nothing but the best property in the district was worthy of housing the government engineers ready and willing to begin rebuilding damaged roads, culverts, creek dams and even Redwood town itself.

Time, only time, was the enemy. So much to do and only six months in which to do it.

Kim was up before dawn in the morning and gone out to the paddocks, the training ground, or the dam in the back paddock before it was quite daylight.

Two days later Mrs. Baxter and Tuffy came back. Jill welcomed them with rose bowls everywhere, and a roast dinner cooked to perfection. She was so glad to see them she nearly cried. In spite of all that activity the homestead had been lonely. Never for a moment could she quite get that tall, silent tired image of Kim out of her mind.

He was tired. Something more than mere physical exertion weighed on him. Desperately Jill put from her the thought that he might be regretting that he hadn't taken the fun with Vanessa instead of the reliability, and that separated life, with Jill.

" Well now, Jill ! " Mrs. Baxter had said within five minutes of coming into the homestead and taking off her hat. " We must get to work and find that house for me in Darjalup. Of course with the place full of do-gooders . . ."

" There isn't a house to spare at the moment," Jill finished for her. " Never mind, we'd hate to lose you for quite a while yet. Best to look around and wait." She smiled and pleaded. Mrs. Baxter gave in.

" For the time being———" she conceded.

Tuffy, once she was out of her " town " clothes and happily back to the grey alpaca with the round white collar, went to her kitchen. She stood in the middle of it, her hands folded in front of her, and her mouth pursed.

" Well, I must say . . ." she said. " You know how to keep a kitchen nicely . . ."

" Oh Tuffy dear," Jill said. " How could I wreck it in three days ? "

" I've made up my mind about you, Jill," Tuffy said, wagging her head and making for her flour bin. She must start making bread at once or the yeast would pop its cork. Jill had made bread, not so very successfully as it was her first try and she thought it best not to spoil Tuffy's enthusiasm. She had given most of her bread to the turkeys.

"And how's Kim ? " Tuffy said, straightening up,

turning and looking at Jill closely. " Have you taken care of him, Jill ? "

Kim belonged to Tuffy and was the sole reason for her existence, so Jill had to be understanding about that question. She would have loved someone to ask—had Kim been taking care of *her*. No use to tell Tuffy the most she saw of Kim was his back going down towards the stables as the red glow of the first sunlight appeared on the tree tops to the east; and his reticent tired face when he came in at night.

Jill was saying . . . " Yes, oh yes ! Of course ! " when it occurred to her Tuffy was looking at her very closely. Tuffy's eyes were telling her that Jill's face was tired and strained, and Tuffy was doing some wondering. This marriage had started off as a " useful " one. But surely the young people had done something about that !

"And how did you like the rooms ? " Tuffy asked. " The painter would have his own way about the colours but I don't think he made a bad job of it. The beds were the best I could do for the time being. I thought you and Kim would go and buy a suite of your own choosing."

Tuffy was back at the flour bins ladling out flour with veteran skill.

" That double bed Kim's set his heart on," she said with the natural ease of one sensible woman to another. " Maybe he'd want to pick it himself. Men are funny creatures when it comes to their rights and their tastes."

Jill didn't say Kim had been too short a time in Perth to go shopping for furniture.

As if Tuffy knew anything about men, Jill thought. But then . . . perhaps she did. Hadn't she underlined that word *rights* a little unnecessarily ?

Jill flushed and turned to go out of the kitchen.

" There's so much to do, Tuffy," she said apologetically. " Now you're home, please may I go ? I've hundreds of notices to send out to the Junior Farmers. Shane Evans and I are having the first meeting with them since the fire on Tuesday night . . ."

" Tuesday night ? " said Tuffy, looking up again. " Kim's too tired at nights to go gallivanting thirty miles into Darjalup. I thought they used to have those meetings at midday. On pig-sale day ? "

" Kim's not coming in," Jill said. " He's handed it all over to Shane, rather thankfully. It's one less job to do and he thinks Shane and I will do it well."

" *Shane and I ?* " said Tuffy. " I don't understand this *Shane and I.* I thought you were Kim's off-sider."

" So I am. Doing this job is really off-siding for Kim. One of the Junior Farmers who lives ten miles farther up the track is calling for me; and will bring me home."

" I still don't understand why it's got to be at night-time," said Tuffy, shaking her head, disapproving. Jill laughed because she knew Tuffy was wedded to the idea that work began at daybreak and ended at sun-down.

" It's a social meeting," Jill explained. " To start everything off with a swing. Full of good-will and all that sort of thing. Gets them in, Tuffy. You'd be surprised. Shane told me . . ."

" Here we go again . . . *Shane told me . . .*" said Tuffy. " If I were Kim I'd keep that young man out of bounds."

Jill laughed.

" He's too useful," she said. " Now Tuffy, I've done all the explaining. Please can you spare me to go and write my notices ? "

" Well . . . I dare say," said Tuffy. "If it was Kim's notices now, I wouldn't mind."

Jill laughed as she went through the wire door. Dear Tuffy. She adored Kim.

Well, she wasn't the only one who did that, was she ? A shadow fell on Jill's face again. Then she shook her head. Work. That was the thing. If one kept working one didn't think, and one day? Who knows? She and Kim might stop working just long enough to mean something to one another that touched their hearts.

Mrs. Baxter was too preoccupied with picking the drooping blooms from her roses, wondering distractedly what she would take with her and what she would leave behind when she got *that house*, to notice anything odd about Jill and Kim. But Tuffy's canny old eyes moved from face to face, and now and again she wagged her head.

Kim, who had as much second sight as Tuffy where Tuffy was concerned, noticed it. He smiled at her, that slightly school-boyish, half-mischievous, half-intimate smile he had specially for her behind other people's backs, and shook his head slightly from side to side.

No use to worry, Tuffy! that smile said. *I'm not telling, so don't ask.*

His old friend knew him too well to ask . . . just yet. But she knew also that all was not well. That absence from the homestead all day; that quiet aloof reticence. These were not the signs and portents that all was well.

When Shane rang up in the next two or three days, and he did this several times, Tuffy was very short with him on the switchboard.

" Tuffy, you all but cut us off," Jill complained half jokingly on the following Saturday.

" Why not ? " said Tuffy shortly. " When I hear that voice—*Shane Evans, Tuffy. I want to speak to Jill*—I want to say . . . Mrs. Baxter to you, Mr. Shire Secretary. She happens to be Kim's wife, not yours."

" Why, Tuffy ! " exclaimed Jill, wanting to laugh outright but afraid of hurting Tuffy's feelings.

" Ringing you up about this and that ! And you going off to a Social with him ! Can't think what Kim's think-

ing about to allow it." Tuffy stopped short and stared at
Jill, who was doing the flowers on a piece of newspaper
on the kitchen table.

" Come to think of it, Jill. What does Kim really think
of it ? "

" Why, Tuffy, he's pleased. We're doing something
big . . ." She saw the expression in Tuffy's eyes. Was
Kim pleased ? What did he think ?

Jill put a long-stemmed rosebud down on the table and
stood thinking herself. She had turned her back to Tuffy
now but the older woman had seen that rosebud go down
and that now Jill's hands were still.

Why, Kim wouldn't think . . .

Jill stared with unseeing eyes at the flower-strewn table.
It wasn't possible ! But if he did . . . ?

Very slowly Jill picked up a bowl of flowers and turning
round went out of the kitchen with it, not even noticing
that Tuffy was watching her ; in fact forgetting that
Tuffy existed at all.

The flowers were intended for the hall but Jill forgot
this too. She went down the side passage to the office,
put them on the cedar table amongst her litter of notices
without knowing she did it. She sat down on the bentwood chair by the telephone table because the only other
chair in the room happened to be occupied by the postal
directory from which she had been taking addresses.

He couldn't possibly think . . . ? But supposing he
did ?

Jill put her elbow on the table and rested her head
in her hand.

It was fantastic. Everything about everything was
fantastic. She would have to tell Kim.

She sat upright, staring at the telephone bracket on the
wall and not seeing it.

She would tell him. She would tell him everything.
She would tell him she loved him, she'd been jealous . . .

she'd been wrong. Yes. She would tell him she loved him.

It wouldn't matter if he looked at her with those strange uncommunicative blue eyes of his, and said nothing. It wouldn't matter if he rebuffed her. Nothing mattered except that she told him.

She would have him on his own terms, any terms—but she would put an end to this silence. It only seemed to matter, at that moment, that Kim knew she loved him.

She would tell him Shane was nothing more than a kind person who had given her something important to do . . . to take her mind off herself. That he, Kim, was the only person in all the world who mattered to her.

Mother, Father, Bal-Annie—nothing mattered, except that one day those eyes might look at her with a smile and real kindness; and that once again she might be cradled in those arms, happy in a dream of love, even if it was no more than that.

Jill stood up.

She would go and tell him now before she became afraid to do so. She would catch Gem. She didn't care where she told him—on the race-track, in the middle of a paddock, out amongst the men at the dam in the back paddock—She would tell him *now*.

Suddenly Jill felt as if she was filled with light. Once she had told him, she would be at peace.

She had reached the door when the telephone rang. " I won't answer it," she said. But she had faltered.

Again there was that awful old dilemma, as compelling as that summoning staccato ring of the telephone. Supposing it was something vitally important for Kim?

She turned and went slowly back, knowing for the first time why Mrs. Baxter called that black thing on the wall " *an instrument of torture.*"

She lifted the receiver.

" Yes, Tuffy ? " she said.

" It's a long distance call, Jill," Tuffy said. " They're waiting for you. It's Mount Sterling."

Mount Sterling ? Jill felt as if someone had hit her, and her heart clanged to the ground with a sound as if a gong had struck it there.

" Yes ? " she said, her voice dead and flat in her own ears.

A man's voice answered. From the quality of his voice Jill could almost see the man who was speaking at the other end. He would be elderly, rich, self-indulged. His voice was positively *fruity*.

" Hallo. Is that Mrs. Baxter ? . . . the young Mrs. Baxter I should say ? . . . It is ? Well met, my dear ! I knew it was someone young, and darn pretty too, by that voice . . . Well now, listen, my dear. I'm going to borrow that husband of yours. Can you get a message to him ? I don't suppose he's in the homestead . . . You can ? Bravo. Well, here it is. I've had a word with the Member for our district and we're to have a big rally of the landed people down here. We're all coming to the rescue of those Redwood people . . . not to mention Darjalup as a whole . . . You got that ? Good. Kim's the key man and we must have him here. Tell him to come down to-night. He can get here by midnight in that big car of his . . . you'll tell him ? We can get straight to work in the morning. Have you got all that ? . . . Splendid, little lady. I can see Kim's bought himself a jewel in you. Here's the rest—Every man on a parcel of land south of the thirtieth parallel will be here sometime to-night or during the morning—Got it ? . . . Kim's the big man so we can't do without him. He knows that. Tell him we'll take the leg-rope and halter off him about Monday night or Tuesday morning. Three days away from Bal-Annie won't wreck the place . . ."

Very slowly Jill put down the receiver. Three days at Mount Sterling, with Vanessa Althrop serving drinks, coffee and physical charms !

Kim wouldn't do anything, but Vanessa would. Oh yes, Vanessa *would*. Then how could Kim come home and take a repentant Jill in his arms and pretend to like it ? Whose image would be in his mind then ?

Jill looked up. Heavy footsteps were coming down the passage. She knew it was Kim before he came in.

" There was a message down at the stables that Mount Sterling had been trying to ring the line down there," he said. " Do you know anything about it, Jill ? "

" Yes," said Jill slowly. " They want you down there. By to-night. The district Member of Parliament will be there . . ."

She looked up at him, incapable of seeing straight as she gave him the message. There wasn't any hope in her heart that he would say no. He couldn't be the one defaulter when the troubles of his own district and town were being nobly shouldered by those farther afield.

Kim cart-wheeled his hat on to the shelf on the other side of the room. He was suddenly alert, his eyes keen.

" That's the best news I've heard for a long time," he said.

CHAPTER SEVENTEEN

JILL FOUND it was Tuffy's prerogative to pack Kim's overnight bag. She let her do it. She didn't want to know what he was likely to wear. Anything he wore would charm Vanessa.

The recurring picture of Vanessa hostessing that party of landed notables wounded Jill's mind. She had to try and think of something else.

Shane Evans rang up and said there wasn't anything doing this week-end as the big drive to help the Junior Farmers would start at the meeting before the social on Tuesday night. She could go to golf. Anyway, he was going himself.

Mrs. Baxter, who had by this time been away from Bal-Annie near on a fortnight, had quite a pile of her own correspondence to sort out. Jill offered to help her.

" Dear girl ! You're not an off-sider now. Not that I wouldn't just love you to take the wretched stuff off my hands. I would. But I do have to keep remembering you're Kim's wife."

If Mrs. Baxter found it so easy to forget, Jill wished she herself could.

" Wives are always off-siders," she heard herself saying. " I like doing it, and I can type."

" Yes. We must get Kim to buy you a new typewriter. I believe they have electric ones."

" I believe so too," said Jill. " But I wouldn't know how to use one."

By this time they were sitting at the occasional table in the front room and Mrs. Baxter was sorting the private letters from those relating to all her committees. She glanced up in surprise, almost as if she had caught a note in Jill's voice that was puzzling.

"My dear," Mrs. Baxter said firmly. "I think you're quite wonderful. Do you know, Jill? You could do anything, if you set your mind to it? Even find out how an electric typewriter works."

Jill's eyes moistened over.

"Thank you for having such faith in me," she said. "And thank you for being so kind to me too, Mrs. Baxter. It's not everyone who would take a daughter-in-law in with such a good grace."

"Nonsense," said Mrs. Baxter, quickly sorting letters again to hide the fact that although she was embarrassed she was also touched. "Pure selfishness on my part. You've taken Kim off my hands; and Bal-Annie." She looked up quickly. "But Jill. There's one awful problem. *Donald*. You know this is his home too? He'll be such a hair-raising ordeal for you. Of course I'll keep him as much as possible in the Darjalup house, when I get it."

Jill smiled, the first real smile she had had to offer anyone for hours. Certainly she had not had a smile since Kim's car had roared away with him down the drive.

"I think we'll have a fight after all," she said to Mrs. Baxter. "It will be over Don. Do you know, Mrs. Baxter, it was Don who first showed me lovely Bal-Annie? And whom do you think I'm schooling those brumbies for?"

"Yes, come to think of it, you did get on rather well with him. You know he'll be home for Easter. Plus ..."

"Yes, plus Dick and Harry. I'm looking forward to it. It'll make Easter for me."

Like Shane makes life in Darjalup possible for me, she thought.

"It mustn't be all work and no play for you," Mrs.

Baxter said firmly. " You must come out and have a game of golf."

Jill looked eagerly across the table.

" To-morrow ? Do let's go and have a game of golf to-morrow. Somehow I feel the long walk and that maddening ball will clear the cobwebs away."

" Well, of course," Mrs. Baxter said. " Do you think we have time, Jill ? Look at all this correspondence. And Kim said something about you sending out dozens of notices."

" We'll make time," said Jill. " Do please say yes, Mrs. Baxter. I've always more energy after golf and I'll finish all this to-night, then the notices to-morrow night . . . if only we can have a game of golf to-morrow afternoon."

" You do sound keen. What is your handicap, Jill ? "

" It was twelve," said Jill. " But I haven't had a game since last winter."

" Twelve ? Good gracious. A young girl like you. We'll have to do something about getting that down. Of course we'll go out to-morrow."

Jill was a little taken aback at Mrs. Baxter's reaction to that twelve handicap. Twelve was supposed to be a very good score for a girl who only learned and played on a public golf course.

" What is your handicap, Mrs. Baxter ? " she asked tentatively.

" Nine—which is a disgrace, of course. All these town committees——"

" Nine ! " said Jill, her eyes widening. " Why, Mrs. Baxter, you must be in the Pennant class."

" Yes. Country Women's championship, but that was ten years ago."

She leaned forward and tapped Jill's arm with an unopened letter. There was a little gleam of amusement in her eyes.

"Now you know why I want my little town house," she said. "Committee once or twice a week, but golf three times a week. Regularly."

Jill leaned back in her chair and laughed.

Mrs. Baxter went back to her mail.

"Of course Kim and Tuffy are always so *earnest* about Bal-Annie, I felt just too guilty golfing too often."

"But Kim would have wanted you to go."

"I know. But I still felt guilty. Ah well, Kim and Bal-Annie are your problems now. All the same, Jill, we must get that handicap of yours down. I'll have to speak to Kim about it."

Wonders would never cease, Jill thought. And she would never cease learning something new about Mrs. Baxter.

They had an eleven o'clock lunchette the next day and then Mrs. Baxter drove Jill to the golf course just outside Darjalup.

It was a beautiful course, carved out of the forest. The long holes ran up and down a beautiful grassed valley. At a glance Jill could see that one would have to play straight. The trees stood in splendid array on either side of the fairways, and that meant a hook or a slice would be fatal to a score card.

Inside the clubhouse Mrs. Baxter seemed quite proud to be introducing her daughter-in-law. All the ladies, in between changing their shoes, polishing balls against their skirts and pinning tees in their hat bands, were charming to Jill. She began to feel happy again. She knew this was only temporary.

Anything, she thought, *anything* to play, and not think of that high-powered gathering at Mount Sterling with Kim the centre of attention, and Vanessa the donor of that attention.

As they emerged from the club door Jill almost walked into Shane.

He grinned at her a little wickedly.

" I thought that seed might fall on fertile ground," he said. "And sprout, of course. I heard about Kim's shoot through to Mount Sterling. The blighter had to go, you know."

" He's my husband, and I miss him," said Jill staunchly. Better get this straight with Shane, at once.

" Of course you do, but it's mixed doubles to-day and I haven't got a partner. Couldn't book up one because I didn't know whether I'd be roped into that meeting too. When I wasn't . . . well, I thought of the grass-widow who also wouldn't have a partner. Right ? "

The grin was mischievous but kindly. Jill knew there was nothing more than good nature in Shane's heart.

She smiled readily.

" I'd love it, Shane. But what about Mrs. Baxter ? Has she a partner, do you know ? "

" She's the Women's Captain. She ought to know. Anyhow, she always plays with old Daddy Riddle. He's ancient but he's a classic player."

" Mrs. Baxter is the captain ? Oh no ! " said Jill. " Not one more committee."

" Don't hunt round Mrs. Baxter's life too much, dear child. You'll find a committee round every corner. Anyhow I'll go and find out how she's fixed."

It was a lovely afternoon's golf. It was warm but not too hot. Jill played the first two holes poorly but struck form on the third then holed out on the short hole for a lovely two. Shane played brilliantly but erratically but he had enough good holes to cancel the very bad ones and they came in to win the trophy for runners-up.

Mrs. Baxter was delighted that Jill had made such a good début.

They drove home through the sundown both feeling more at peace with the world, Jill still trying to keep her mind away from Mount Sterling ; and some of the time succeeding.

Mrs. Baxter's correspondence was finished and Jill's own notices were signed and sealed ready to be picked up by the mail man in the morning and be delivered straight away to all the young farmers on his route. The Junior Farmers already knew about, and were coming to, the meeting-then-social but these later notices were subjects to give them food for thought in their discussions.

On Monday night there was no word from Kim, and all Tuesday morning Jill had her head turned to hear the sound of his returning car. On any pretext whatever she went through the hall to the front veranda and looked down the long, long drive leading to the stock trap.

She felt as if she would die if she didn't soon see that dust cloud and hear the thrum of that engine.

When afternoon came and she couldn't bear that waiting any longer she went down to the brumbies. This time Snubby did come, faltering step by faltering step right up to within reaching distance of her out-stretched hand. Moving only her fingers, and nothing else about her body, she gently caressed his nose.

Snubby investigated this pleasant sensation and Jill's warm kind fingers for quite two minutes, then throwing up his head he wheeled and cantered away down the paddock. His mates were no longer throwing up their heads and shivering in anxious contemplation of this slim human being in her golden-yellow slacks with the be-guiling grey-green eyes. They came very close to watch what went on with Snubby and the visitor. Jill smiled happily to herself. To-morrow she would have her arm round Snubby's neck and probably her fingers on the noses of at least two of the others. A week from now they'd bear their saddles again. Don would have something really schooled by the time Easter came.

Jill walked up to the homestead slowly. If Kim had come home she would have known. She could see the drive from the brumby paddock. Nothing had come that way. The track had lain brown and still in the warm afternoon, bare of life of any kind.

Jill came up to the homestead by the path from the stables and on to the back veranda. Tuffy, or Mrs. Baxter, had been doing flowers on the table-tennis table, and the leaf and petal debris was still there on a piece of paper. Jill began to gather it up.

Tuffy, who had been watching through the kitchen door as Jill approached, came to the back door. She had seen that strained, white face. Off and on she had noticed all day how Jill had gone to the front veranda and looked out. She had noticed that half-listening attitude of Jill's head even when they'd been in the kitchen after lunch and washing up; with not much likelihood of hearing anything above the clatter of dishes.

"You go into your own sitting-room, Jill," she said quietly. "I'll bring you a cup of tea."

"Isn't it a bit late?" said Jill, parcelling up the remnants of the flowers in the paper.

"You've been out in that paddock in the sun. And you're going out to-night. Go and have a rest, old Tuffy'll bring you some tea."

Jill looked up and saw the lurking anxiety at the back of Tuffy's eyes.

"Did Kim ring up and say he was not coming home?" she asked. She could hardly bear to wait for the answer and knew she would hardly hear it for the thrumming of her heart-beats in her ears.

"He didn't ring," Tuffy said, trying to sound matter-of-fact. " There was a call from Mount Sterling. It was Mr. Althrop himself, I think. No, it was to say Kim had left. He wasn't sure at what hour exactly he'd get home."

" I suppose I will have gone to Darjalup by then," Jill said sadly. Suddenly she wasn't able to hide, even from Tuffy, just how she felt about that Mount Sterling visit. She put the parcel of rubbish back on the table. " I think I will go and have that rest . . . and yes please, I will have some tea, Tuffy."

She went into the house through the passage door then down the cross passage to the office and into their own small sitting-room.

The window was open and the soft warm air was flooding in. On the table, on the mantelshelf and even on the window-sill were bowls of flowers . . . some Tuffy's dahlias, some Mrs. Baxter's roses.

Tuffy, or Mrs. Baxter, or both had made the room beautiful and sweet scented.

Jill sat down in the comfortable chintz-covered arm-chair and wondered why. It wasn't anybody's birthday. Perhaps it was because Kim would come home some time to-night and this was their way of making homecoming kind for him. Jill couldn't remember that, when she first came to Bal-Annie as Kim's off-sider, there had been flowers put about for him anywhere. She wondered if, man-like, he would even notice now.

It didn't occur to Jill that Tuffy had done this for her. Tuffy had seen a white-faced girl, suffering for her husband's absence, and hadn't known any better way of making something beautiful and comforting for that girl.

Jill put her head back against the head-rest and closed her eyes.

Tuffy was being so kind.

Had Tuffy lied too ? Was it Vanessa who had rung up ?

If Kim could lie anyone could lie.

Tuffy brought the tea in and Jill opened her eyes and sat up.

" There you are," said Tuffy. " I told you you were tired. Why, you're almost asleep."

" So I was," said Jill. She too could tell lies. Was no one ever honest in the world of love ?

Jill had early dinner that night because the young farmer calling for her would be early. She was dressed in a simple black lace dress, short but, as Tuffy said admiringly, she had such nice legs she ought never to wear anything long. The deep black, with the pretty squared neckline, suited Jill's fair tanned skin beautifully. She wore no jewellery except the diamond engagement ring and wedding ring and a single string of pearls that had been Kim's wedding present. They were beautiful pearls perfectly graded and probably cost Kim a fortune. This was the first time Jill had had the opportunity to wear them since she was married.

She ought to have been with Kim on that first occasion.

" But pearls are for tears," she thought. " What does it matter ? "

Mrs. Baxter and Tuffy both exclaimed with admiration when Jill came in dressed up.

" Why Jill, you're a beautiful girl," Mrs. Baxter said. " I thought you were far too nice-looking for an off-sider when you first came, but to-night—in that dress. Why, dear girl, you are beautiful ! "

Tuffy thought so too but she only nodded her head.

And that Shane Evans is going to get the benefit of all that beauty; and those lovely pearls, Tuffy thought. There was something wrong at the heart of Bal-Annie when Kim's young wife went off dancing with another man, harmless and all though that Shane Evans was. Of course, it was supposed to be called a meeting followed by a social, but if Tuffy knew anything about young people, specially the young people of the Darjalup district, there'd be dancing too.

She shook her head. Tuffy wasn't very happy either.

The meeting part of the social went off with a great flourish and enthusiasm. The only danger was that the cross-fire of talk and ideas would have gone on all night if Shane hadn't decided there had to be a Social too. Business was very important, but so was fun. It was ten o'clock when he called a halt to discussion, commandeered a team to put away the trestle tables and chairs and clear the floor for dancing.

Two of the young farmers brought out their piano-accordions and a third produced his fiddle. Within no time everyone was dancing. At the end of the hall the township " Ladies " auxiliary had spread a table of good things for supper. A small keg of beer was tapped for the older members, and a keg of ginger beer for the younger ones.

Jill found herself rushed, for not only were these young farmers attracted by her lovely appearance in that black lace dress with her fair skin and charming widely spaced eyes, they had all taken a great shine to her because of her enthusiasm and willingness to help them. The shyest and clumsiest of the young men in everyday life on the farm knew all about country dancing at night time. Jill found herself waltzed off by one partner after another. They were too shy to utter one word but they held her, and danced with her, as experts.

It was a lovely evening and her eyes were shining, partly because she loved all these kind gawky lovable youths and partly because the music, the jolliness and the expert dancing whirled her out of thoughts of herself.

Shane had to devote himself to the kegs, where it was

he who had to decide who was old enough for beer and who wasn't. And he was as firm as a policeman about that.

Towards midnight when Jill was sitting talking in a circle of the girls, some of whom were the most expert and helpful amongst the Junior Farmers, he came down the floor to her.

" Our dance, Jill," he said. " This is the last . . . and some of them with miles and miles to go are already off. We've got to have at least one dance together just to demonstrate the executive agrees on all subjects."

He was tired but his smile was still cheerful. Jill jumped up with readiness.

" Of course," she said. " I've thought for quite a long time what a shame it was you had to work all the time."

They danced away into the thinning group of dancers.

" When this is finished," Shane said, " we'll jolly well sit down with the rest of the committee and have a drink together. Nothing like a post-mortem on a party."

"Agreed," laughed Jill. "As long as my chauffeur doesn't go without me."

" He won't. He's on the committee. He'll go when I tell him. Not one single dazzling minute before."

CHAPTER EIGHTEEN

IT WAS TEN o'clock when Kim pulled his car into the Bal-Annie garages. He switched off the car light and then shut the car door behind him with a slam. He was tired. He knew in advance that Bal-Annie had a certain emptiness for him to-night. Jill would have gone to that social in Darjalup.

He hadn't hurried home. Though he was a fast driver he didn't believe in taking risks at night. There were other people on the road doing that and the twisting roads through the forest could be very deceptive when headlights twisted and turned with them.

Anyhow he was too tired to drive fast. That sort of driving took too much concentration.

The veranda light was on. That was Tuffy, he knew. Tuffy always left the light burning in the ingle-nook. She'd done it since he was a small boy finding his way home from Boy Scout camps down in the forest.

For the first time in his life Kim did not feel that he was coming home because Tuffy would be there.

In spite of the light on the front veranda he chose to go into the homestead the kitchen way. There was a light there too. Perhaps Tuffy was up, and would give him a cup of tea.

Tuffy was not only up, she was waiting for Kim.

As she heard his step she put down her knitting. When he came into the doorway her eyes watched him closely.

Yes, there he was ! Her Kim. Home, the way he always came, into the kitchen for a cup of tea with old Tuffy.

It should be the other way now. He should be coming home to that young wife of his.

Something was wrong with Kim. Tuffy could tell by that quiet air, those eyes that found it an effort to smile, even at her. It was her business to find out, and find out she would.

" Sit down, Kim," she said. " The kettle's on the boil."

He put his hat on the table, kicked a chair round with his foot and sat down.

" It's always on the boil, Tuffy, isn't it ? Like the light on the veranda ? "

" Habit," said Tuffy, non-committally. She was not going to be soft-soaped by Kim till she had found out what was on his mind. Then she was going to give him a piece of hers.

He took out a cigarette and lit it while Tuffy poured the boiling water into the teapot and let it brew. She put a plate of finely cut sandwiches on the table and some buttered scones. Then she poured his tea.

" Tell me about that honeymoon," she said, pouring herself a cup of tea too, and then sitting down at the other end of the table from Kim. " Where did you go ? "

" Come Tuffy, you can't go walking into a man's bedroom like that . . ."

" Can't I ? " said Tuffy fiercely. " You'd be surprised what I can do when I want to find something out."

Kim looked up at her in surprise.

" Why should you want to find anything out ? " he asked carefully, stirring his tea, then lifting it to his lips. It was too hot and he spluttered.

" When will you learn to sample your tea first, Kim," Tuffy said severely, " I've never seen you take a cup of tea that you don't do that—burn yourself ! "

" Go on, Tuffy ! " Kim said flatly. " Why should you want to find anything out."

" Because I want to know what's wrong with Jill. Why she's got a white face, and why she's gone off to that social with a young farmer from up the bush, instead of with her husband."

"Is anything so noticeably wrong with her?" Kim asked quietly. " Shane Evans is looking after her. And as she's addicted to Shane's company I don't think she'll suffer from boredom at that social, or any other one. She's an attractive girl, isn't she, Tuffy ? And Darjalup is full of willing partners. She'll dance . . ."

" So now we're getting down to it," said Tuffy. " You don't like Shane Evans and you don't like him paying so much attention to your wife. Well, if you want to know the truth, neither do I. So let's get down to the cause of it. What happened on that honeymoon ? "

Kim didn't look at her but rather at his sandwich, or the cigarette which he smoked while he drank and ate.

" Nothing much," he said. " We got there, late at night. Jill went upstairs to get undressed. I had a double whisky and sat in the arm-chair in the lounge to give her a chance to be free for a few minutes. Then a telephone call came through that young Phillips had overturned the car. I had to go out and find him. There was no alternative to that. I'm afraid it was morning before I got back."

" So ! " said Tuffy. " Go on. What happened the next day ? "

" We went swimming. It was glorious." Kim stopped, broke a sandwich in two then looked up at Tuffy. His eyes were dark, and there was an odd weariness about his manner. Tuffy did not take her eyes from his face.

"After the swim we found Vanessa on the beach nursing our togs for us. I'd seen her name in the hotel register the night before. I half expected her to do that, but hoped we'd be able to give her a wide berth."

Kim smiled a little wryly. " You know what Vanessa is, Tuffy. Amusing, but cloying I'm afraid."

" I certainly do know," said Tuffy. "And so does everyone else from the Equator to the Antarctic. But does Jill know? She's a stranger to the south and a stranger to our kind of life. Does she know what Vanessa is ? "

" She had a pretty fair example of it," said Kim. " Vanessa was at her best. You know . . . hardly any clothes on and a wobble when she walks. She also monopolised my arm as she monopolises any man's arm if it gets in the way."

Tuffy folded her arms and leaned back in her chair. " Don't tell me any more, Kim Baxter," she said. " You've told me all I want to know and I don't know why I don't go out there and pick up your shooting gun and take a good accurate shot at you."

Kim stopped mutilating his sandwich beyond all possible use and stared at Tuffy.

" What exactly do you mean by that ? " he demanded.

" There's a girl . . . and a lovely girl too . . . with her brand-new husband and he dallies about downstairs when he ought to be up unhooking his wife's dress for her. Then the next day he lets someone like Vanessa Althrop start her clinging act. What are you thinking of, Kim ? How was Jill to feel ? "

Kim was silent a minute, his eyes fixed on Tuffy's eyes.

" How . . ." he said, speaking very carefully, " was I to know exactly how Jill would feel ? We went into this marriage in a rather hard-headed way, as you well know, Tuffy. Whatever I did in those first forty-eight hours I was endeavouring not to affront Jill with too much ardent attention; and certainly not to hurt an old, though admittedly pestiferous, friend like Vanessa. How was I expected to know what Jill would feel ? "

It was Tuffy's turn to stare at Kim.

" She loves you," she said. " Even if she hadn't told me I'd know by the look on her face. Any girl, love or no love, has a terrible feeling of insecurity on her wedding night. That's the crucial time to win her confidence for all time. I know, Kim. I was married myself once."

" Just a minute, Tuffy," Kim said very quietly. " You said Jill told you. Told you what ? That she loved me ? "

" Certainly she did. You came out here to the kitchen and told me you had found the girl of all girls for Bal-

Annie, but no mention of love. This was a strictly sensible marriage. Remember? And I gave you the rounds of the kitchen about marrying for Bal-Annie only. It wouldn't work out, I said. And you went off smiling to yourself. Very pleased with yourself you were that day. But I wasn't. Not for the first hour anyway."

Kim had finished his cigarette and stubbed it out. He pushed his half-finished tea away and took out another cigarette and lit it. He did not look at Tuffy.

" Go on," he said. " What happened next, after you'd given me the rounds of the kitchen ? "

" I washed my face and put on a clean dress and did my hair, like the Spartans before battle, and I went right in to tell that girl the same thing as I'd told you. Then I didn't. I took one look at her face and I knew. She was positively pleading with me; and not saying a word."

" Go on," Kim said again.

" So I looked her in the eye and asked her straight out. ' Do you love him,' I said, and she answered straight back, honest as those clear window eyes of hers. ' Yes,' she said. ' I love him '."

Tuffy stopped speaking and sat and watched Kim. He had looked up now and their eyes met.

" It wouldn't be a bad idea if you fell in love with her yourself," she said a trifle sagely. " Late in the day though it might be."

" Don't be a damn' fool, Tuffy," Kim said. " I have —and I did. At the time I asked her to marry me, I think. No. I believe it was when I first saw her in the hotel. She was so fresh looking. The way she carried her head—so different from any other girl I'd met. She's got lovely eyes, Tuffy." He drew on his cigarette suddenly, as if by this action he might camouflage the expression in his dark eyes. It didn't fool Tuffy.

She bent her head and picked up her knitting.

" I didn't tell you before, Tuffy," he went on, " but

I once saw her at Jukes's Riding School when I went along there to sell him a couple of brumbies for beginners' hacks. Jukes told me she'd been grooming for him since she was a schoolgirl. She was some distance away . . . riding one of Jukes's fast horses. There was just something about her . . . I remembered."

Kim stopped.

"Go on," said Tuffy.

"Jukes told me she was doing a physical education course in a college, or something. I remembered that straight back, and the fair hair; the sheer youthful enthusiasm. When she was posted down here Jukes sent me a letter. He wanted me to be of assistance, if necessary . . . You know the sort of thing, Tuffy. Then that damn' school was burned down."

"Not so damned as that," said Tuffy. "You got yourself a nice wife out of that little bonfire."

A wry smile flitted across Kim's face. He looked up at Tuffy for the first time for quite a while. His eyes had been concentrated on the tip of that cigarette for most of the time.

"In a contradictory sort of a way—because she was such a delightful person, I suppose—it put me off wanting to employ her as an off-sider . . ."

Kim drew on his cigarette furiously. "Damn' fool name that is, if ever there was one," he added. " Off-sider! Another one of the Shire Secretary's 'ideas'!"

Kim was getting nicely angry and Tuffy was beginning to feel rather pleased with herself. But she had more fat to throw in the fire.

"Talking about the Shire Secretary," she said. "He's certainly having himself a wonderful night to-night. You ought to have seen Jill before she went out! Mrs. Baxter and I just looked, and *looked* . . ."

Kim's eyes were on her now, listening. There was a kind of dark suppressed anger in them.

"A black lace dress, it was," said Tuffy. "And her hair was shining. And those pearls ! Kim, that was a lovely present to give her. You ought to have seen them on that dress . . ."

" You have a dove's voice, Tuffy," Kim said sardonically. " But you roar, in a muted way, like a lion."

" Lioness ! " Tuffy corrected him.

Kim pushed back his chair and stood up.

"All right, Tuffy ! " he said. " I get your point. You can go to bed now and sleep your troubles off. I'm going to Darjalup to get *my wife*."

He was as far as the door when Tuffy spoke again.

" You're not going like that, Kim. Shouldn't you change your clothes ? It's a social, and they're all dressed up in their best suits . . ."

Kim had been in a sports jacket and tan trousers when he came in. His hat was on the table and his jacket now hung across the back of his chair with his tie.

He tucked his shirt into his belt and gave Tuffy a last baleful look.

" I'm going for my wife just as I am," he said. "And she's coming home with me. Black dress, pearls, and all—just as *she* is ! "

Before he had finished speaking he had gone through the door, the wire screen banged behind him. Tuffy could hear his footsteps as he leapt down from the veranda and strode across the gravel square to the garages. A minute later she heard the car rev up, pull out and roar away down the drive.

Tuffy pulled the teapot towards her, then going to the stove she added boiling water to it. It was time, she thought, to pour herself another cup of tea.

Forty-five minutes later Kim pulled up in front of the Roads' Board Hall—soon to be glorified by the name of Shire Hall. He got out of the car. With an effort he refrained from slamming the door;   and walked into the doorway of the hall.

Most of the dancers had gone home but at the end of the hall, chairs pulled round in a circle, sat a group of the last of them. They were talking volubly, excitedly, as if they had all the rest of the night—and next day too—to discuss their momentous affairs. Shane Evans was handing one of them a drink. Jill sat back a little from the group. She had a drink in one hand and a cigarette in the other.

Kim remembered it was he who had said that petty vices were humanising.

Shane Evans leaned over and said something to Jill. She laughed.

Kim walked down the middle of the hall. The sound and purposefulness of those footsteps made everyone turn his head. Jill looked up. Her heart stopped, then started again. But she did not move.

Kim walked right up to the group.

" Good evening, everybody ! " he said, unsmiling. He eased his way between the chairs into the circle. " Excuse me," he said. " I've come for my wife."

He leaned over, took Jill's glass from her and put it on the ledge of the platform behind her. He stubbed out her cigarette in the ashtray. Then he took her hand.

" Let's wrap this up, Jill," he said. " Come home." For a moment their eyes met, and held. Then lamblike, a little stupefied, Jill stood up and followed him.

At the door she pulled on her hand to bring him to a halt. He had walked down that hall with long masculine strides, Jill nearly running because of the grip he had on her hand.

" I must tell Ernie Riddle," she begged him. " He was to drive me home."

" He can see for himself," said Kim.

" But what will they think . . . ? "

" That I am a man who has come for his wife. Period."
Kim took her to the car, opened the door and packed
her in.

He walked round to the drive seat, slid in, revved up
the engine and let go the brake. Jill watched him, her
heart somehow failing now to do anything but beat
slowly and painfully.

" Did you have a nice time at Mount Sterling ? "
she asked carefully. Anything to break this awful
silence.

" Nice enough. It was busy."

The car was roaring up to a good speed.

She had to ask it. " How was Vanessa ? " Jill had
thought her voice would choke on the question, but it
didn't.

" Vanessa wasn't there," Kim said. " She left the
Southern Ocean Hotel late the night before you and I
left. On that honeymoon." Kim sounded almost bitter
on those last three words.

" She came out while I was having a cigarette after you
had gone upstairs—to tell me," he went on. " She had
changed her mind about the south coast and was driving
across to Bunbury for a more lively time." Kim stopped
then added thoughtfully: " It seemed to me, at the time,
she had woken up to the fact she was one too many for
that hotel. After she went inside I walked along the
waterfront to make some arrangements for young Phillips,
the stable boy, to get a lift home to Bal-Annie. I didn't
tell you, Jill, but it was he who overturned the car. I
didn't want you worrying about him. He only had a
shaking-up."

" So Vanessa went to Bunbury," said Jill, almost
dazed by what Kim had just said.

" Yes. And as far as I know, she's still there."

Jill was too stricken to say any more. That honeymoon

ruined, and all for nothing ! She could have cried out at the pain of her own folly.

They drove for a mile in silence.

" How is the Shire Secretary ? " inquired Kim. " I hear you won some sort of golf trophy with him yesterday. They told me at Albion when I drove through to-day."

" We did," said Jill. "And I hardly know how he is. He's been busy policing the kegs all night."

"And who danced with you ? "

" Most of them. Ages ranging from seventeen to nineteen."

There was a minute's silence and Kim's head turned and he looked at Jill. Her eyes clung to his.

" Kim, why did you come for me like that ? What are you going to do now ? "

" I came for you because, in spite of the warm weather, my bed's damn' cold. And what I'm doing right now is taking you home to put you in it. That damn' dress, pearls and all ! If necessary."

Jill wasn't sure, but she thought she heard the bells of heaven ringing far off.

" What's wrong with my dress, and the pearls? " she asked carefully.

" Nothing, except you look beautiful in them. Why should that Shire Secretary and those farming kids be looking at you when you're beautiful ? You belong to me, not them."

Jill's breath had been packed up inside her a long time. She let it all go, sighing like a small happy child. She slid down a little in her seat.

There was another silence. She glanced sideways at his profile. He wasn't smiling but he wasn't grim any more either.

" Kim . . . " she said gently. " Shall I light you a cigarette ? "

" Yes. They're in my shirt pocket. Up here on the left-hand side . . ."

Jill turned a little in her seat and put her hand in Kim's pocket.

" You mean the pocket over your heart, Kim ? " she said softly.

He slammed on the brakes and the car slid to a halt. He had caught Jill's hand against the pocket with one hand while he swung the car off the road with the other. He held it pressed to him. Then he switched off the lights and they sat there a long moment, neither saying anything. Jill's hand felt the thump of his heart under it, the pressure of his hand over it.

" Jill," Kim said at length, his voice uneven. " I'm sorry for what happened. I loved you so much and I hadn't asked you to return it. I didn't want to frighten you with that kind of love——"

" Kim. I'm sorry too. All the time I was terribly in love with you. And I wondered—and *doubted* . . ."

His arms went round her and he held her pressed to him, his hand cupping the back of her head, her face buried in his shoulder, her lips touching his bared throat where the open-necked shirt left it exposed.

" What fools we were," he said with a groan.

They stayed like that, not moving, a long time.

" Let's go home, dear," Kim said, at length.

" Yes," Jill said. " Home to bed."

"Jill," his lips were less than a paper's width away from her lips, his voice very tender. " To-morrow, we'll go into Darjalup and buy a new suite of furniture for our room. I can't stand that stuff Tuffy's cluttered round the place."

Jill sighed in sheer bliss. That awful little lamp table wedged between herself and Kim !

They *were* the bells of heaven she could hear. They rang very sweet and clear.

Kim's arms were tight around her, and his mouth was on her mouth. He had said—" *Let's go home!* " ; but Jill forgot for quite a long time that Time itself, like a river, passes by.

Soon another dawn would streak the sky behind the jarrah forest. But it would be a *new* dawn; a different one.